Sign up for our newsletter to hear
about new and upcoming releases.

www.ylva-publishing.com

OTHER BOOKS IN
THE SUPERHEROINE COLLECTION

SHADOW HAND

SACCHI GREEN

Ylva

THE
SUPERHEROINE
COLLECTION

ACKNOWLEDGMENTS

It took the superpowers of two fine editors, Gill McKnight and Alissa McGowan, to drag an entire novel out of this set-in-stone writer of short stories. I will be forever grateful to them, and to Astrid Ohletz of Ylva Publishing for giving me the chance to take my characters on this long, exciting journey.

DEDICATION

Dedicated to all women who find the superpower
within to do what must be done for their
families, their countries, and the world.

PART ONE

CHAPTER 1

TREMORS UNDERFOOT ALERTED CLEO BEFORE she heard the growl of distant engines and saw plumes of dust rising across the desert. Motorcycles—not on the road, but racing in leaps and jerks across rough terrain.

Ash saw them an instant later. "Cleo! Ours?"

"No. Not ours." Cleo and engines shared a common language, learned as a child raised above her uncle's automotive repair shop. She shaded her eyes against the unrelenting sun. "Coming too fast for us to make it back to the jeep and get it going."

She'd disabled the vehicle herself as an excuse to drop behind the convoy and spend an hour or two exploring the ancient ruins of a walled palace built over a thousand years ago and deserted for centuries. Ash had read about El Ukhaidir when she'd studied anthropology in college, knowing she'd be deployed to the Middle East and figuring she might as well know something about its history.

The turrets in the wall and the graceful, elegant arches within— some crumbling from the weight of years—were fascinating, and the courtyards still showed traces of great clay pots where flowering fruit and nut trees might once have grown. Probably almond and apricot, according to Ash. There were even remnants of a low wall that would have encircled a shallow pool.

A place well worth visiting, exploring, even fantasizing about, although Cleo's fantasies ran more to envisioning harem girls lounging beside the pool, while Ash kept talking about a famous woman who'd discovered and mapped ruins like this, an eccentric British explorer who'd become an expert on the desert and its tribes, and been called by some "The Desert Queen." Cleo had listened, but more to the point as far as she was concerned—even more than imagined harem girls—was the chance to be with Ash. Alone. A chance they'd taken as much advantage of as they could in the limited time they'd dared to stay.

But now enemies were approaching, and Cleo and Ash were less than halfway back to the jeep. As easy as repairs would be, no way could she do it fast enough to be gone before the oncoming motorcycles arrived.

Damn! Cleo knew better than to believe morning reports that a sector was secure. Why had she chosen to believe them today? Hope overriding skepticism, that's why.

The stone ruins were already too far away to reach before they could be seen. Besides, that would be too obvious.

"This way!" Ash ordered. She veered from the path and bolted across sand and gravel toward the dry ravine, a *wadi* in Arabic, that must once have provided water for the palace in the brief rainy seasons. Cleo gripped her rifle close and slid down the steep bank behind her. No need for Ash to look back to make sure she followed; they both knew by now that Cleo would follow her lieutenant anywhere, even to the depths of hell—which this might very well be.

The undulating *wadi* was wide and shallow, the bank just high enough to hide them if they stood erect, but not from an observer on the edge looking directly down. There were overhangs left by erosion in many places, some deep and cave-like. One hollow, where the dry streambed turned sharply, looked big enough to hold them. They scrabbled inside, making it still deeper and higher, clawing desperately at the packed soil and gravel, glad of the dirt that collapsed behind them across the entrance and provided more concealment.

"Behind me," Ash panted, wriggling so that Cleo was shoved further into their burrow. "That's an order, Sergeant Brown!"

"I'm the one with the rifle!" Not to mention the one with sharpshooter rating. But when the lieutenant called her "Sergeant" in that tone, arguing was out of the question, so she crouched behind with the gun angled across Ash's shoulder. If they were discovered...

By the noise and clouds of dust, there were too many cyclists to defend against. Cleo knew what the fate of two captured woman soldiers could be. Her own skinny ass might have no more than propaganda appeal, if they even noticed her sex before shooting to kill. She'd been mistaken for a teenaged boy often enough. But Lieutenant Ashton, an officer and most definitely a woman for all her tall, strong frame, would be a rare prize.

The growls of engines rose to a roar, louder, closer, closer—Cleo estimated a dozen machines—and stopped.

They'd found the disabled jeep.

Ash shifted in the confined space, trying to draw her sidearm. The slight movement triggered a shower of sand and stones from above. Cleo felt Ash flinch as something struck her right hand. Body pressed hard against Ash's back, head against her thick, dark hair, cheek against her face, Cleo steadied her. Enough light came into their hiding place to show a trickle of blood along Ash's hand, already beginning to crust over with the dust that covered every inch of them. Sweat trickling down their faces turned into gritty mud. Ash reached down with her left hand, groped for the stone that had hit her, and stared at it in the dim light. Cleo strained to see it too, without success.

Voices carried through the dry desert air—shouts, questions, orders, all too far away to make out individual words. The convoy Ash and Cleo had lagged behind had left plenty of tracks, so the newcomers might conclude that the jeep's occupants had gone on in another vehicle. Or they might not. The women's own boots wouldn't have made much impression on the hard ground, but a really skillful tracker might notice something. Cleo herself would have noticed.

The voices came gradually closer, paused for some sort of discussion, then moved on toward the arches and turrets of the ruins. Ash and Cleo dared to draw a few breaths, then froze as boots—more than one pair—crunched over pebbles until they stopped not far away near the rim of the *wadi*.

Two voices, arguing. The others must have gone on to search the interior of the fortress while these men checked out the *wadi*. One of them cursed and moved off to follow the rest, but the other could be heard starting down the bank and then, after the first step or two, setting off an avalanche of dry soil.

Under cover of the clamor outside, Ash tried again to get at the holstered sidearm at her hip. Cleo's leg was pressed so hard against the pistol that it bruised her knee. There was no room for her to shift—but suddenly the gun wasn't there anymore. It was in Ash's injured hand. A hand that hadn't moved, and couldn't possibly have reached for the pistol.

The sound of boots on gravel moved away.

"How…?" Cleo murmured.

Ash's hand began to shake. The lieutenant's hands *never* shook. They'd been in tight spots before, with their whole squad in danger, and she'd stayed cool as an October breeze in Montana.

"Something's…strange."

The faint quaver in her whisper scared Cleo, but she didn't let it show. "Later. It's okay. Hold steady."

Cleo felt Ash brace and take command. "Sergeant. I'll save two bullets. You know what to do, if it comes to that."

"Yes, ma'am." One for each of them. They would not be taken alive. Cleo'd be the one to do it, as she'd promised once before, when it hadn't quite come to that.

The sound of boots approached again. No more time for talking. Maybe no more time for living. Cleo drew in a slow, silent breath, and held it—a breath filled with the aroma of Ash's sweat, the lemon soap she used, and an essence all her own that only Cleo knew. If there'd been rumpled lavender-scented sheets beneath them instead of acrid desert, it would have been almost like that tiny room in Paris where they'd spent a glorious secret week of leave. Add in the musk of their lovemaking, just Ash and Cleo together, no barrier of rank, no sense of shame; and their reflections in the wall mirror

4

framed by carved wooden curlicues and cherubs, with Ash's dark, tousled hair just long enough to brush her jaw and Cleo's cropped coppery hair pressed against her cheek. A memory to cling to. All the more if it would be the last memory ever.

A breeze had sprung up outside, sending little puffs of dust through the slit at the cave's entrance. Anyone looking there directly would notice the opening. Cleo let her breath out slowly and drew another one.

The pistol appeared suddenly in Ash's left hand, while the stone had shifted into her right. Bit by bit, with quiet rustlings and scrapings, the entrance to their hideaway changed form to allow them both a better view—yet Ash still hadn't moved.

Cleo tensed. She must be hallucinating. Stress, heat, dust-filled air, fear for Ash, all screwing with her mind. *Focus! Concentrate! Brace for whatever you have to do!*

There was a hint of movement outside. Now she could see, clearly, the man pausing just beyond them under an overhang that jutted out like the prow of a ship.

He began to turn. Ash's hand didn't move, just stiffened, and a tremor shook the overhang. She raised a finger, and a clod fell. Another twitch of her finger, and a bigger clod fell, then another, and another. With a loud crack the whole formation began to capsize, stones and dirt pelting down, almost hiding the man. He yelled and struggled, lurched as though he'd been shoved from behind, and managed to stumble away before the full brunt of the landslide hit. When the noise and dust subsided, he could be heard some distance downstream scrambling up the side of the *wadi*.

The returning silence felt louder than the turmoil just past. What had happened? What had Ash done? And how?

Ash kept on staring at the object in her hand. Cleo, with no idea what to say, said nothing. Eventually, the men who had been searching the ruins could be heard on the path back to the road, but it was a while before they revved their engines and roared away. Cleo knew all too well what they'd probably been doing in the meantime.

At last, desperate to move her aching joints and feel more air and space around her, she lifted the end of her rifle and began to knock bits of dirt and pebbles out of the small opening in front of them. Ash looked up, and all at once great gaps appeared, as though some giant hand was punching through the wall.

Ash lurched forward and scrambled out on all fours, dropping the pistol along the way while favoring the hand still holding the hidden object. Cleo tumbled out behind her. They sat a few feet apart in the dry streambed, gulping fresh air, dazed, but not so much so that Cleo wasn't on alert for any sign that someone had stayed behind.

"Cleo," Ash said at last. She hesitated. "Sergeant Brown."

This was serious. Cleo waited. Usually when Ash shifted into full lieutenant mode her clear gray eyes took on a steely glint, but not now. This time they begged for reassurance.

"Sergeant Brown, what...what did you just see?"

"I saw you save our sorry asses, ma'am. I don't claim to understand what happened, how things moved the way they did, but I saw it."

"So if I'm hallucinating, so are you."

Cleo could get away with a lot when it came to most folks, but she could never lie to her lieutenant. To Ash. "We're not hallucinating. Just because we don't understand something doesn't mean it isn't real. I know plenty of things for sure without understanding them. Objects moved, and from what I saw, you made them move. How did it feel to you?"

"It was...strange. Things happened because I thought about them, but it wasn't just me. It was this." She opened her right hand at last and showed what she'd been holding, what Cleo was pretty sure had fallen on her in the cave and drawn blood. "Her."

Not stone, at least not any kind Cleo had ever seen. Ivory, maybe, yellowed by age. Whatever it was made out of, the carved figure was clearly, extravagantly female, four or five inches high, with three pairs of full breasts springing from her torso. Some kind of ancient goddess. She wore a sort of high crown that must once have been even higher but had been broken off. Her legs were obscured by a skirt incised with unidentifiable designs. Her face had lost part of its nose, but was otherwise intact, with a regal look about the chin and the direct gaze. Her arms, too, were mostly missing, although you could see where they'd been, and there was enough left of one of them to form a sharp point where it had broken—a point stained with recently shed blood.

Ash's blood. All that mattered to Cleo right then, besides the unlikely fact that they were still alive, was Ash. The lieutenant was… shaken. Not scared, not confused, not angry, exactly, but struggling with something made up of all of those, and more.

"She's stuck in my mind," Ash blurted out at last. "Trying to control me. She may have saved us, but I want her out. I get all the orders I can stand from my commanding officers."

Defiance! Cleo nearly shook with relief. Ash was going to be all right.

"Toss her to me, Ash. See how you feel then."

She held out her hand, then tried to duck when the figurine shot up and hurtled toward her head, stopping with a sudden jerk just before it hit. Ash's face was taut with strain. A fierce heat flowed from the hovering figure, feeling as though it would sear Cleo's skin. Then all at once the goddess, or whatever she was, vanished. A few pebbles could be heard dropping inside the cave. Maybe she'd burrowed back into it.

Cleo's whirling mind took refuge in crude humor. "Guess I'm not this particular Desert Queen's type. Just as well. She wants somebody like one of those Hindu Kali statues, with a bunch of extra arms and hands to do justice to all her extra boobs."

"What she wanted," Ash said, standing somewhat stiffly, "was to hurl herself right through your head. I struggled to stop her, and I won. Now she's gone. I made her go away. It's over."

Cleo got to her feet with an effort. It seemed like they'd been scrunched up in that cave in fear for their lives an hour or more. "So it was only your ass she intended to save, and mine was just collateral non-damage? I can live with that."

7

"If you're lucky," Ash said. "She may be bound to this place. Not to the palace over there—that's only about 1,300 years old—but to something much older. Astarte, Ishtar, Ashtoreth—many names for more or less the same goddess. Maybe some temple was here thousands of years ago that left no trace—except for Her."

"A real Desert Queen, then? But 'Ashtoreth'? Really? That name?"

"Don't go there! It's just a coincidence. Besides, in this area her name would most likely be Ishtar." Ash's irritation was an improvement on worrying about possible hallucinations. "A hundred years ago the clerks at Ellis Island didn't bother with figuring out how to spell immigrants' names. My great-grandfather's name became 'Ashton' instead of 'Athanasiou.' Greek. A whole different crew of goddesses." Her expression warned Cleo not to mention her actual first name, Athena. "Anyway, enough of that. She's gone now. End of story."

"Sure." Cleo watched Ash bend down for the pistol she'd dropped, now half-buried in gravel. The gun rose to meet Ash's hand. "If you say so."

"It'll wear off," Ash muttered, still looking down.

Cleo groped for words. What must it feel like, some impossible, unnatural power being thrust into you without your consent? Something that couldn't be explained by experience, or training, or instinct? For that matter, was Cleo herself suffering from shellshock, to willingly believe in a stone goddess controlling her commander?

Right now it didn't matter. She found her words. "Whether it wears off or not, you're still you." She reached out, and Ash's hand met hers in an entirely natural grip.

"We're still us," Ash said.

What flowed between them when they touched needed no explanation at all. Ash rested her gritty cheek against Cleo's until a stronger breeze sprang up, signaling the lowering of the sun toward the vast desert horizon.

Ash stepped back. The lieutenant in command resurfaced. "It's time to get back to the jeep and out of here."

Cleo didn't have much hope that it would be that easy. There was nowhere anyone could hide between where they were and the jeep, and Cleo was sure, as much by instinct as by sight, that no motorcycle lurked behind its low profile. One man might be hiding there, prone, but with no motorcycle left behind she doubted that. They'd have thought of a different plan. She held her rifle ready just in case.

"They've booby-trapped it. Or maybe planted the explosives on the periphery. Let me check it out. If they've just left a few IEDs in the road, I can find and avoid them, and we might yet be able to drive out of here." This was one of Cleo's areas of expertise. She'd developed an instinct for it. For all kinds of explosives, in fact, even guns; she knew when a gun was about to fire, and from roughly what direction. Just something you picked up from experience, she figured, if you were wired like that. So she was sure there was no gun aimed at them from behind the jeep—and equally sure that there were explosives nearby.

She led the way slowly, carefully, focusing intently on the terrain, not even looking away at the sound of another vehicle coming fast.

"Ours," she said briefly. "Signal him not to come too close." She knew which vehicle it was by the sound, and who'd been driving it in the convoy. Somebody must finally have noticed that they were missing and sent Corporal Jones back to check on them. Not a good choice. He was new to the country, ignorant of the terrain.

Cleo didn't need to look to make sure Ash would signal, but the new arrival was speeding faster than he should, and not braking soon enough. Ash shouted. Cleo looked up and shouted too, but of course he couldn't hear them.

"Stay back!" she yelled at Ash, and began to run right toward the oncoming jeep. Jones braked at last, went into a spin, slid toward their disabled jeep—and suddenly the earth fell away under Cleo's feet. Or, no, she'd been lifted high by some strong, invisible hand, then set down hard against the ground at least twenty feet from where she'd been.

Jones's brakes squealed. He slowed way down in a cloud of dust, but there was no way he was going to escape a collision. Cleo, still holding her rifle, lurched toward Ash to protect her, to shield Ash's body with her own. The lieutenant evaded her and extended her right hand toward their jeep, which leapt suddenly high into the air, flying at least fifty feet while a series of explosions shook it. And then a surging mass of flames erupted, far more than the gas in the tank could account for.

Yeah, it had been booby-trapped. Cleo's head pounded with the frantic beating of her heart, or the explosions echoing off the stone walls of the distant fortress. Or maybe both. She found herself crouching on the ground at Ash's feet, and noticed the lieutenant beginning to slump just in time to catch her and ease her down.

Jones, staggering out of his undamaged jeep, hardly registered in Cleo's consciousness. Ash in her arms was all that mattered.

"I don't know how..." Ash muttered. "I thought she was gone, but it's not over after all."

"Shush. It'll be all right." Cleo stroked her back. Being able to do what Ash could now do might not be such a bad thing. This didn't seem like a good time to say that, though. Cleo's arms tightened around her. The hell with what Jones would think. Technically it wasn't illegal anymore to be lesbian or gay in the Army, but they could always get you for something. Fraternization between officers and enlisted was high on the list.

Ash pulled free and stood. So did Cleo. By the time Jones started toward them with questions, Ash was every inch Lieutenant Ashton, and Cleo was Sergeant Brown.

"Are you all right, ma'am?" he asked.

"Just a little shaken. How about you?"

"All in one piece, I guess, but what..."

"That was really something, wasn't it?" Ash said casually. "Those guys are getting mighty creative with their explosives." Then, sternly, "You'd better learn to approach any possible booby trap situation more carefully. If they'd buried IEDs out at a distance from the disabled vehicle you might not be all in one piece."

"Yes, ma'am. But what..."

She ignored him, moving off toward his jeep. He turned to Cleo.

"What was all that, Sergeant?"

She outranked him, but he'd had a big shock, and was honestly curious, so she let him get away with questioning her.

"My fault. Clogged air filter. I always check, but didn't today, so I had to stop to clear it, and then we saw a gang coming fast on motorcycles. Lieutenant Ashton and I managed to hide over in the *wadi* until they were gone. The rest you've seen." She turned away and followed Ash.

She'd actually fiddled with a different system to disable the jeep, but nobody was ever going to find out anything from that still-glowing hunk of twisted metal. A hunk of twisted metal that had been her jeep. Her responsibility. She knew better than to get sentimental about machines, but this was the one she'd driven the lieutenant in for two years, the closest thing to a home together they'd had.

Her eyes stung, but it couldn't be tears. She hadn't cried in twenty years. Well, except that once, in Paris, with Ash, but that wasn't the sad kind of crying. Anyway, she wasn't crying now. It was just all that sand and grit getting into her eyes.

But it *was* her fault. She shouldn't have believed the all-clear report, shouldn't have given in to the lieutenant's obsession with ancient ruins, shouldn't have let their mutual desire to steal some time alone together make her expose Ash to such a risk.

Guilt kept her quiet on the ride to rejoin the convoy. Cleo generally couldn't stand to ride with somebody else driving, but this time she put up with it. She deserved it. The lieutenant sat in front with Jones, while Cleo sat in back, simmering with guilt and trepidation. How much had he seen? Had he believed Ash's quick-witted story about the enemy having "creative" new explosives? Who might he tell?

Above all, what was happening to Ash? Would the kind of power she'd shown, if it lasted, turn her into somebody entirely different? Somebody who wasn't the Ash who was closer to Cleo than she'd ever thought anyone could be? Wasn't the Ash who could love her? The Ash who could sometimes read Cleo's mind, as Cleo could read hers.

Ash turned a bit to look over her shoulder. "Hot enough for you?" she asked.

They were going to be all right. "Hot enough for you" was their private code phrase, almost the first thing she'd ever said to Cleo, just a casual, clichéd remark that had come to mean so much.

Cleo had been sent to pick the lieutenant up at the airport in the capital city, and yeah, it had been hot, but it was always hot. Cleo was used to it. Her sweat and foul temper had been due to a hit-and-run fender-bender on the way and then an altercation over a parking space, not the temperature. It hadn't helped that even travel-worn and jet-lagged, Lieutenant Ashton was all too attractive. Not beautiful, exactly, except for the swallow-wing curve of her dark eyebrows, but definitely intriguing. That didn't matter, couldn't matter. As an officer she'd be strictly off-limits even if by some miracle she were interested in dating women.

The greeting her and schlepping of luggage had gone okay, but Cleo had been overly forceful heaving the duffle bag into the jeep, and had to wipe the sweat from her face before turning to open the door. At her passenger's casual, "Hot enough for you?" Cleo had decided she was too dumb to care about one way or another. But some perverse impulse that got her in trouble now and then had made her want to see if she could shock the new lieutenant.

"You bet. Hot enough to steam my clams."

One eyebrow had gone up. "Sounds like you must come from near the ocean. Where I come from we have prairie oysters, but I've never taken much interest in those."

Cleo's mouth had dropped open. Somewhere in her varied past she'd heard that term for fried bulls' testicles, but coming from this woman it was a shock. She'd just mumbled something about being from upstate New Hampshire, not exactly on the coast. Lieutenant Ashton had said that she was from Montana, and they'd conversed sporadically and impersonally all the way to the base where they were stationed.

Just as she was getting out, though, while Cleo was handling her luggage, the lieutenant had said casually, "I've heard that clams are good raw, too, with just the right tangy sauce."

Cleo had hoped there was nothing fragile in the bag she'd dropped. And while the lieutenant had sauntered toward base headquarters, the sergeant had watched her eloquent backside and realized that, for better or worse, she'd met her match. And, as it turned out, her soul mate.

CHAPTER 2

THE SUN SET IN A shimmering red haze well before they approached the multi-national base. Under a crescent moon, the desert lay still and serene, as though never swept by storms of war or nature. The land sloped gently down toward a river flowing from distant mountains, a mere trickle at this time of year.

From a distance, the rows upon rows of tents inside the walled perimeter of the camp glowed golden with interior light. Ash and Cleo had been stationed there for three months before the mission they'd just completed but had never approached by night before. To Ash, nearly dozing, it looked like a palace from some fantastic Arabian Nights tale. Or like a futuristic outpost under an invisible dome on a far-off planet like Mars.

Once through the gates, they were back in the military world they knew so well. Corporal Jones dropped them off in front of Headquarters, one of the few permanent buildings in a city of canvas. Staff and vehicles were coming and going in spite of the late hour; there was no chance of a private conversation.

"I'd better go file my report with the motor pool office right away and face whatever I have coming." Cleo sighed. "I'm responsible for letting my jeep be destroyed." It went without saying that she wouldn't bring up the flying-through-the-air parts, either hers or the jeep's.

Ash nodded. They knew without discussion that Corporal Jones was a problem. Had he been distracted enough not to notice Cleo being raised so far and dropped? Or Ash with her arm outstretched toward the jeep as it lifted? He'd certainly been jittery during the rest of their journey back, casting all too many sidelong looks at Ash, but that could have just been a reaction to seeing Cleo's arms around her. He hadn't actually said much of anything beyond comments on the weather.

"Good luck, Sergeant. I'll take some of the blame if it comes to that."

"No worries." Cleo's flashing grin said more than any bystander could have understood. Her guilt was fading, and she headed for the motor pool with a jaunty stride that would have convinced anyone else of total confidence. Ash watched her go, wishing they'd dared at least a quick hand clasp. Her arm twitched. If she really tried, could she just yank Cleo back to her? She suppressed the urge, but barely. Impulse control was going to be a problem.

Ash did worry, but not about Cleo's standing in the Army. Nothing short of a dishonorable discharge would bother Cleo much, and that wasn't likely. Nobody could handle motor vehicles like Sergeant Brown, or diagnose their problems, or come up with creative ways to fix them. Command had been pressuring her to rethink her decision to quit as soon as her current (and fourth) tour of duty ended in three months.

Ash was getting out, too, in about eight months, when the obligatory years of service for her Army ROTC college scholarship were completed. Both of them had thought about making the Army a lifetime career, but that was before they met, before sparks flew between them as intense as whatever had happened to Ash in that cave. Laws or no laws, being a lesbian couple in the military would be uncomfortable, to say the least. They had other plans. Cleo could easily get a civilian job with a contractor in the capital to keep her in the country until Ash was free, and then they'd be off to make a life together.

But now, in spite of Cleo's reassuring grin, Ash had other worries. If this mysterious new power turned out to be permanent, what would that do to their plans? Their lives? Everything they thought they knew about the world? She didn't even know if she was the same person she'd been all her life. There was something new going on inside her, something she could feel if she focused on it, a buzz verging on a burn in her joints, her skin, her mind.

"Lieutenant?"

Ash had stopped at the foot of the walkway to Headquarters. She swung around and stepped aside. "Sorry!" She'd been standing in the path of two men trying to carry a load of long steel pipes up the walkway. A truck bed on the roadside was half-full of similar pipes. Looked like something to do with heating, hard as it was to imagine that this desert could get cold. The load was heavy, and while trying to work his way around her one of the guys stumbled. A couple of the pipes began to slide off his shoulder, down his upper arm, totally out of his control. He let out a loud curse, and suddenly, impossibly, the pipes retreated back into balance. It wasn't until then that Ash noticed she'd raised her arm. The realization shook her. *Impulse control, damn it! Get a grip!*

She followed the men through the door, then turned to the office on the left, steeling herself to report to Colonel Rogers if she was still on duty this late—and hoping she wasn't.

This time luck was on her side. No report possible tonight. And tomorrow all she'd really be expected to report on was the successful mission they'd completed before joining the convoy for safety on the way back. Their all-female squad of Army nurses and doctors from the capital city, along with escorts and a mobile medical facility, had gone from village to village in a district where a UN relief worker had persuaded the tribal leaders to let their women be treated by other women. Ash had plenty to say about that, and the explosion near the end could just be tossed in casually. Remembering it all, though—if you could call it remembering, when she'd scarcely been conscious of what was happening—set off a burn in her right arm and side and, in fact, her whole body.

Just an effect of all that riding with no chance to limber up, she told herself. After grabbing a bite at the Officers' Club and then strolling briskly along the walkway inside the perimeter wall, she did feel better, mentally and physically.

There were manned watchtowers at the four corners of the wall and at regular intervals in between, and a walkway all along its top, with now and then an angle where the terrain was especially uneven. In some of those angles, sandbags were heaped, ready for filling gaps in case of explosive attack. Ash had a favorite shadowed spot where occasionally at night, feeling unbearably penned in, she climbed the sand bags, hooked her fingers over the edge of the wall, and scrambled up. It was no harder than some of the obstacle courses where she'd trained.

Being on the wall wasn't strictly forbidden. Ash had trained, in fact, for back-up status as a leader of extra observers in case of emergencies. Whether she could be there whenever she chose was a gray area, regulation-wise, and the closer she got to leaving the Army, the more inclined she felt to push the military envelope. Sure proof that she wasn't career-officer material. If all her duties were like the successful medical mission, she might have reconsidered, and so would Cleo—but that wasn't going to happen.

From her position on the wall, Ash could look behind to the bright ant-hill bustle of the camp and enjoy an illusory freedom from it all, but more often she'd gaze out over the darkened desert toward a horizon where, if the moon were full or a faint glow still lingered from the sunset, she could see an irregular line of mountains.

Cleo knew about the place on the wall, and had joined Ash once, but the apparent privacy was deceptive. Resisting temptation was too hard, and Cleo hadn't come again. Tonight, though, after Ash had been there for half an hour practicing tossing pebbles in the air with her mind and making them move in unlikely ways as they fell, Cleo came.

She hauled herself up, sat cross legged several feet away, and eyed Ash's progress. A pebble left Ash's hand, hurtled toward Cleo, stopped just short of her nose, then slowly returned to Ash. Cleo never flinched.

"Nice yo-yo effect," she commented. "I thought you might be up here figuring out how to move mountains." She gestured toward the range far to the northwest. "Moving them pebble by pebble might be the best plan, though. Sneakier. Stealth terraforming."

Ash flipped another stone toward Cleo, who caught it in the natural, old-fashioned way, then hurled it outside the wall. It fell, in the old-fashioned way, and could be heard hitting the sandy earth below.

"Try that again." Ash dug another pebble from her pocket and tossed it to Cleo. "Surprise me."

Sitting high above both desert and camp, bantering with Cleo, accepting everything about themselves, loosened the knots of stress that had been binding her. The tension of watching for Cleo to throw the stone wasn't stress, it was just play.

Cleo tossed the pebble upward over and over, keeping the timing between flips as random as she could, whistling softly all the while. Her actual throw, when it came, went straight up over her own head, fell back toward her, and veered off into Ash's hand at the last nanosecond. Cleo didn't look up to watch it coming. "You could be handy to have around," she said lightly. Then, as if it had just occurred to her, "Hey, they finally got that enclosed firing range finished while we were gone. Want to meet up there tomorrow afternoon? Shooting under a roof without getting sand in your eyes or your gun barrel. Pure luxury."

"Sure. I'll call you when I know my schedule. The colonel wasn't in tonight, so I have my whole report to get through."

"I figured. Nobody will read mine until tomorrow, and then I may get hauled over some coals. Or maybe not." Cleo shrugged. "Whatever." She shifted toward the inner edge of the wall "I'd better get back before somebody comes looking for me. They've been saving all the most fucked up jeeps and trucks for me to diagnose all the time we were gone." She flopped on her stomach, swung her legs over the side, and poised facing Ash with her weight on her elbows and arms. Ash moved swiftly on hands and knees until she was close enough to get her lips on Cleo's, gently, not wanting to knock her off the wall, but Cleo raised herself into a deep, passionate kiss, held it for half a minute, then slid down out of sight to the sandbags below.

Ash was at Headquarters early the next morning, but not early enough to be the first to get to Colonel Rogers. When Corporal Jones came out of the office, saluting on his way past without meeting Ash's eyes, she knew luck wasn't on her side after all. There was still a wait before she was called into the office. She could hear someone talking and wondered who else might be there, but the colonel was alone when Ash was finally admitted. She must have been talking on the phone.

Colonel Rogers, behind the desk in her small office, did meet Ash's eyes, but with a perceptible effort. "Glad to have you back, Lieutenant Ashton. I've had excellent reports of you and Sergeant Brown from the medical team you accompanied. What was your impression of the mission?"

So they'd get the easy part out of the way first.

"My impression, Colonel, is that more missions like that would get us a whole lot further than any combat actions. It's not just the 'honey catches more flies' thing, but a way for all sides to see the others as real people not so different from themselves. And in spite of all the tribal restrictions, the women here have significant influence in their own ways. Winning them over would be better than winning a battle."

"You'll get no argument from me." The colonel sighed. "As I told you before you left, though, this was a one-shot affair. We can't get funding for more. There was a trial program like this several years ago, and I was involved, but in spite of being clearly successful, the budget for it was scrapped." She shook her head in disgust. "Plenty of funds for weapons, almost none for humanitarian purposes. Don't quote me on that." She and Ash were on generally friendly terms, but Ash was still surprised that she'd spoken so frankly. Possibly she, too, was uneasy in this formal interview. "Well, write up your report in detail, and we'll hope that a time comes when we can use it as support for a new program."

She stood and moved to look out a window, dusty from the sand outside. Ash could see the tension in her shoulders, and feel it in her own.

Colonel Rogers turned back. "Enough about that. I hear you had some excitement yesterday on the way back, but Corporal Jones's account seemed confused. What was all that? Tell me about it."

Ash was weirdly relieved to finally get down to it. "Yes, ma'am. It was pretty intense, and I'm hazy about some of it. All that time hiding, cramped up, breathing dust..." Her shiver at this point was entirely genuine. She went on through the part about the disabled jeep. "I think Sergeant Brown said something about a clogged air filter. Anyway, when we saw the motorcyclists in the distance, she knew by the sound of their engines that they were the enemy's. There were some ruins nearby that seemed too obvious as a hiding place, so we went down into a dry *wadi* and managed to crawl into a sort of a cave under an overhang. We could hear them stopping by our jeep, and then passing by on foot to search the ruins, but one of them came down into the *wadi* and nearly found us. We were there, in the cave, for a long, long time, firearms ready if it came to that."

The colonel's brief nod showed that she understood. "So. What then?"

"They finally left. Sergeant Brown suspected a booby trap or peripheral IEDs, so we approached cautiously, with her in the lead. She's had a great deal of experience in mine detection."

"So I've heard. One of her many useful talents."

Ash eyed the colonel sharply. Was there an implication of more intimate skills? Did it matter? "While still some distance from the jeep, we saw Corporal Jones coming at a high speed. I signaled him to stay back, in case of IEDs, but he ignored me, so Sergeant Brown ran toward him at risk of her own life to slow him down. I'm not entirely clear about what happened next. All I can tell you is what I think I saw."

Did that flicker of the colonel's eyes mean she sensed an evasion? Ash forged ahead, closing her own eyes to focus on what she had actually seen. "His jeep swerved, and skidded, and looked like it would hit ours. Sergeant Brown ran toward me as though to shield me. Just before a collision, our jeep seemed to leap high up and sideways, then exploded on landing. To my shame, I think I passed out briefly right about then. Sergeant Brown seemed certain that it had been booby-trapped. I think she's filed a complete report."

"Yes. I've seen the report. Much like yours, but with speculation as to what new explosive techniques the enemy might have developed."

"As I said, I was pretty much in a daze by then, so that's all I remember."

The colonel began pacing slowly back and forth between the window and her desk. "Corporal Jones tried to reach me here last night, as did you, apparently, because he saw you outside. He particularly remembered because a strange thing occurred just then. Did you notice two men carrying steel pipes on their shoulders, one stumbling, and several pipes very nearly falling off?"

Oh, damn. Here it came. "That was my fault, Colonel. I'd been, well, daydreaming, and was in their way. He tripped trying to get around me."

"Did you observe the pipes roll back up onto his shoulder in a way that can't be explained?

"Yes, ma'am, I did. It startled me."

Colonel Rogers stopped in front of her desk and leaned back against it. "Lieutenant Ashton. 'Dazed' and 'daydreaming' and being 'startled' are not terms that I would associate with you. Your record has been exemplary, especially your cool competence in dangerous situations. The medical personnel on your mission had high praise for how you handled some very tricky confrontations. I have to ask, are you feeling quite well?"

Ash was in fact feeling suddenly strong, and confident. The colonel's words were like a switch that connected who she'd always been with exactly who she was now. "Quite well, thank you. Yes, I was shaken by yesterday's occurrence, but I think I've completely recovered."

It was true. There was no point in worrying, in questioning. She thought about how much more she could have done on the medical mission, actions in her power now but not then, like moving an injured child into the X-ray van without causing pain. While there was still much to learn, she knew without a doubt that she had people to save, and missions to carry out that were far beyond anything she could do in the Army.

"I'm glad to hear that." Colonel Rogers sat back down at her desk. "I'm required to report yesterday's incident to a special unit where they take an interest in things not easily explained, like your jeep leaping high up and away before exploding. That level of weapons technology must be investigated, and, if it exists, used for our side. I expect them to send an operative here to interview you, possibly even this afternoon." Her expression relaxed. She very nearly smiled. "Take the rest of the day off, Ash." The informality would have been routine for the Officers' Club, but was seldom used in the office.

"Thank you, Colonel." Ash saluted and began to turn away, but the colonel went on, "Just one more little detail in Corporal Jones's report that I've been curious about. Are you in the habit of raising your arm in front of you when inexplicable things are about to happen?"

Ash had no power to deflect this kind of missile, but she took it without flinching. "Something reflexive, I guess. Do you suppose there's such a thing as an instinct for self-defense that kicks in even before a danger is apparent?"

"Who knows? But if such occasions arise in the future, it might be just as well if that reflex isn't so obvious to onlookers. In some cultures that might even suggest, say, witchcraft. Just something to consider carefully."

Ash nodded, saluted again, and left to find Cleo, mulling over what had been said. Just how many of the colonel's statements was she meant to consider carefully? *"Plenty of funds for weapons?"* *"Weapons technology put to use by our side?"* Was she herself in danger of becoming a human weapon? *Get a grip.* More likely paranoia had come with whatever that cantankerous goddess idol had injected into her. In any case, Ash had already resolved that she alone would be the one to decide how and when she used this questionable gift, in the Army or out of it.

Cleo was puttering around outside the motor pool's repair facility, sitting in a patch of shade and poking at some bit of mechanical gadgetry. She set it down when Ash approached.

"Hot enough for you?" Ash murmured. Then, a bit louder so that anyone nearby could hear it, "You said they'd finished the enclosed firing range here, Sergeant. How about it? If we're going to get into any more messes, I'd better do something to sharpen my marksmanship."

"Firing range" was another turn-on phrase for them. Places where most people are wearing earplugs are good for private communication if you know how, and if your timing is right, there might not be anybody else there at all.

"How did your report go over?" Ash asked on the way.

Cleo was nonchalant. "There'll be some flak to face, but I can deal. You?"

"Corporal Jones was coming out as I was going into the colonel's office. Things are hitting the fan. She asked about the medical mission, and wanted to know about the 'incident' yesterday, and how I was feeling, and then said someone from a special unit was flying in to interview me. They want to figure out what the hell kind of technology could have sent that jeep flying."

"I'll just bet they do."

"I need to figure it out for myself, but I'd rather leave them out of it. Whether it's technology or some woo-woo power, whatever it is, it's mine, and I've still got it." She stared at the canvas flap leading to the firing range twenty feet away and lifted her hand just a little. The flap rose slowly in a series of jerks, then folded itself back to let them in.

"Can you do that with no hands?"

"Let's see." Ash clenched her fists at her sides and concentrated on the canvas. It twitched upward a couple of feet, but that was all.

"You just need practice. C'mon. Whatever this thing is, we should take it for a spin and see what it can do. What you can do." Cleo led Ash into the tent. Nobody else was there.

"I've been doing that already. As far as I can tell, I have to be able to see something to…to affect it. My aim isn't always good, either, and I can't lift anything much bigger than a suitcase. Yesterday must have been…I don't know what. Maybe it will all fade away after a while."

"Like some kind of virus? Do you *want* it to fade away?"

Did Cleo want that? Ash didn't dare go there. Did she wonder why the power had come to Ash, but not to her? And why had that goddess figure had it in for Cleo? Maybe she'd been a strictly feminist goddess and was fooled by Cleo's boyish impression. Ash shook it off. The important question was whether it would change things between them.

"No, I don't want to lose it," she said bluntly. "That whole affair was my fault, wanting to explore those ruins, and I couldn't stand it if you'd been…hurt. If I'd lost you. Just the same, I don't want to lose this now that I've got it. I want to make it even stronger. There's no going back. I almost get the sense that she's still watching to see what I'll do. It's like she's in my blood." She rubbed her hand where the cut was already mostly healed. "I honestly don't know what happened with the jeep; maybe it was the motivation. And adrenaline. I couldn't do it now. But I'm going to learn."

She still had her sidearm and began to draw it out, then paused, concentrated, and the gun rose by itself, executed a wobbly flip, and settled in her hand. She gave a rueful laugh. "Not too smooth with the old-time gun slinger tricks yet. I'm hoping working on target shooting will help my focus on more than one front."

The best part of target practice was always when Cleo stood behind with her body pressed close, reached her arms around, pressed her cheek against Ash's hair, breathed in her scent, and guided her stance and aim. It hadn't yet done much for Ash's so-so marksmanship, but it did a whole lot for both of them just the same.

This time, when Cleo backed away and Ash started firing, at first she was missing as much as she ever had. Gradually, though, she learned to focus, not hitting the bull's eye, but at least nudging the bullets into its neighborhood. Cleo was impressed, but not deceived.

"Hey, you're really working it, aren't you?"

"Yeah, focus is exactly what I need. I could affect the damned bullets better if they didn't go so fast, but I'm getting the hang of it."

"Keep it up, and maybe you'll be able to launch them just as well without benefit of the gun at all." Cleo's tone was joking—or maybe not.

"That'd look suspicious, wouldn't it?" Ash turned, grinned, and held out the gun. "Here, you take over and see if you can beat my score."

Cleo returned the grin, clearly glad that the cocky lieutenant she loved was back. Ash knew there was still a hint of brittleness to her own mood, but what the heck, they'd both been through some severe trauma. Not that Cleo would cut her any slack when it came to marksmanship. She'd always beaten Ash's scores right into the ground. She'd know what that challenge was really about.

Cleo's first three shots centered or edged the bull's eye. The next one barely clipped it. When she missed by an inch, first to the right and then to the left, she stopped and set down the gun.

"Impressive," she said. "The real challenge is whether you can divert a bullet coming right at you. Better yet, stop it in midair. But we're sure as hell not going to test that notion."

"Maybe with a Kevlar vest? But I'd need to be able to see the bullet, and that wouldn't be possible."

Cleo ignored her. "You couldn't actually see our bullets in flight just now, but you knew their trajectory well enough to divert them. Maybe you don't have to literally see a thing."

Ash thought about that. "Maybe it just has to be in my line of sight."

"How about if you know exactly where something is, even if it isn't entirely in your line of sight?"

"Hmm. Let's just see about that." Ash drew back a few feet. Her mouth twitched into a little smile and there was a subtle movement in Cleo's right pants pocket where she kept her key ring, attached by a chain to her belt. For a moment, it felt exactly like when she'd slid her hand deeply into that snug space and teased Cleo's all-too-sensitive thigh while they'd strolled through a Parisian evening, but now Ash was standing four feet away with both hands in her own pockets.

Cleo, startled, drew a sharp breath. Ash's smile widened. She extended her hand with the key ring dangling from one finger. Cleo grabbed reflexively at the chain, still attached to her belt. Very slowly the key ring drifted through the air between them until it almost reached her, then blinked suddenly out of sight, secured once again to the chain.

"Show off!" Cleo blurted, and then, "What does it feel like, doing what you do?"

Ash considered. "At first, in the *wadi*, it was like pulling strings, or pushing buttons. I felt something like a vibration, and things would move the way I wanted them to. The jeep thing was so sudden I didn't think at all, an explosion in my head before the actual explosion. I may have been thinking when I threw you out of the way, but I'm not even sure of that."

"What about the target shooting? Can you really move the bullets the way you want them to go? That's some major voodoo!"

She shrugged. "Focus. Bearing down, sort of boring a hole through space and sending orders through it. I worked on focus this morning when I was sure nobody was looking, opening and closing things, making pencils float around. Just moving things through the air feels different from making them disappear and appear somewhere else, but I don't know exactly what the difference is."

"How about taking the keys out of my pocket?"

Cleo had looked like she'd felt something more than just the keys moving. Ash was sure of it. Was it only because she wanted to be sure of it?

"That was..." Ash paused. "What did it feel like to you?"

26

"It felt like your hand, your actual hand, in my pocket, feeling me up. The way you did in Paris."

"I felt it, too. Like real touching. Nothing else I've moved felt like real touching."

How far could that go? Ash guessed Cleo was wondering that, too. She focused again on the hand deep in her own pocket, and imagined it reaching out invisibly to stroke down Cleo's back and over her tight butt. By the way Cleo twitched, that butt must be tingling. Ash's actual hands moving in her pockets made her own flesh tingle, too.

"Ash! How far can we take this?"

Ash smiled. Cleo's keys began to move again—and then the canvas flap lifted. Someone peered in.

They stood immobile, still four feet apart, but clearly not shooting at the targets. The intruder backed out without a word.

Ash sighed. "I'm being followed. They'll want to know where to find me when that specialist arrives."

Cleo got her breathing under control. "So maybe playing hide-the-keys isn't our best strategy right now."

"It was your idea," Ash said reasonably. "You challenged me to move something out of my line of sight. And you said we should take this power thing for a spin. Why not have some fun?" Her tone changed. "There's so much to learn, so much I don't know. And I don't dare let anybody but you know too much."

"There was this movie a while back," Cleo said carefully. "Something like *Men Who Stare at Goats*, about trying to use people with psychic powers in the military. Stupid damned movie, but I just wondered whether that specialist flying in to interview you might be involved with something like that, instead of regular technology."

"Of course he is! Probably some character who thinks he can read minds. But there's no way I'll let them use this...this thing, for destruction, no matter how noble they think their motives are." Saying it to Cleo strengthened Ash's resolve. "I have to use it, not let it go to waste. It's going to be *me* deciding what's worth doing. I've given the Army everything they asked of me up to now, willingly, but this is different."

"No disagreement there, except…" Cleo sank onto the bench behind them, looking like she was envisioning some grim possibilities. Ash sat too, her head drooping into her hands. So much for cockiness. She wished Cleo hadn't shot down her good mood, but knew they had to face things squarely.

"I was just wondering," Cleo said after a while. "You moved me away from the explosion. Could you move yourself like that? I mean, if…"

Ash raised her head. "You mean if I were restrained somehow? In prison? Or worse?"

"Right." Then Cleo went on, clearly trying to divert her, "Hey, how about we experiment now? I'll try to restrain you, and you see if you can get away without a physical struggle."

"You'll do anything to get your arms around me, won't you?" The mounting desire that had been derailed by the momentary intruder came surging back.

"Absolutely," Cleo said, and didn't say more because then, snoopers be damned, their arms wrapped tightly around each other, no brittleness at all in their eager bodies, and their mouths got too occupied savoring whatever skin was within reach to bother with words. Ash nearly managed to subdue the fear that this might be the very last time she'd ever have a chance to kiss Cleo, and hold her, and be held.

They'd paused for breath by the time they heard the approach of people, maybe really coming, this time, to use the range. All at once Ash was three feet from Cleo and aiming toward a target, revolver in hand. She thought for a moment that she had moved herself away until she remembered what their relative positions had been. She'd moved Cleo away from her instead. She glanced sideways, gave a subtle shake of her head, and shrugged. One question, at least, answered; she couldn't use her power to move herself. Not yet, anyway. It didn't much matter as long as she could move an attacker away, but prison walls could be a problem.

A few more practice shots to make things look normal, and then they left, walking slowly.

"What are you going to do when this hotshot specialist gets here?"

"Get out of here as fast as I can."

Cleo must have suspected that already, but she looked as though hearing it was a punch to the gut.

"I can't do it on my own," Ash went on, "out here in the middle of nowhere. He may even arrive today. I'll just say as little as possible, like, 'I don't know what happened, everything was a blur. Maybe it was one of those things you hear about people doing under extreme stress. Maybe it really was some super-strong explosive we've never heard of'—you know the kind of thing. And if I have to, I'll pretend to go along with whatever they want, whatever tests they have in mind, and learn all I can from them. If he's flying in, chances are he'll need to fly me out to whatever headquarters they have for things like this. Who knows, they might even want to use me for some humanitarian cause that I can't refuse, but if not, I'll take off before they can get much of anything going."

There was another possibility she hadn't mentioned. "They might want to talk to me, too," Cleo said, "as a witness. Or something. From what Corporal Jones saw, they might even think it was me doing some fancy mechanical tricks."

"But it wasn't. You can't take the rap for me, any of it. And you can't outright lie to them."

"Wanna bet? I'm good at it. I won't tell them anything about what happened in the *wadi*. I'll just say pretty much what you said you'll say. 'All a blur, don't understand, extreme stress, yadda yadda yadda.'" Cleo looked behind them, then all around. "I'm surprised they aren't keeping us apart so we won't collaborate on what to say."

"No surprise to me. We're being watched. Those two at the range? One of 'em is a file clerk at Headquarters. Look, she's just walking behind that tent over there. Mighty short shooting practice. I'll bet she never willingly touched a gun in her life."

Cleo began to look over that way, then suddenly, intently, stared into the too-bright sky. A few seconds later, Ash caught the pulsating soundwaves, too. A chopper. And another one quite a bit farther away.

"Could that be your guy already?" Cleo asked. "Seems too soon."

Ash shaded her narrowed eyes. "That's a medevac, with both patient transfer panniers filled. I hadn't heard that there was any fighting today in this sector!" She started off toward the hospital landing pad, Cleo following.

There was a crowd there waiting. Ash saw a nurse she knew. "What's up?"

"Village kids," the nurse said bitterly. "Stumbled over old landmines while they were herding goats. I've seen this before, but it never gets easier." She couldn't say any more. Ash put a comforting arm around her.

"That chopper has problems," Cleo said urgently. "The rotors are out of sync. Just a little, but I know by the sound, and it's getting worse." People close enough to hear her looked up, and others caught the tension and looked too. By then the helicopter was jerking and shaking so much that anybody could tell it was in big trouble. A transfer pannier was even drooping at one end, some of its supports shaken loose. Could the bird manage to land safely? Would the pannier hold on?

"Ash!"

Her body tensed like a bowstring, and she and Cleo instinctively backed away from the crowd. She aimed her focus at the incoming aircraft, feeling power shoot from her like a bright arrow. In the turmoil all around, while emergency fire and rescue personnel swarmed through the crowd of onlookers, she stood straight and still, heat rising inside her, and Cleo stood with her. No one else could have seen the arm at Ash's side reach forward slightly, fingers curving just enough that they could have held something precious, and fragile, if it had been there to hold. The late afternoon sun glaring onto the pavement cast a dark shadow of Ash and that hand, magnifying them to huge proportions warped by the angle of the light, but no one saw that, either, besides Cleo, or would have thought anything of it if they had.

Everyone looked up in horrified fascination. Just two hundred feet above the earth the helicopter began to spin entirely out of control, falling fast—but at fifty feet it abruptly slowed, still wobbling, moved just the amount needed to hover over the landing pad, and settled onto the ground as though some giant hand had caught it and set it gently down.

Ash looked down, saw her own huge shadow, and felt in danger of settling down onto the ground herself, but Cleo was right there to support her.

Her nurse friend, still nearby, came to help. "That was... incredible!" she said. "I'm in the business of praying for miracles, and seeing them once in a great while, but that was something else! It would shake anybody up." She did look rather oddly at Ash, but had to rush over to help unload a patient from a pannier. Ash caught a glimpse of a child cocooned in bandages, a girl with long, bloodied hair.

The second helicopter, the daily Black Hawk transport to and from the major airfield near the capital city, landed at some distance from the first without anyone paying much attention. In a few minutes Ash recovered enough to walk away with Cleo, mingling with the crowd. As far as she could tell, they'd lost their tail, at least for the moment. They strolled around inside the perimeter walls as though just getting some mild exercise.

"Cleo," Ash said at last, "all that with the helicopter—it couldn't have been rigged, could it? To test what I could do?"

"No! That 'copter was about to crash, I guarantee, and everyone in it was going to die, including the little girl being unloaded. There was a malfunction that unbalanced the rotors. I knew by the sound even before the flight got erratic."

Ash picked up on Cleo's icy tone and knew her question had sounded—had been—incredibly self-centered. "I'm sorry. It's just that...if I could keep that huge piece of machinery from crashing, could I learn to make one crash, instead? Maybe even bring down low-flying planes?"

"I don't know, could you?" The chill lingered in Cleo's voice.

"I don't know either." Ash shook her head slowly. "I don't know what I could do if it mattered enough to me. Like keeping you from blowing up with the jeep. But if that guy is really coming from some unit where they study this sort of thing—telekinesis, I guess they call it, or something paranormal, anyway—who knows what they might want me to do?"

"Having second thoughts? You said you were going to see what you could learn from them, at least for a while."

"I am. I have to. But I've got to move on pretty soon. This guy may be my ticket, at least part of the way. Wherever he's coming from, it has to be somewhere other than in the middle of endless desert. I agree to go along with what they want for a while, find out what, if anything, they can teach me, and then I get lost, disappear, hit the road, and figure out what's really worth doing with what I've been given."

"Sounds like a bad case of save-the-world syndrome." But Cleo didn't sound so upset with her anymore. "Most of that makes sense, except assuming that you can scarper off whenever you decide it's time. Not that I'd bet against you." She laughed a little. "Did you read superhero comics when you were a kid?"

It felt good to be joking around again. "Not much. My brother did, but I was more interested in the girlie magazines he hid under his mattress."

"Well, of course! But next thing you know you'll find yourself in a skin-tight onesie, a mask, and a billowing cape."

"What, no sparkly bikini with boots? Just as well. And I draw the line at wearing a cape."

"It could have a have a big dark silhouette of a hand on it." Ash flinched at that, but Cleo didn't stop. "A Shadow Hand! And you could have cards printed with a black hand on them, to leave at the sites of your victories."

"Forget the costume. And the cards." Ash got serious again. "First I'll have to figure out where I can do the most good. I'm damned sure not going to be bringing down planes or helicopters, no matter what."

"That's good to know, in case I get an urge to fly someplace myself."

Ash gave her the mock swat that comment deserved.

They kept on, together, but Ash couldn't help wondering whether they could ever be together again the way they had been before all this weird drama came along. She was sure Cleo wondered that, too.

There was a limit to how long they could take to walk around the base, and somewhere along the line the clerk who had been sent to follow them picked up their trail again. By that time, they were approaching Ash's tent, and there was no more good excuse for them to be hanging out together. Neither had approached the issue of what role, if any, Cleo could play in all of this.

Through two years of being together in the jeep almost daily, carrying out missions that could go from routine to deadly in an instant, they had opened themselves to each other bit by bit. They'd grown closer, laughing, sharing memories, bonding, becoming more than comrades-in-arms, much more than friends. Those days and years were over now. The jeep was gone, and Ash was, one way or another, going. Even camaraderie seemed to be draining away.

Cleo jerked her head sharply in the direction of the dutiful spy lurking behind a trash bin. "How about putting on a show worth watching? What have we got to lose?" Her tone was harsh, not disguising the emotion beneath. "How about I fuck you up against a wall?"

"Don't." Ash's voice felt rough, too, in her throat. "Keep it together until your tour is up and you're legit to leave. I'll probably have disappeared by then, and they may follow you to see if you know where I've gone."

"So I don't get to know."

Anything more Ash might have said—not that she could think of anything—was cut short. Colonel Rogers was waiting at her tent.

"Lieutenant, your contact is here, and wants to see you right away." She glanced at Cleo, her expression sympathetic. "Maybe Sergeant Brown can help you pack your bags. I'll send someone to pick them up. You're being transferred for an indeterminate period."

"Ma'am, but I'll be out of the service in eight months. Is that long enough to bother...?"

"Lieutenant, I'm sure you've read the small print. You serve at the pleasure of the president. Your tour can be extended for purposes of national security." She seemed about to say more, but instead turned aside to let them enter the tent alone.

What did it mean that the colonel had come herself instead of sending a messenger? It did seem like she wanted to let Ash and Cleo have a few last minutes together.

"Transferred!" Cleo folded what few bits of clothing Ash had unpacked when they'd returned to base and shoved them savagely into a duffle bag. Everything in the jeep had been destroyed, but most of their gear had been in a baggage truck ahead in the convoy. "How do they know already that you have what they want? Does this guy think he's some kind of psychic?" She slumped onto the stripped bunk. "Maybe he really is."

Ash grasped both arms and pulled her up, squeezing hard enough it had to hurt. Something in the back of her head that wasn't quite her own mind, something like the buzz that came with using her power, urged her to move away from Cleo. She tried to resist it. "Cleo, you're the best, most real, true thing in my world, even though I have to do this. You know I do. Maybe someday..."

But the colonel lifted the tent flap, Ash gave Cleo one huge damn-the-consequences hug, and then she left.

The "guy" waiting in Colonel Rogers's office turned out to be a dangerously attractive major, fortyish, strong and elegantly built, with hair as dark as Ash's except for silver wings at her temples. Her well-cut uniform included a trim, mid-length skirt—as rare as it was impractical here in the desert where minor sandstorms weren't rare at all. She looked like she should have been in an office at the Pentagon.

Colonel Rogers made the introductions. "Mac, this is Lieutenant Ashton, Ash to her friends. Ash, this is Major Margaret McAllister. She and I were in training together, as well as on that trial medical mission I mentioned. We're lucky she happened to be in the country on other business just now."

The major strode toward Ash, or appeared to, even though the office was too small for actual striding. Her energy made it feel even smaller. Ash saluted and then reached out to shake hands, but the major grasped both of her arms.

"Lieutenant Ashton, I have never seen anything like what you did for that helicopter today! Magnificent work!"

It was a statement of certainty, not a question. How did she know? Had someone seen and told her? That might leave some room for denial. Or had she seen for herself? Ash tried to play for time. "When did you get here, Major? I didn't expect you so soon."

"I was in the other helicopter, the one that's waiting for us right now for our first lap on the way to Berlin. I hope never to have such a heart-stopping view of tragedy in the making again, but your extraordinary save almost makes the experience worth it."

This wasn't an interview at all. No questions to answer. Ash figured she might as well ask some of her own. "I was as terrified as anyone else, Major. What makes you think I had anything to do with that?"

"I don't need to think. I know. I have an instinct for these things. That's why I have this job." She turned to the desk and picked up a cup of coffee. "You're wondering whether I read minds, right?"

Something about the woman raised Ash's hackles, but appealed to her anyway. Something about her also made Ash forget about deference due to rank. "*Do* you read minds, Major?"

"No. Not word by word. But I know truth from lies, and I know when a certain energy is present. An energy you might call power. Yours, by the way, is off the charts." She emptied the coffee cup and smiled like the Cheshire cat in Disney's *Alice in Wonderland*. "Yes, there are folks in my department obsessive enough to make charts of these things. Those who can do; those who can't make charts. And those of us in between, like me, sniff out new talent the way a bird dog flushes pheasants."

"So you see me as a pheasant?"

Major McAllister seemed to be enjoying the exchange. "Lieutenant, you're from Montana, right? Do you hunt birds with dogs out there?"

"We hunt bears with dogs."

Colonel Rogers tried to hide a smile. Major McAllister laughed out loud. "Bears! I like the sound of that. My bosses would rather I brought them pheasants, or rabbits—anything timid or malleable. Someone with an inner bear is going to make life interesting."

"As long as it isn't boring." Ash realized that she was tacitly agreeing to go along with this woman. Not that she had any choice. Yet.

The helicopter with the damaged rotors was still on the hospital landing pad, so the bigger, long-distance Black Hawk took off from farther down the field. There were people milling around—mechanics, curious onlookers, MPs. When Ash looked down from a few hundred feet in the air, one slight figure stood out from all the rest. Cleo was gesturing and conversing with a group of mechanics, but as Ash's gaze fell on her, she looked up, stood straight and rigid as a flagpole, and watched until the helicopter banked, turned, and rose high into the blazing sunlight, heading west until Ash could no longer even pretend that she still saw her.

CHAPTER 3

EARLY THE NEXT MORNING, CLEO strode purposefully up the Headquarters walkway, nearly running down a messenger Colonel Rogers had just dispatched.

Once in the office, Cleo saluted, then got bluntly down to business. "Colonel, you've got to find me something to do. Something that matters. I'll go crazy without important work to distract me." By the colonel's expression, she understood Cleo's underlying anguish. Cleo forged ahead, slightly more diplomatically. "That medical mission you sent us…me…on was so rewarding that I'm spoiled for just hanging around the motor pool being the go-to advisor for every little glitch of a fractious jeep." Drat, poor choice of words for someone who'd just allowed her own jeep to be destroyed.

"Sit down, Sergeant," Colonel Rogers said calmly. "We have a good deal to discuss."

Cleo pulled over a metal folding chair and sat on its edge, unable to relax.

"I've read your report, and heard Lieutenant Ashton's, and had confirmation from someone trained in these matters, so certain things are not in doubt. I'd still like to have the benefit of your expertise on one point. Do you consider it really possible that the odd behavior of your jeep was due to technological advances known to the enemy?"

Cleo's mouth opened. No words came out. How much to say?

"Let me rephrase that, Sergeant. Do you consider it at all likely that that could be the case?"

Damn the torpedoes. Full speed ahead. "No, ma'am. Not at all likely."

"Thank you. That's all I needed to ask." She hit the intercom button and ordered coffee brought in for two.

"Now, on to the subject of missions. I've been thinking along those same lines. With only three months left in your tour, it would be a shame to waste your skills."

An aide brought in the coffee, poured it, and left. The colonel shifted gears. "I don't suppose I could persuade you to rethink the matter of re-upping?" Cleo could almost hear the omitted words— "under these changed circumstances"—meaning now that Ash had gone. "I understand you've already been offered promotion if you stayed on. I might even be able to arrange one of greater magnitude."

Cleo's curt, direct "No, ma'am," brought an understanding nod from the colonel, who returned to the previous topic.

"There may be a mission in the works. I've had a dozen messages this morning already that lead me to think that what happened to those children yesterday, common as it unfortunately is, has been some kind of tipping point. Come back at 1700 hours and we'll see what's developed."

Cleo's stride was as brisk leaving as when she'd come, but her mood was less grim. A mine-clearing assignment was just what she needed. Humanitarian mine-clearing—as opposed to the military kind that used big machinery to clear routes for troops to advance— worked best with manual detection, something she was as good at as anyone she'd ever met. At least, anyone left alive. Metal detectors are sensitive enough to pick up most mines, but they also yield about a thousand false positives for every correct identification, and minimum-metal mines are almost impossible for them to detect. Areas that had theoretically been cleared by machines were the most dangerous of all to villagers, especially children, since they'd think the area was safe.

Cleo returned to Headquarters at 1600 hours, a bit early, and was called right into the colonel's office.

"Pack your bags, Sergeant. You'll be leaving at dawn with a combined UN/US Army demining squad."

"Bags already packed, Colonel."

"Why am I not surprised?" Colonel Rogers grinned, and Cleo mustered something closer to a legitimate smile than she would have thought possible eight hours earlier.

Fourteen hours later, she was behind the wheel of a new jeep, part of a convoy of deminers and their gear. Quite a few of the guys were old friends from the days before she'd known Ash, when she'd done demining most of the time. So much territory had been cleared—and the use of whole fields of mines largely discontinued by the enemy in favor of roadside IEDs and targeted rockets—that demining hadn't been high priority any more. She'd been reassigned. This was like a high school reunion, with explosives instead of a cash bar.

The first day, in the province where the kids had been injured, they found and detonated six mines, a couple so old they might have been there for fifty years. Cleo found those two, buried deeper than the others, and signaled to her partner.

"Hey Cleo, still got it, I see."

"Both still just as crazy, right?"

"And lucky," Mitch said, but as the sapper who did the detonating, he was the one who needed the most luck. Cleo could detect a concealed explosive from far enough away to keep mostly out of danger. She'd tried to teach others her methods, but it seemed to be an instinct that couldn't be passed on.

They moved across the province slowly, thoroughly, then on to another further south, eliminating hundreds of deathtraps, not that Cleo kept score.

She did keep score of the erratic mail deliveries—the post office back at base always knew where she was, and would forward any mail—but nothing came from Ash. Not that she'd expected anything.

Two weeks before her tour came to an end, she was summoned back to base, and to Colonel Rogers's office. The colonel wasn't alone.

"Major, this is Sergeant Brown. Sergeant, Major McAllister is with the PsyOps division. She escorted Lieutenant Ashton to one of their training facilities."

Cleo's first thought upon meeting the major was, *No wonder Ash went off with her! I might have done it myself.* Her next was to wonder why she was being questioned, when they already had Ash and must know what she could do. A glance at Colonel Rogers assured her that there wasn't any tragic news involved, so she just waited in at-ease stance to find out what was what.

The major greeted Cleo warmly, commenting on her excellent performance as a mine detector, but that was clearly just a prelude to whatever she'd actually come for.

"Colonel Rogers was telling me that she hasn't heard from Lieutenant Ashton since leaving her at the PsyOps facility," the major said conversationally, "so we were wondering if you'd had any letters."

So Ash had gotten away! And hadn't contacted Cleo. "No, nothing. Nothing at all." Cleo let her pain show through. "I figured you folks were keeping her too busy with whatever it is you do."

"As a matter of fact," the major said, "she hasn't been seen since a few days after she arrived."

"You mean she's either gone AWOL, or been...been..." Cleo pulled herself together. "What happened?"

"I was away on other business, so all I know is what I've heard, but there isn't any doubt that she left on her own accord. Apparently she literally "lifted" documents and a military ID from a staff member who fit her description closely enough to get her on a commercial flight to Amsterdam. From there she transferred multiple times, and effectively disappeared."

Major McAllister watched Cleo keenly as she spoke, obviously to see whether she knew the details of Ash's escape already. She might even have deliberately changed details to see Cleo's reaction, in case it revealed that Ash had communicated with her in some way.

Cleo didn't try to conceal her hurt that she hadn't—or her happiness that Ash had pulled off the caper. Served them right.

Any agency claiming to specialize in paranormal powers that didn't realize what someone with telekinesis could do to evade them clearly had nothing Lieutenant Ashton wanted to bother with.

Neither did Cleo Brown, she thought, then mentally kicked herself. What she didn't know, she couldn't tell. And even though she'd never tell, she might follow, and be followed.

Major McAllister switched the conversation back to Cleo herself, showing an interest in her uncanny talent for detecting even the oldest, most deeply buried mines, and in her record of extraordinary skills with all kinds of machinery. She even made a subtle reference to the possibility of promotion if Cleo changed her mind and stayed on, just as Colonel Rogers had.

Something about the major's voice, her expressions, her apparent warmth, was dangerously appealing. Cleo didn't think she could read minds, and suspected that what she did owed more to intuition and presence than to any paranormal ability, but whatever it was, she was damned good at it. If Cleo did have any idea where Ash was, or even where she might be, would she be able to hide it from this woman? Yes, Cleo thought, she would, but it was just as well she didn't have to try—although that battle of wits might have been highly enjoyable.

By the time their meeting was at an end, Cleo had an odd impression that Major McAllister had discovered things about her that she didn't even know herself.

Cleo spent that night at base, her last before rejoining the squad of deminers and heading toward the capital city, where she'd officially part ways with the Army. She lay sleepless on her cot for a long time, wondering if things would have been different if she'd suggested to Ash that the two of them together could make a big dent in the landmines and IEDs endangering, among many others, children herding their goats. With Cleo's instinct for pinpointing camouflaged explosives, and Ash's power to move them to a safe area for detonation, or disarm them at a distance once Cleo explained exactly how to do it, they could have covered twice as much territory as most squads. Would she have stayed around longer? Would that kind of mission have satisfied her determination to do great work with her new power? Would she have been allowed to? Not likely.

Cleo twisted and turned on the hard bed. The squad's route would take them right past that same ruined fortress, that same *wadi*. The place where her life had been changed, and Ash's, and the lives of who knew how many people in the future. If only she could find that damned statue, smash it, grind it into tiny specks of sand! But it was too late now.

Better, she reasoned, to do what she could with what basic talents she had, and wish Ash well on her crusade to do big, important things—more important, at least, than Cleo ever would.

Reason didn't cut it, though, when she was tossing on her cot in the desert heat, mind spinning through endless loops of memory. She was fixated on desperate longings for what might have been, and useless speculation on what might be happening now. Was Ash safe? Did she think of Cleo at all, or had power made her so full of herself that there was no room left?

"Stop it!" Cleo told herself severely, and eventually managed to obey. She must have slept, because dreams came—dreams of Ash, in the little room in Montmartre, where the whole world had contracted into just the two of them, together, touching, loving. Ash's hand stroked Cleo's cheek, moved down over her neck, shoulder, all the way to the warmth between her thighs, and Cleo was brought to a shuddering peak. She woke slowly to a sense of joy. A good dream. And what harm was there in thinking of how it had felt when Ash had probed her pocket for the keys with her mind, and said she'd felt it, too?

Only a dream. Cleo knew that. Ash wasn't dreaming of her at the same time, wanting her, touching her. It might not even be night where she was. Cleo put herself back to sleep trying to compute what time it was in various zones in the world, while still, down deep where reason and common sense couldn't reach, a lingering memory whispered, *"Just like real touching."*

The squad stopped for a lunch break in sight of the ancient ruins. They'd all heard the story about what had happened to Cleo and her jeep there, or at least a small part of the story, and they humored her when she said she'd lost something over in that *wadi* and wanted to take a look to see if she could find it. Alone.

Down in the dry river bed, the area where they'd hidden was pretty much all rubble now. The air was still, but every now and then dust swirled around her head, and pebbles slid and bounced from the bank, some even hitting her. She had a definite sense of being unwelcome, even though her rational side knew it must be her imagination fueled by memories.

Ash thought the damned statue still kept an eye on her. Did that mean the goddess would know where she was? Cleo had about got over wanting to smash the figurine, but why not give in to imagination and try making use of it? Not so easy, since the bitch had taken a disliking to her, but Cleo had been wondering for a while whether that was a case of mistaken identity. Maybe the goddess had been fooled by her boyish looks.

A quick glance up at the rim of the bank showed that her privacy was being respected. "Look, you!" She unbuttoned her shirt and wriggled out of her sports bra. The dust stopped threatening to get into her eyes, at least. She cupped her small breasts in her hands and turned in a circle to display them, torn between laughing at her own absurdity and longing for the touch of Ash's hands instead of her own. "Look, you," she repeated, "whatever you are, I'm a woman, and Ash needs me whether she realizes it or not. If you know where she is, tell me right now!" She unbuttoned her belt and let her pants drop. "See?" Then she thought all those words again as hard as she could in case the goddess didn't speak English. After all, why should she?

A very small opening appeared right about where they'd been able to see out when they were hiding, and no more pebbles rolled down the bank. Cleo stared, wondering whether it would expand, what might come out of it, until she began to feel dizzy. Her vision clouded, darkened, then suddenly cleared, but what she saw wasn't the *wadi*. It was an opening, like an airplane window. It *was* an airplane window! She could look down through a widening gap in the clouds and see the earth beneath, close enough that the plane must be planning to land within the hour. The landmarks below—the oxbow of a river, a short, low line of green hills, a sprawling reservoir—were as familiar to her as any in the world.

The vision faded slowly, and before it was gone completely Cleo had pulled up her pants and buttoned her shirt. There was no way some ancient piece of stone or bone far in the Middle East could have made up that scene. She needed to believe, *had* to believe that it was what Ash was seeing right now—which meant that Cleo knew exactly where Ash was, and where she was going, and where she herself was going to go as soon as she possibly could. If Ash was going to Boston, it could only be because she hoped to find Cleo there. Because Ash needed her.

CHAPTER 4

As THE HELICOPTER ROSE FROM the base and headed west, Ash twisted and turned, keeping Cleo's straight, still form in sight for as long as she possibly could. The hollow feeling in the pit of her stomach was standard for the rising aircraft, but the emptiness in her heart, her mind, came from leaving Cleo behind. And there was more to it. Ash suddenly felt that she was leaving herself behind, the self she'd always known. All the selves she'd been. The young tomboy on her grandfather's failing ranch. The teenager working nights and weekends in a diner and summers with horse trek outfitters guiding tourists up into the Absarokee Mountains, where she would look out over the seemingly endless plains and long to discover the world beyond. The student struggling to hold a job and still keep her grades up enough to get and then keep her scholarship to Montana State in Bozeman. The newly-fledged lieutenant off to see the world, and the seasoned soldier who'd seen altogether too much, without flinching, so often with Cleo at her side and in her heart. All of those were herself, the self she knew. But who was she now? Had part of her been left back in that dratted *wadi*, or changed forever? More to the point, what had been added, and what could she do about it? How much could she do, if she only knew what that should be?

Major McAllister sat on the right side of the chopper, with Ash on the left. Two officers behind them were riding along to the airfield on their own business. The major stared through the small window toward the north, and just before the chopper banked again to turn southwest, Ash caught a glimpse past her of the distant mountains. Then they were out of sight. The major straightened, an intense, brooding emotion lingering on her face that quickly vanished when she saw Ash watching. Those mountains meant something deeply personal to her. Ash was sure of it. She was no mind reader, or—what was the term, empath? Still, you couldn't be a good officer without learning to read your companions' moods to some extent. If a young soldier under Ash's command had looked like that, she would have reached out, and listened if they needed to talk. Had she herself looked like that while she watched Cleo's straight, lonely figure shrink into invisibility? If so, the major, so intent on those mountains, couldn't have noticed, which was a relief. Ash had no desire at all for sympathy from this woman. What she did have was a need for information. What was their ultimate destination? *"On our way to Berlin,"* McAllister had said, but that might not be their last stop. Wherever it was, how restricted would she be?

Conversation was next to impossible with the din of the Black Hawk's rotors hammering their ears. The major, all traces of deep emotion erased, flashed a wide, aren't-we-having-a-jolly-adventure grin, produced a packet of chewing gum from a pocket, and held up a stick with a questioning quirk of her eyebrow.

Ash nodded. She was about to reach out across the narrow aisle between them when the major deliberately tossed the stick of gum too far forward for her to easily catch.

Ash didn't even try. What a stupid trick, with other passengers behind them who might notice if the gum moved toward her on its own, although a quick glance over her shoulder showed both officers leaning back and apparently dozing. She stared stonily across the aisle. The major shrugged apologetically, unbuckled her seat belt, and leaned forward to retrieve the gum. Ash waited a few beats to make her point. Then, with McAllister straight in her seat again, her body blocking the view of those behind, the gum blinked out of existence in her hand and back into existence in Ash's. It didn't take spoken words to get the message across: *Screw your little tricks.*

After that, Ash pretended to concentrate on the land below, in all its monotony. She'd traveled much of that sandy earth, breathed it in and coughed it out when sudden winds sprang up, shaded her eyes against its glare when the sun was high, and come to find an austere beauty in its sweeping vistas. But the view from above held little interest, she'd had very little rest last night, and the noise of the rotors, annoying as it had been at first, was so unrelentingly regular that she soon dozed off like the others.

More than dozed. She was deep in sleep when the regular throb of the rotors altered enough to be noticed. As she rose slowly toward wakefulness, resisting, resenting the noise, she fuzzily envisioned the rotors, wanting to make them stop. The muscles of her hand began to tighten...

"NO!" McAllister was instantly on top of her, pressing her hands down with a savage grip. "Wake up! We're about to land at the airfield!"

Consciousness came like a hard, vicious slap. From the major's expression, it would have been an actual slap if she hadn't been using both hands to restrain Ash.

"What? Did I...?"

"No, but you came too damned close!"

"How could you tell?" Ash didn't try to deny it. There was a hint of a tingle in her right hand.

"I could feel your energy gathering. For God's sake, learn some control before you kill yourself and everyone around you!" At such close quarters, it was all too easy to hear the major's fury even though she kept her voice low. She eased off, releasing Ash's hands. "I'd been wondering whether taking you to the PsyCenter was the best plan after all, but you've clearly got a whole lot more learning to do." Her tone slumped from anger into frustration. "I'd hoped..." She shook her head and swung back into her own seat. In the whole attack-and-retreat maneuver, Ash didn't think the major's sleek skirt had once slid above knee level. That took talent.

Ash felt too wrung out, too ashamed, to ask what the major had hoped for. She knew, had known all along, that she had to learn to control a power that could be deadly. If they had only left her alone, with Cleo to support her, steady her! Cleo had already been helping her to test herself—subtly, carefully, feeling out what she could do and how to control it.

But she'd left Cleo behind without even a struggle. It didn't matter that resistance wouldn't have done any good. She'd owed it to Cleo to try. She could have pointed out that Cleo had been with her at the start, and every time she'd done something major—the jeep, the medevac about to crash. Maybe Ash couldn't do as much without her. In spite of how strong the thrill of power made her feel at times, maybe she really, really couldn't.

Before meeting Cleo, Ash had been more or less on her own since her early teens, but she'd never felt as alone as she did now.

They transferred to an Army plane headed, Ash noticed, to Munich, not Berlin. Whatever their actual destination, the major didn't want it widely known. Ash wasn't surprised. She didn't bother to ask where they were going, but turned to her companion once they were at cruising altitude.

"Major, I apologize for my negligence. But I want to assure you that I couldn't have damaged the 'copter's rotors even if I'd tried. I need to see things before I can affect them, or at least have them in my line of sight." It didn't seem necessary to mention the key ring in Cleo's pocket. That was something else entirely. Something profoundly private.

"Don't count on that. You haven't known before what you could do until you did it. There'll be more times like that. Just be damned well prepared to stop yourself if your impulse is wrong." McAllister didn't sound angry anymore, just tired.

"I will. I'll learn whatever they can teach me." That much, Ash thought, was absolute honesty. How she used what she learned would be her own business.

The major sighed, then startled Ash by nearly echoing her thoughts. "Lieutenant, I'll be honest with you. You'd better manage to learn more than they can teach you. They'll have no idea what to do with you. Oh, they'll have plenty of ideas about things they want you to do for them, but not how to train you to do them. We've never found anyone with quite your talents before. Nobody who could do more than move a chess piece or flip a card, although we have some hotshots who can read your mind enough to know what cards you're holding. Don't get suckered into any poker games."

The major's odd lack of military formality in spite of her immaculate uniform had been evident from the start, but the way she was talking now to a junior officer was astounding. How did she get away with it? Maybe she didn't, entirely. If she'd been in training with Colonel Rogers, she hadn't been promoted as far, as soon.

"What you'll get, I hope," she went on, "is space to experiment, try things out, without worrying about panicking bystanders. There are more places in this world than you might think where you'd be accused of witchcraft."

"If they can't help me, why couldn't I do all that experimentation someplace else?" Someplace in Montana, in the mountains, Ash thought wistfully, with a cabin in a forest-ringed meadow, an Appaloosa mare grazing out back, and Cleo to share her bed and her life. And, knowing Cleo, a couple of old junkers out front to tinker with until they became stealth race cars.

"Reg-u-la-tions, of course." McAllister's tone was mocking, and more than a touch bitter. "Besides, it's my job to deliver you there. My 'patriotic duty' as an officer and a, well, whatever." For a couple of minutes, she was silent, then said abruptly, "Hell, I may be wrong about what they can do. There are a couple of other PsyCenters, much farther away, and this one has been declining for the last year. A new director has just been appointed, though. I haven't even met him yet. Maybe he'll do better. I hear through the grapevine that he's a bit of a loose cannon, which isn't necessarily a bad thing." She must have noticed Ash's expression, half shock and half barely suppressed laughter. "You're thinking I'm pretty much a loose cannon, too. Why not? None of us involved with Psy research are what you'd call normal. What use would we be if we were?"

Now Ash did laugh. "Then Cleo—Sergeant Brown—would fit right in. You should have brought her along, too."

McAllister turned serious. "I thought about that. But something tells me that she has more important things to do where she is, for now."

In Munich, they boarded a much smaller plane. When it headed approximately north by northeast Ash was even less surprised than she'd been on the first flight. This was a route she'd flown before.

"Hohenfels?" she asked, but it wasn't really a question.

"You got it. Familiar territory, right?"

The Joint Multinational Readiness Center at Hohenfels was a major base for training soldiers before they were sent to assignments in the Middle East, although the Bavarian hills and villages weren't at all like the terrain and culture where they'd be going. Four years ago, Ash, already missing the forested mountain slopes in Montana she'd been so eager to leave behind, had taken full advantage of all the running trails steep enough to be challenging, and even managed a couple of trips for Alpine skiing in the south. The training had been rough, and Ash had been glad enough to leave, but life since then had been even rougher, and the green woodlands would be a welcome change. If, that is, she'd be allowed the freedom to enjoy them.

"I never heard of the PsyCenter. It must be pretty hush-hush, which makes sense, I guess."

"It's only been there for about three years. I never did know who pulled what strings to get the funding, but they've had just about enough in the way of results to keep it going."

"What do you consider 'results'?" Ash figured she might as well be as frank as the major. "Psychic warfare?"

"Hah. They wish. Nothing proven yet. A guy who can tell what card somebody in another room is holding might be able to read a document somebody else is reading, but strings of words are more complicated than numbered cards with simple pictures. Besides, they'd have to get the card-reading guy in the room next to the document guy, when he was actually viewing the document, and that's not about to happen any time soon. And predicting the flip of a coin even three times out of four is still poor odds when they need to know which way a tank is going to fire next. Naturally, the prime form of entertainment there is betting on or against each other." Her tone became more thoughtful, and a bit sad. "There are also some seriously gifted people there, and a couple of seriously disturbed ones who should be getting help instead of being made to perform, but no actual weaponization has been worked out. Yet. Not that they aren't trying."

Ash hadn't missed her use of "they" instead of "we," yet McAllister was the one forcing her to join this ominously screwball group. Probably just a trick along the lines of "good cop, bad cop."

"So you think I could move the document itself into *your* hot little hands, if I could be, say, in the same building? I already told you I have to be able to see the objects I move."

Ash's emphasis on "your" didn't escape the major, whose lips twitched into a near smile. She gazed at Ash thoughtfully for a long minute. "Not even if the object is in someone's pocket? Someone very…close?"

So she was more of a mind reader than she'd let on. Ash gazed levelly back at her and didn't answer. Finally, the major shook her head. "Just a very fuzzy impression I got. Once in a while, when someone's on a wavelength very close to mine, I can see a few things." She paused again, then shrugged. "I've never told them that at the Center, so I'd appreciate it if you don't, either. And don't, whatever you do, show them more about what you can do than you absolutely have to. Official questions, direct orders if you can't avoid them, yes, but don't make things too easy for them too soon."

This time Ash came right out with it. "'Them'? You've got this 'good cop' thing down pat."

"One of my many talents." McAllister's grin was wide but brief.

CHAPTER 5

THE PSYCENTER TURNED OUT TO be in a looming stone building high on a hillside and set partially into the earth behind it, bunker-style. Barbed wire–topped concrete walls surrounded it, but there was no other indication of it being an Army facility.

The heavy gate opened for the military car that had met them at the airfield. An armed sentry waved them through.

"This place!" Ash shook her head. In her many times climbing the trails nearby, she'd never noticed any signs of life here at all. "I always figured it for some kind of abandoned insane asylum."

"How appropriate," McAllister said dryly. "It was a summer lodge for one of Hitler's minor flunkies. A lot of that kind of thing in these hills and down toward the Bavarian Alps."

"Oh, great." Ash couldn't figure out what the major's game was, but she clearly had one, and it concerned Ash herself in some way. Just then, though, they stopped at the entrance, grim in spite of elaborate stucco ornamentation, and guarded by two more armed sentries. Why all the security? But she had no more time to ponder.

An orderly took their bags and disappeared into an antique gated elevator, while the major took Ash on a tour of the main floor.

"Introducing you around will let me assess what's going on with new director here."

Ash let herself be used. She wanted to assess what was going on, too.

In a spacious room furnished with cushioned sofas and chairs, a billiard table, and a well-stocked bar, several card games went on at green baize-covered tables. McAllister nodded to a few men who looked up.

One said, "Hey, Mac, who've you got there? About time we had more ladies around here." At that, most of the others looked up, too.

"Gentlemen, this is Lieutenant Ashton, who'll be training in this fine establishment for a while. I suggest you be very, very nice to her. And very, very careful. The lieutenant knows how to handle herself."

There was general laughter, except from a couple of men who never raised their eyes from whatever they were studying—cards, books, or in one case, a bare tabletop. One with sergeant's stripes on his sleeve stood and saluted, but the rest appeared to be civilians, and even the sergeant wore jeans with his Army-issue shirt. Ash returned the salute, looked the group over, and gave them a casual nod.

"Ladies?" she asked. "Are there not many here already?"

The men looked at each other like teenage boys waiting for somebody else to field a question. "Just one," the original speaker said at last. "Mona Litvik. Two, if we can count Major Ratlaff's secretary." This brought sly grins and subtly shuffling feet.

I have GOT to get out of here soon, Ash thought as McAllister steered her toward the hallway.

"Let's go see how Mona is doing, shall we?"

Mona, it turned out, was lurking just around the corner. The major gave her a gentle hug, and Ash, noticing the pale, wispy hair and narrow face lined with anxiety, thought she must be one of those disturbed souls who needed help.

"Hello, Mona, I'm Ash," she said, and Mona, looking over the major's shoulder, gave her a tremulous smile.

"You'll be good friends." McAllister stepped back and gave Ash a look that said she'd damned well better be a good friend. "How are things going, Mona? What do you think of the new director?"

Mona's face tightened. "Major Ratlaff is crazier than anybody else here." Her low voice shook from time to time. Her slight accent might have been Polish, or from one of the Baltic states. "He takes me through the cellars and the tunnels and out in the hills looking for where things might be buried, things from the Nazi officers, or even from very ancient people. Bodies too. And if there's treasure he wants it for himself."

"Come on, we'll talk upstairs." McAllister led them to the room allotted to Ash, who didn't miss that the door could be locked from the outside, but not the inside. Maybe this building had been an insane asylum after all. Maybe it still was. The major saw that too, frowned, then went on in.

Ash's bags had already been set on the bed. There was only one chair, so she amused herself by making the bags rise from the bed and tuck themselves underneath it so she and Mona could sit there. No point in pretending when everybody else here had talents too.

"Cool!" Mona gazed at her, wide-eyed. "I wish I could do that!"

"What *do* you do?" Ash asked, then wished she hadn't.

Mona bent her head, looked down, and muttered, "I find dead people. And places where things have been buried."

"But...don't they have dogs for that?" Ash blurted. "And metal detectors and X-rays or something?"

Mona looked up and said, simply, "I do it better."

"Yes, you do," McAllister said. "But the director has no business using you for his own purposes."

"He wants to take me to the mountains, to the Untersberg, where there is a legend that Charlemagne is sleeping in a cave of ice deep inside the mountain, waiting for the time when he will be called back to save the Holy Roman Empire."

"Wow," McAllister muttered. "Okay, *that's* crazy. I may have to pull some strings in high places. We'll see."

Ash decided that if the major didn't handle things, she herself would take drastic steps to keep poor Mona from being abused. Her sad talent was hard enough for anyone to bear.

"Meanwhile, Mona, have there been any messages for me?" McAllister shifted in her chair, nervous in a way Ash had never expected to see.

"Oh, yes, two days ago. Hidden in the usual place." Mona fumbled inside her shirt and brought out a folded paper.

"Maybe I should go, um, stretch my legs." Ash stood, but the major shook her head.

"No. Stay." The paper she unfolded looked, from what Ash could see, like a crossword puzzle in some language using foreign characters. Not Arabic, but vaguely similar.

McAllister studied it. A guttural sound deep in her throat was quickly stifled. She stood, grasping the back of the chair for a moment, and Ash began to step forward in case she staggered, but the major waved her back. "I have to leave. At once. Mona, stay close to Ash. Ash, take care of Mona. Let your inner bear loose if necessary."

Then she was gone, and minutes later they watched through the window as she strode across the driveway, duffel bag in hand, wearing not a skirt but full desert camo, boots and all. The car that had brought them was still there, and its driver came running out of the building, got behind the wheel, and they were off.

"What's that all about?"

Mona shrugged. "I just save the messages for her. She's never run off that fast, though. And just before dinner time!"

So I'm left holding the bag, Ash thought, *with no idea what's in it.*

By the end of dinner, though, she had a pretty good idea. There were other people around besides those she'd seen in the card room, mostly civilians, mostly keeping to themselves. There were also staff members who appeared to do nothing but watch the…well, the inmates. The new director gave off creepy vibes, and from the way several guys eyed him—or avoided looking at him—he'd already given cause to be hated. His secretary, a specialist with the same build and coloring as Ash herself, was pretty clearly having an affair with him, and glowered at the way he was blatantly checking out Ash.

After dinner, Major Ratlaff summoned her to his office, closing the door in his secretary's face.

"So, Lieutenant, I hear you have some major chops. Bringing down a helicopter!"

"No, sir, holding up a helicopter. It was an emergency. I couldn't do it again."

"Up, down. What's the difference? Bringing one down should be easier. We can't requisition one to practice on right away, though. We'll just have to work closely together on useful exercises. Very closely."

She'd throw him over one of those rocky cliffs out back before she'd work "closely" with him. "Sir, it's been a very long couple of days. I don't think I can work on anything right now, so I'll just say good night." She swung around, made the door open well before she reached it, nodded to the secretary lurking outside, and went to her room.

Mona knocked softly a few minutes later. Ash let her in and got right down to business. "Do you want to get out of here? Do you have somewhere to go?"

Mona shook her head slowly, sadly. "No place I could get to. I don't have any money, and all my documents are locked in the office."

"So that bastard doesn't give you a cut of any treasure you help him find?"

"All I've found here so far is a hidden room full of wine bottles in the cellar, and a cave in the hills that somebody had already cleaned out. Just a couple of coins in the rubble. He did offer me a drink of wine, but his eyes scared me and I wouldn't take it."

"So you'd go if you could." Insane, to try getting Mona out as well as herself, but Cleo would have done it without hesitation. Someday, maybe she'd be telling Cleo all this, and she didn't want to have to admit to abandoning Mona. She might even be useful.

"Is there any way out besides the front door and any others likely to be guarded by gunmen?"

Mona's face brightened a little. "Not really, but I've thought—I detected—well, I know there used to be an opening at the end of one the tunnels leading from the cellars, but it's been closed up with heaps of dirt and rubble and nobody knows about it but me. I didn't tell Major Ratlaff." Her expression dimmed. "I don't like to think about it much. There's too much sadness there."

"Dirt and rubble is my specialty." Ash's spirits soared in spite of Mona's change in mood. Their situation was dangerous, escape chancy, but she saw it as a game, too, and one she had a chance of winning. "Where in the office do they keep your documents?"

"Everybody's are there, in the deep drawer at the left of the desk. The secretary keeps the key on the ring in her pocket."

Ash's documents hadn't been taken yet—service ID, passport— but they probably would be soon.

For three days, she exercised as though she were training for a marathon. How much could she lift without the adrenaline of a crisis? Considerably more on the third day than on the first. Could she focus on something she couldn't see but knew was there and had seen—say, in a drawer—and move it out in spite of a lock? Sometimes. More often each day. She didn't want to think about anybody's pockets except Cleo's, but maybe she could get around that.

The director approved of her efforts, noting that they were great for a spy's work, and she managed to evade him when he seemed about to get too close. But that got harder and harder. She began moving the chair up against the doorknob in her room, for what good it might do. At least there had been no attempt to lock her in. Yet.

In the evenings, she exercised other skills. She followed Major McAllister's advice and avoided the poker tables, but billiards was another matter. She'd been good at pool, back in college, so the first night she asked if anybody wanted to place some small bets, and with careful alternation of wins and losses, ended a couple of hundred dollars ahead. Apparently not everyone had known about her particular talents. They all used theirs in similar ways, though, so nobody made much of a fuss.

The secretary did, in fact, ask for her documents, "For safety, you know. Some of the people here are, well, not entirely trustworthy." Her look made it plain that she didn't consider Ash trustworthy, either, but on personal grounds. Ash complied without hesitation, lingered in the office to ask questions about the general operation and customs of the facility, and noted the big leather case in the drawer where her papers were inserted along with a thick stack of others.

"So many?" she asked casually. "I didn't realize that many people were here. Kitchen staff's and the director's and yours and everyone's?"

"Not the director's, of course!" The secretary's eyes shifted almost imperceptibly to the briefcase she always kept with her. Now Ash knew where the woman's own papers were probably kept.

The office door was locked when the secretary wasn't there, but Ash noticed that inside, the door had a somewhat old-fashioned handgrip instead of a knob, a grip that when turned downward opened the door even if it had been locked from the outside. She tried to memorize the exact shape and position of that grip.

Late on the third night, she moved noiselessly through the halls to the office door. She concentrated, envisioning the handgrip on the other side. *Focus, focus!* Her fingers twitched, almost feeling the smooth metal, and slowly, slowly she pressed the grip downward, heard the click of the bolt retracting, and pushed open the door. She entered, closed the door as silently as possible, and faced the desk. The drawer opened with a little persuasion. She riffled through the contents to find Mona's papers and her own.

Ash relocked the office, leaving it in its usual condition. She then proceeded to the secretary's apartment, right next to the director's. She'd suspected, from some interchanges between them at dinner, that they'd both be in the director's bed that night, but she was as careful as possible in opening the secretary's door, which had the same sort of lock arrangement as the office. Bingo. The briefcase was there, and the woman wasn't. Soon the woman's papers, with an ID photograph that could pass for Ash if her luck held, were no longer there, either.

Mona was ready with a small bag. The tunnel out of the cellar branched in several places, but Mona knew where she was going. After twenty minutes, they reached the pile of rubble, which looked just like all the other piles along the way that Mona had said weren't the right one. "There is something very, very old, though, beneath us here, very deep, very sad," she'd said at one point, in a shaky whisper. "I didn't tell Major Ratlaff. I wish... The old ones should be left in peace."

Ash figured they were far enough away from the main building by then that nobody was likely to hear her work, so she lit right into the pile, moving pebble by strategic pebble at first, then making big areas slide down into the tunnel and along it. Mona hung back several feet, pointing her flashlight unsteadily, as though her hands were shaking.

When the light showed a small dark gap ahead of them instead of dirt, Ash knew where to concentrate her efforts. There appeared to be a passage, once lined by flat stones, some of them missing, so that dirt and pebbles had spilled in and partially blocked the way. She cleared the rubble, and when she knew they could crawl through, she turned back to Mona. The girl's face was distorted with despair.

"I can't! Not any closer...not where the dirt can fall in..."

"It's all right," Ash said softly. "My power is from an ancient one stronger than anything here. Will you let me guide you? You can close your eyes."

Mona scrunched her eyes shut and nodded.

"I won't go without you," Ash said. "Go ahead of me. I'll hold on to you the whole time. There's cool clear air coming in from outside, and with me behind there's nothing to fear."

Moving someone fearful through a narrow, slanting passage called for a whole new level of her skills. She didn't dare to panic Mona by physically pushing, but she found that she could feel Mona's body with her mind and move her this way and that, hoping that Mona could feel her as well, and take comfort.

It couldn't have taken as long as it seemed, but they emerged at last into a still night lit by a full moon. Mona lay unmoving on a grassy slope while Ash looked around at the trees and hilltops, clear in the moonlight, and knew pretty much where she was. There would be a trail in a nearby hollow at the foot of a cliff.

"Ash..." Mona sat up. She stared, wide-eyed, at the outdoor world, and then the sky. "This feels like being born!"

"Maybe." Ash hoped fervently that she'd never come any closer than this to anything concerning childbirth. She turned her attention to caving in their exit and smoothing the earth outside, but if anyone looked even moderately closely they'd be able to tell something had happened there. By the time she finished, Mona was standing and brushing herself off. Once they found the trail, she moved along surprisingly swiftly, so Ash didn't have to reduce her own strides all that much.

They caught an early bus to the nearest major town, changed to another one there, and reached Munich by late afternoon with enough money for a cheap hotel and some left over. Mona's German was fluent, and Ash had picked up a fair bit when she'd been in training at Hohenfels, so they toured the city's Rathskellers and seedier dives, and between pool and billiard tables and various games of chance involving dice or other objects moved by Ash, by that night they could split the equivalent of $800 between them.

Mona did seem reborn. She handled their finances, placing bets on Ash's pool games with the innocent air of a girl who was new to the scene as well as to drinking, and didn't quite know what she was doing. Ash felt guilty at getting Mona involved in what was, when you came down to it, cheating, however necessary.

They knew they should keep moving. The second night in Munich, in a smoky dyke bar, after Ash had cautiously won a pool game or two, Mona tugged at her arm and whispered, "Over there. That one who resembles a bulldog."

Ash looked. The woman was very large, and deliberately fierce-looking. Quite a handsome bulldog if your taste ran that way. She was arm-wrestling another who looked nearly as strong, but not strong enough, and the bulldog won. Money changed hands in the group huddled around them. Ash, making a good show of resisting, let Mona hang on her arm and steer her in in that direction.

"So." The woman stared directly at Ash. "Who has the guts to challenge now?" She swept her stack of winnings from one side of the table to the other.

Ash tried to balance on the line between reluctance and pride. "What's in it for me?"

"What, impressing the little girl isn't enough?"

"Hah. I have better ways of impressing my girl."

Bulldog, with a guttural laugh, raised her right hand and flexed her thick fingers. "Oh, I'll just bet you have!" The various onlookers laughed, and others left their pool games and barstools to join the crowd.

"So you also want to bet that I can't force your hand right down onto the table." Ash hoped she'd managed the right tone of dubious bravado.

"Sure you can, honey." Mona rubbed up against her. "You can do anything! I'll bet on you." She looked vaguely around the gathering crowd and pulled an untidy stack of bills out of her purse. "Let me…oh, I think I'd better sit down." Somebody offered a chair at a nearby table. Mona stumbled a step or two with Ash supporting her, sat down, and lay her wad of cash on the table while Ash muttered something nearly inaudible, only a few words reaching anyone nearby. "Not too much…don't know…"

"So, hotshot, does the girl go with the bet?" Bulldog was having too much fun.

Ash raised her head. "The lady," she said in a steely tone, "goes wherever she pleases. Got that?" She pulled out her wallet and slapped her cash down on the table, an approximation of what Bulldog already had there. "This is just between you and me."

Bulldog's heavy eyebrows went up. "Fair enough."

Ash could tell she was reassessing the situation, but it was too late for either of them to back out.

It wasn't, in fact, just between the two of them. Mona, still in her drifty, half-drunk role, was taking bets from observers, and some of those who'd heard Ash's tone started making side bets.

Ash wasn't, in fact, sure that she could win. She hadn't tried her powers on anything like this before. Her rolled-back sleeve revealed a well-muscled forearm, but her opponent had much more heft all around. More experience, too, although Ash did know the importance of making sure the bout went on long enough to provide maximum entertainment to the onlookers.

They tested each other for half a minute. Ash could hold her own legitimately up to a point, but that point came soon. Her arm began to slant backwards. Time to cheat. She couldn't afford to let her opponent force her too far down, and she couldn't be too obvious in exerting her powers. It had to look natural.

Trying to move herself, or parts of herself, had never worked, so she focused instead on Bulldog's arm, with its taut, bulging muscles. Slowly, slowly, she moved that arm, millimeter by millimeter, clenching her jaw with the effort, letting her strain show, beginning to sweat and even grunt. *Ease off just a little…lift again just a little more…repeat…*

She had the feel of that arm firmly enough in her mind now that she could look up. Glaring at each other was good for the show. Bulldog's face was fierce, intent, maybe even a bit puzzled. She inhaled just before giving a quick, expert twist that regained her lead and more and nearly broke Ash's concentration. Nearly, but not quite. Ash clenched her teeth, braced hard with her whole body, and pushed harder with her mind. Bulldog's arm moved back up by centimeters instead of millimeters. Just as their arms reached vertical, Bulldog inhaled again, and this time, Ash, forewarned, forced her back so far that no twist could interfere. Bulldog's teeth were gritted now, too, and Ash took another half minute that seemed like forever before launching her final drive. As Bulldog's arm flattened on the table, there were gasps and exclamations all around them, but Ash and Bulldog still held each other's gaze.

"What the fuck was that all about?"

"Your guess is as good as mine." Ash loosed her hold and extended her hand. Bulldog shook it with a grip that came close to making Ash yell, but she didn't try to stop it. Fair enough.

Mona scooped all the bets into her bag, letting a few notes and coins drop to the floor to keep up her fluttery image. "Save some out to buy a round of drinks for everybody," Ash told her, and gave the bartender enough and more for that, providing plenty of distraction for them to slip out without much notice.

Their bankroll had nearly doubled, and it was clearly time to get out of town.

"Is this enough to get you somewhere safe?" Ash asked the next morning. "They'll be searching for us, and it's better if we split." It was bluntly put, but the truth. They had pushed their luck far enough.

"Somewhere, yes." Mona looked mildly hopeful. "I never count on real safety."

They parted with a warm hug, and Ash watched Mona board a train, feeling a bit guilty for not making absolutely sure she would be okay. "I tried, Cleo, really," she muttered under her breath. "I did what I could." Then she rushed to the international airport, hoping that her theft hadn't been discovered yet, and managed to get an expensive plane ticket to the States. So far, so good. Except that now she was AWOL, nearly broke, had no idea what to do next—and felt as far from Cleo as though they were on different planets.

PART TWO

CHAPTER 6

Renegade Lieutenant Athena Ashton gazed down from the plane onto sunlit clouds blanketing the earth. Or maybe Rogue Lieutenant would fit better. Ash wasn't feeling like any kind of hero just now. If she had to be cursed with some unasked-for superpower, why couldn't it have included the ability to fly through the air like Superman? Would that involve having to wear a stupid cape?

That made her think of Cleo—not that she wasn't already thinking of Cleo. That dream early this morning! Touching, feeling, loving, all so real…

If Cleo were here, it would be fun to pass the time moving things in subtle ways that no one else would notice. Like the clouds. Ash picked out one white mass and stared at it until the billows moved far enough apart to show a wide swath of the earth far below. There was a river, and green hills illuminated by the sunlight streaking through the gap she'd made, and just beyond them a large, narrow lake, or reservoir.

Cleo wouldn't act impressed. She'd just come up with more ideas. Ash eyed the opened packet of salted peanuts on the tray table, made it float upward, tilted it so that the nuts started to fall out, and whirled them around in a circle. Boring. She looked around to see whether anyone would notice if she tried something more dramatic. The plane was less than half full.

Two seats ahead, a middle-aged, sharp-faced man sat with a young girl Ash thought looked like Cleo might have at sixteen or so. Cleo would never have worn her red hair in long waves, though. Then the girl walked unsteadily back toward the restroom with the guy close behind gripping her arm, and Ash was sure Cleo's green eyes had never been dull like this girl's, to the point of showing barely a glimmer of life.

The girl, although her face was unmarked by anything beyond a few cute freckles, looked mentally scarred. She never seemed to speak for herself. When the flight attendant had come by soon after take-off, the guy had snapped, "No, she doesn't want peanuts or juice. Just some water." Ash hadn't thought anything about it at the time, but now...

Something felt wrong.

She could just imagine Cleo saying, "This looks like a job for Shadow Hand!" Beneath the teasing, Cleo really did seem to think Ash was some sort of superhero. Ash had to admit that she herself had felt that way for a while, but now she felt more like a one-trick pony who'd been given, or cursed with, just a single party trick kind of power. In sudden crises she'd reacted without conscious thought, but nothing like that had happened since the helicopter incident at the base. Getting out of the PsyCenter with Mona had been less dramatic, but more...satisfying. She'd made plans, and decisions, and carried them out, instead of reacting automatically.

The girl and her "keeper"—Ash automatically thought of him that way—returned along the aisle. Ash looked right at the girl and smiled. The wan face didn't turn toward her, but Ash had the impression of a glance out of the corner of an eye.

She had to help this girl. The situation called for plans, and decisions, and resolve. Some heavy piece of luggage could be dropped on the keeper guy's head, but they'd still all be confined together. Better wait until landing, in about—she looked at her watch—another half hour. Getting rid of the guy wouldn't be much of a problem, but what could she do with the girl then?

There'd been plenty of minor adventures that Cleo would have termed "jobs for Shadow Hand" since Ash had reached the States, but none had involved somebody to look after once the bad guys were defeated. Ash knew better than to take the few superhero comics she'd read seriously, but it did seem unfair that the heroes generally fought mega-villains in a fantasy world with no connection to the evils going on in this one. The people they saved from whatever or whoever weren't their responsibility after the rescue.

At first there hadn't even been any outright villains, although Major Ratlaff and his secretary had come close. Her shenanigans after probably made Ash herself a villain, but she'd had to get a grubstake together, as her grandfather used to say. Money was necessary in order to survive, travel, and be prepared for whatever might happen. She felt a lingering guilt at sending Mona off with less than half of what they'd scrounged in Munich because her own plane tickets—a short hop to Amsterdam and a long flight to Miami—cost more than Mona's trip to relatives in the UK.

At the airport in Miami, there'd been tourist flyers promoting a shipboard casino. Just what Ash needed. Some of her winnings had even been legitimate, but gaming the roulette wheel had been so easy that she'd had to move on quickly from casino to casino and state to state in order to stay anonymous.

The fact that so many casinos were owned by Native American tribes made her feel guilty after a while; her own Montana heritage included a sixteenth or so of Absaroka bloodline. She'd decided after a while to go to Las Vegas in spite of the tight security there.

After raking in a substantial amount, she got out just in time. A croupier was watching her a little too keenly and spoke a few words into his headset. Her description must have been getting around. A quick trip toward the restroom, a fur stole appearing suddenly on her shoulders while its oblivious owner was engrossed in a blackjack game, and Ash was out the door. The fur, having served its purpose, reappeared right back where it belonged.

The casinos had given her a chance to encounter a few truly nasty characters and separate them from their ill-gotten gains, with some punishment on the side. She'd learned to tie sturdy knots in ropes from a distance, and even to activate items like fancy canes or pool cues. Being beaten by inanimate objects that seemed to have wills of their own was even harder on the recipients' minds than on their bodies. But she was coming to realize that to do any real good, to have a far-reaching effect, even a superhero needed organization, and assistance. And she needed Cleo.

She'd chosen Boston because Cleo used to reminisce about knocking around the city and hanging out in bars on Dyke Night when she was scarcely old enough to get in. Maybe, just maybe, Cleo would visit those old haunts when she got out of the Army. Assuming she'd even continued with her plan to get out, with Ash gone. Any reasons she'd had for leaving Cleo didn't matter anymore. Ash wished achingly that she hadn't done it.

Well, what was done was done. Now to figure out how to help this girl, and fast. If she could get her away, where would she take her? What was Massachusetts like? Back in Montana, Ash had assumed that all of New England was densely populated, one big city, but Cleo had told her about the forests and farms and small towns of New Hampshire and Vermont and western Massachusetts as well as the enticements of Boston.

The Fasten Seatbelts light came on. The flight attendant moved along the aisle to make sure trays were back up and carry-ons stowed securely. Ash heard her speak pleasantly to the girl, and the man answer sharply.

The plane's angle of descent increased briefly, then flattened out. They came out of the cloudbank so close to the ground that nothing of the city could be seen but the airport itself and the dull glint of a harbor.

Then they were down, standing up, gathering their gear. The man and the girl had no carry-on baggage at all. Ash followed them through into the terminal and looked around for inspiration. The women's restroom just down the hall—a steady stream of travelers pulling huge rolling suitcases—yes. One suitcase rolled suddenly away from its owner and hit her target hard enough in the shins to knock him over.

Ash grabbed the girl's unresisting hand and pulled her into the well-populated restroom. "Do you want to get away from him?" Ash muttered in her ear.

"Yes! But..." And then they were in a relatively roomy handicapped stall. "He'll kill me, miss! Ma'am!"

"Not if he doesn't find you. Do you have somewhere to go if I get you away safely?"

The girl looked blank for a moment, trying to process the situation. "I think so...I've a sister in Dublin would take me in for a bit." A bit of color returned to her cheeks. "Scold the skin off me, but take me in." Her accent revealed her origin as much as the mention of Ireland. "But I've no money for an airline ticket!"

What a relief. Somewhere to send her. "Don't worry about that part."

"And he keeps my passport!"

Okay, a minor challenge. "Where does he keep it?"

"In the pocket inside his jacket, ma'am." She touched a hand to her adolescent left breast to indicate the position.

Good. No waiting for the baggage to be unloaded.

"Will you just trust me?" Stupid question. What if the girl said no?

But she just shrugged, as though whatever happened couldn't be any worse than what she'd already been through. "I guess. Just don't let him get me."

"I won't. I promise. Wait here."

Ash got to the restroom exit just as the man tried to shove his way in. She stepped one way and another, pretending to try to get out of the way while actually blocking him.

"Bridget, you fucking bitch," he yelled. "Get out here!" He pushed further into the room, Ash still blocking him. The other women there saw his contorted face, heard his torrent of profanity, and shrank back or surged forward, depending on their natures.

Ash backed him into a corner by a hot-air hand dryer. "Somebody go get a security guard!" Several somebodies did. The guy tried to beat her off, but she didn't let any of his blows land with much impact. It was all she could do to resist physically grabbing him in a neck hold and twisting until something broke, but there had to be some semblance of an accident, so by the time security guards arrived the intruder had mysteriously managed to bang his head against the towel dispenser hard enough to knock it off the wall, and was unconscious and bleeding on the floor. Ash herself had been seen to step back just before this happened, so when the guards questioned witnesses they all agreed that he had fallen and struck his head all by himself. "Drunken bastard!" was the general opinion.

In the chaos Ash grabbed Bridget and got her out of there. "Any baggage to pick up?"

"No, but... Ma'am, my passport!"

"No problem." She flashed the packet of documents that had been in the scumbag's pocket, then slid it back into her own.

In the taxi pickup area, a cab pulled right up to the curb for them. The driver looked startled, but when Ash shoved fifty bucks at him and told him to take them to any hotel within two miles of the airport, he seemed just as glad his cab had stopped where it did.

The hotel was glossier than Ash would have liked, but no irritating questions were asked, and she paid in cash. Her ID, forged in Miami since she knew the one she'd stolen in Hohenfels would have a trace on it by then, was the best money could buy.

Bridget was wilting when they got to their room. Ash ordered room service and sent the girl to take a shower while they waited. Later, after they'd eaten and Bridget had revived quite a bit, there was the awkward part where Bridget thought she should offer herself in case that was Ash's motive for helping her.

"I wouldn't mind with you," she said, when Ash gently turned her down. "I used to get...no, I didn't get anything. Harry got a hundred dollars an hour for me early on. Sometimes more, but those times when the fucker wanted something...extra, those were the worst." She looked away, trying to hide her face. Ash stifled an impulse to hug her, for comfort. In this touchy situation, the gesture could be misinterpreted.

"Now, though," Bridget said, her voice so low Ash could barely hear her, "now that I'm so... used up, he said the high rollers in Vegas won't pay so much, so he brought me to Boston 'cause he said they like an Irish look here. He could get twenty bucks a shot for me in a hotel, twenty times a night. Better than selling drugs." She searched Ash's face for disdain, saw none, and went on. "And there's a big football playoff going on at the end of next month, with great crowds, and girls are delivered in vans to pay-to-play parties. But if I didn't do well enough, he swore he'd sell me to a guy who works the truck stops—no rooms, just the back of a van, and that would finish me off." By then her voice was shaking.

"He won't get anything now." Ash's throat was tight. "You get some sleep. We'll see if we can get you on a plane to Dublin tomorrow, and if there's time we'll get some clothes and a suitcase for you first."

She tucked the girl into one of the beds and sat on the other one, wondering whether she should ask more of the questions raging in her head, or wait for morning. At least the girl showed no signs of being on drugs.

"Ma'am," Bridget said sleepily, "excuse me for asking, but are you some kind of nun? One of the other girls said in America, some of the nuns, and other ladies like them, try to help our kind."

"Um, no, not a nun." What was Ash getting herself into? It looked like she'd stumbled into the edges of something big enough to be the major mission she'd been looking for, and she'd figured out roughly what was going on, but in a way she felt like a first-timer, a virgin just discovering how cruel and complex the world could be. Strange, considering all the things she'd seen and done, in the Army and out.

Sex trafficking. She knew thousands of women were captured as sex slaves in the various conflicts in the Middle East and Africa, but hadn't thought much about it happening in the US. "How about you tell me about yourself. What made you come here from Ireland?"

"Just stupid. A rich lady offered me a job as an *au pair*, got me a passport and all, but once we'd come here she turned me over to Harry, and I never saw her again."

"Probably not rich, at least not legitimately, and certainly no lady."

Bridget nodded despondently. "I know, but it's too late. A lot of girls do the same, some from abroad, some from here, runaways met at the bus station, like that. And now we're all nothing but trash."

"No!" Ash mentally kicked herself for getting the girl going. She should be drifting toward sleep. "You're safe now, and you'll never, never be trash." Bridget's eyes closed tightly, tears leaking out between her eyelids. Ash did hug her then, and stayed with her, but on top of the covers, stroking the red hair that even felt like Cleo's except for its length, until the girl slept. Ash herself stayed awake for hours thinking of what she'd learned, what she should do, and how; and wishing desperately that she could talk it over with Cleo.

In the morning they went by taxi to a chain store to buy clothes for Bridget, and a suitcase to hold them. Over lunch, Ash made one more low-key attempt to get additional information, but Bridget had no idea where exactly Harry had been taking her, just that they usually stayed in hotels, run-down ones lately, occupied by other girls like her with their keepers and guarded by guys looking like ex-wrestlers who had got the worst of all their matches. All she knew about how customers found them was that there were classified ads online.

That evening, Bridget boarded the plane for Dublin, nervous but resolved. Just before getting in line she turned and hugged Ash, the way people all around them were doing to each other.

"You'll be all right?" Ash asked, then wished she'd made it a statement rather than a question.

Bridget shrugged, then said timidly, "Could I write to you?"

"I'm sorry. I don't even have an address right now."

The line moved on. Bridget looked back once, her face set, probably thinking she'd been deliberately cut off. Ash felt a surge of guilt, knowing she was glad to shed the responsibility. She could at least have asked for the address of Bridget's sister, but it was better not to fuel any expectations. At least she had sent the girl off with enough money to get by for a month or two. On a remorseful impulse, she made another couple of months' worth transfer from her wallet to the pouch Bridget had sewn inside her blouse. Out of habit she put her hand in her pocket in the process, even though it was all done with her mind, and found a piece of hotel stationery there. Bridget must have managed to slip it in while Ash was showering that morning.

"Ma'am," she'd written, "I know it was a sin, but I opened the door a crack and saw you in the shower when you dropped the soap and made it float up through the air to you. I thought already that you might be an angel, and now I know for sure. Please forgive the sin. And thank you."

An angel? No! Absolutely no. But when Bridget found the extra cash, she'd be even surer. If Ash had to be seen as some supernatural being, she'd rather go with Cleo's Shadow Hand gimmick.

Well. Now for Boston, and all those locales Cleo had mentioned in her stories of youthful wild abandon. Things would have changed in the years since, but there'd still be a community, a network; and sooner or later, just maybe, there'd be Cleo.

Over the next couple of weeks Ash found several women who remembered Cleo. When they heard how Ash had met her, the most common reaction was amazement that Cleo had ever signed up for the Army. The manager of the Galaxy Bar shook her head. "Can't see that firebrand taking orders."

Ash hadn't mentioned rank, but she couldn't resist a casual, "Well, she took them from me. Twisted them to suit herself, but took them." That got her a round of laughs.

"Impressive," the manager said. "You're not from around here, are you? Idaho?"

Ash had noticed their similar accents, though both had been muted by years away from their roots. A far cry from the Boston voices around them. "Western Montana. Pretty much the same thing, right?"

The manager laughed and thumped her on the shoulder. "Damned right. Well, if you run into Cleo again, tell her Mags asked after her." She held out a big hand, and they shook with a subtle, affable testing of each other's grip.

Mags was a classic salt-and-pepper butch with an infectious grin, a square jaw, and ice-blue eyes that didn't miss a trick.

"Glad to meet you, Mags. I'm Ash." She glanced around at the half-dozen women sitting at the bar. "I'm brand new to Boston, but I can sure see why Cleo used to get so nostalgic about the city and the people."

That got her some instant pals, and an invitation to a party, which she turned down with a laugh and "maybe another time."

On Ash's second visit to the bar, it was Dyke Night. She stood watching the dancers and tapping her foot to the music until a gaggle of drunk straight guys paused outside, hooting with laughter and trying to push each other through the door. Finally they managed to shove their way in and started shouting lewd insults.

Her military training kicked in. She was instantly right up in their faces. "Out! Now!" she ordered, her Lieutenant-Who-Takes No-Shit tone making some of them back off and out. Two stayed, bristling with bravado in spite of the unsteadiness of their feet. She sent one to the floor and rolled him right through the door, tripping up the other on the way and tumbling them both out into the road.

For effect, in case anybody had been watching closely, Ash dusted off her hands—hands that hadn't actually touched them, not that she couldn't have handled them physically with her martial arts skills. She looked around. Folks were certainly staring at her, but they'd all been drinking, so she could hope that no one had seen too much, or at least not enough to be sure something weird had happened.

But maybe Mags had. She came around from behind the counter with a funny look on her face. "Hey, what just happened? Great work, but how—"

"Oh, you learn in a lot of useful stuff in the Army. Tricks of the trade."

"Got any more tricks up your sleeve? How'd you like a job here as a bouncer? My last one went off to a cabin in the Maine woods to write the Great American Lesbian Novel." She shook her head in disgust.

"Sure. I'll try it for a while." Ash figured it was as good a way as any to win the confidence of the community. Besides, rousting those bastards had been fun. Good exercise.

The community of Boston-area lesbians turned out to be much more extensive and more welcoming than anywhere else Ash had been. She maintained a stance of confidence without challenging anyone except would-be troublemakers in the bar, and soon had a wide range of casual acquaintances. Most of her time, though, was spent alone, researching information on sex trafficking in newspapers and magazines at the public library and searching online sources on the iPhone she'd literally picked up in Miami. She felt that she was getting a handle on the sex-trafficking situation in New England, but it was maddeningly diffuse. Where was Cleo to help her sort it all out?

Massage parlors, nail salons, classified ads—hundreds of small outfits that would need one-by-one attention, and even then required the police department to take notice. In the massage parlors and nail salons, many of the girls didn't speak English well enough to understand that you were trying to help, or even to tell you if they wanted help. Fictitious superheroes got to battle with super-powerful individuals or criminal rings, so if they put just a few villains out of commission they won the battle.

Real life was a lot more complicated. No single villain had a monopoly on evil. Greed was everywhere—greed for power as well as money—and knocking off bastards who'd risen to power just made room for others to pop up from the same ground like venomous mushrooms.

Just the same, Ash's own power nagged at her to find, uproot, and smash the villains who trafficked in sex slaves. Until she found out how and where to accomplish this, all she could do was vent her frustration on the everyday minor evils common to city life.

In her first three weeks in Boston, she flattened and rolled to the curb a shitbag stealing money out of a handicapped panhandler's cup, slung a bicycle thief over the limb of a stately tree on Boston Common, and administered invisible punches where they would do the most good to a dozen or so guys harassing women on the street. Useful in their way but small change. That wasn't all she should be doing.

If only she'd gotten more information out of Bridget. But Bridget had been just arriving in Boston. She didn't know the territory. She only knew the usual way things went—and what happened to girls who didn't do well enough. Truck stops. Not even a room, just the back of a beat-up van.

Ash had seen plenty of truck stops in Montana, had stopped at some for a quick meal, a restroom, coffee to keep her awake while she drove. Had there been vans there in the shadows between trucks where anonymous men waited in line for their turn to hand over their money, climb in, and come out fifteen minutes later fumbling to zip up their pants and fasten their belts? Maybe. Probably.

A wave of rage and nausea swept her as she lay awake one very early morning. She should hit the road, roar through every truck stop in America, an avenging angel smashing the vans and scouring the predatory filth from the face of the earth.

Full daylight brought unwelcome logic. *How many truck stops? You and what army?* But she had a couple of days between shifts at the bar, so she rented a car and drove north on the highway into New Hampshire, figuring she'd travel until dusk and then look for trouble. Surely there wouldn't be any action before then.

She stopped for a bite at a major rest area shortly after noon, automatically scanning the separate lot where trucks parked, but not expecting to see anything out of the ordinary. In fact, the old pick-up truck fitted with a camper top between two twelve-wheelers looked so ordinary that she wouldn't have thought much about it if the guy leaning against its back hadn't looked like such a scumbag, and hadn't peered into her car with a suggestive smirk as she went slowly by. The smirk vanished as soon as he saw, she assumed, that she wasn't a man.

Ash parked and walked back. By the time she reached the camper he was shifting nervously.

"Lookin' for somethin'?" Then, with an attempt at a grin, "You a cop?"

She let just a hint of Montana cowboy accent through. "Nope. Not me. Far's you can get from a cop." Which was true enough, in its way.

He looked her over slowly, a practiced leer emerging. "So, you lookin' for something?"

"Depends on what you got in there." She made the camper shake a little from five feet away. At the faint sound of a whimper from inside, she yanked the tailgate open, making its owner stumble forward, and before he could turn to shut it she saw a tangle of brownish hair, a startlingly young, scared face, and a slight body wrapped in a blanket.

The guy squealed as he felt himself lifted high against the side of the neighboring twelve-wheeler and pinned there by an invisible force.

It was all Ash could do to keep from slamming him against the big truck again and again until he was just a sack of splintered bones and slushy flesh, but she had to get information, something that might let her save more than one poor girl. "Where'd you get her? Who do you know in the business?"

"Nobody! I dunno!" He drummed his heels against the metal. She shook him hard. "Just…just this dude…he come by and passed 'er along to me for a hundred bucks. Said she was worth more but tried too hard to run away."

"Not enough." She turned him upside down. "How'd he know you'd buy?"

"I might…might'a told another dude I was lookin', you know, over a beer or somethin'."

She flipped him again and slammed him against the truck's side, but she was pretty sure he didn't know anything else. Who'd trust somebody like him enough to let him identify them? The girl might know more.

"C'mon out, honey," she called, and then was almost bowled over by the blanket-wrapped form tumbling out over the tailgate, picking herself up, and dashing away with a bundle of clothing clutched under one arm and a metal box under the other.

Ash was so startled she didn't try to grab the kid before she was out of sight among the trucks. She even let the guy drop, but when he scrambled up and yelled, "The bitch got the cashbox!" she picked him up again, shoved him roughly inside his own camper, and slammed the tailgate shut. Then she turned his whole rig upside down, bounced it hard, and suddenly realized that the commotion had attracted the attention of a couple of drivers returning from lunch.

Ash channeled her steely-eyed military persona, close enough to pass as a policewoman. "Move along, guys. Official business."

They shrugged and moved along, looking back a time or two. They'd have some story to tell when they hit the road, which might even do some good if they knew what had been for sale in the pick-up. But by now it was too late for her to find the young girl who had bolted, although she tried. At least the kid had had the presence of mind to take the cashbox, so maybe she'd make out okay. Small comfort.

Back on the road, Ash's mind was a chaotic whirl. *I should have killed him. It's a good thing I didn't kill him. Maybe I did. Murder gets so complicated!* And then, over and over, *I can't do all this alone. Where's Cleo?*

She drove all the rest of that day and through most of the night, checking out half a dozen truck stops without any more signs of sex trafficking, at least any she could recognize. It would make more sense to get to the sources, like the places where girls were kept between the pay-to-play parties Bridget had mentioned.

She headed back to the Boston area, got some sleep, and by the next day had enough of a grip on herself to think about who might be able to help her. She was pretty sure she could trust Mags, up to a point, but not yet to the point of revealing her true self. If she even still had a true self.

Back at work in the Galaxy Bar, Ash was getting plenty of offers for dates, some quite tempting, but so far she'd remained congenially apart. In the fourth week, on duty at Dyke Night at closing, she didn't even turn around at first when she felt a tug on the flannel shirt she'd draped across her back, its sleeves tied around her neck. People were always claiming her attention.

"Nice cape you've got there," came a familiar voice. An oh-so-familiar voice. For a moment Ash didn't dare look, in case she was imagining things. "Super outfit, too," Cleo said. "Levis and white T-shirt. Classic. All it needs is a single black glove."

Ash waited a few beats to get herself under control. "Hey there, Cleo." She turned, super cool, fighting the stupid grin splitting her face. "Come here often?"

"Not lately. How about we go someplace else?"

"I'm on duty here for…" Ash looked at her watch. "Twenty more minutes." She felt dozens of eyes on them.

"Go on." Mags waved them toward the door. "It's quiet enough tonight." And to Cleo, "Welcome back, kid. I'll catch you later."

They went.

CHAPTER 7

THE FIRST CLINCH WAS UP against a tree around the next corner. Fortunately, it was one of those city-hardened trees that can take anything short of a direct hit by a delivery van, but the way the branches shook above them made Cleo wonder, briefly, whether it could take a hit by Ash. Then she had no time or breath for anything but Ash herself.

Touch said it all, without words. Arms and hands gripped whatever they could reach, mouths found each other with a force as close to pain as pleasure. Ash pressed Cleo's back into the rough bark at first, until Cleo swung around and did the pressing, figuring it was only fair. Finally they eased off, exploring each other with gentler touches in ways that weren't suited to public viewing. Ash clutched Cleo's hand, gasped, "C'mon!" and dragged her along the street.

A second, briefer clinch came at the foot of the outside stairs leading up to Ash's small furnished room. At the top of the stairs, though, with the door already opened from below, Ash paused. "You weren't surprised at all to see me, were you? How come?"

"I knew you were somewhere in Boston, so I've been making the rounds. Were you expecting me?"

"Just hoping. I didn't know where else to look." Ash shook her head. "I've been such a damned idiot, thinking I could go it alone, feeling like I'd been...chosen or something, special, given some great mission— Hey, wait a minute! How could you know I was in Boston?"

"*She* told me." Cleo was enjoying the hell out of Ash's confusion. "C'mon, aren't you going to invite me in?"

Ash backed into the room and sat down heavily on the bed, which took up most of the space. A light switch clicked, and a stark overhead bulb went on without any apparent human intervention. "'She'? The major? How did she know where I was?"

Cleo pulled the only chair out from the folding table and straddled it, arms crossed on its back. "You mean my good pal Major Margaret McAllister? No, as far as I know she hasn't tracked you. It was that other 'She.' The one in the desert. Your own personal goddess."

Ash's mouth hung open for a second or two before she pulled herself together. "You're telling me that Ishtar is your good pal now, too? The one who wanted to kill you?"

"You might put it that way." Cleo wriggled to get more comfy. "I stopped by her lair on my way to be mustered out and get a flight to the States. The mine-buster squad I traveled with went along that same road, and they humored me when I said I'd lost something with sentimental value over in that *wadi* and wanted to take a few minutes to look for it. Good guys. We'd worked together for three months, and they'd all heard the story about when we hid there.

"So we stopped for a lunch break, and I wandered alone over to the *wadi* and down to where our cave had been, pretty much all just rubble now. I could feel her anger right away, by the dust blowing into my eyes and the pebbles bouncing off my head, but I stood my ground, stripped naked, and yelled, more or less, 'Look you, whatever you are, I'm a woman, and Ash needs me. If you know where she is, show me right now!' After that we got along just fine."

Cleo stood, stretched, ambled over to the sink, and drew a glass of water. She drank it slowly, drew another, and nearly choked when the glass moved out of her hand and landed over on the table.

"Sergeant Brown!" Ash snapped. "Finish your report! That's an order!"

"Yes, ma'am!" Cleo saluted and went back to the chair. "Since you ask so nicely. I don't really know precisely what happened, but I had a vision right then, clear as anything, of an airplane window. It was like I was right there with you. I could see the ground through a space in the clouds. You were passing over the Connecticut River and the Holyoke Range and the Quabbin Reservoir. I've been on enough flights into Boston to recognize those landmarks. Could be our goddess didn't know where in the world that was, but it was what she could see when she looked for you, so it was what she showed me."

Ash balanced at the very edge of the bed, leaning forward with her hands on her thighs as though about to spring up. "So that's it? Without being high or anything? You expect me to believe you challenged her, and she told you where I was?"

Cleo shifted uneasily, her bravado faltering. "I can't swear it wasn't just my imagination. And a whole lot of wishful thinking. But here I am, and here you are."

The tense expression on Ash's face was unreadable. Cleo had always been able to sense her moods before, but not this time. She forged on. "Look, if she didn't tell me, nobody did. Not the major, not anybody, if that's what you're thinking. As far as I know nobody else knows where you—we—are. Maybe it was just a lucky guess."

Ash's tension visibly eased. "You were right about the plane. What I saw out the window." She leaned back, arms braced behind her, and worked her modified cowboy boots off her feet. Then she swung her long legs onto the bed and stretched them out. Those legs in baggy camouflage fatigues had made Cleo's pulse pound. In snug blue jeans they made her crotch damp, too.

A smile flickered at the corner of Ash's mouth. "I was experimenting with moving the clouds apart so I could see below, and wishing you could watch me doing it."

"Wow!" Cleo was appropriately awestruck. "Do you think you could make the clouds give rain?"

"Always one step ahead of me! But there are too many factors involved in that besides movement. Besides, there's the whole unintended consequences thing. What if I couldn't make it stop?"

"I dunno, you've always been so good at making things *not* stop." Cleo wriggled in the chair again, this time with clear erotic intent. "I was kind of wondering, if it was a lucky guess that let me find you, just how lucky can I get?"

"I'll have to think about that." Ash looked intently at the dusty Army boots Cleo still wore. Slowly and sensuously, the laces untied themselves. Cleo would never have believed bootlaces could be sexy, but they sure were now. She kicked off the boots.

"You say you stripped for the goddess?" Ash was still five feet away.

"Just my shirt and—ah!" Buttons rapidly unbuttoned themselves. Cleo felt, actually felt, Ash's hand slide beneath her sports bra and cup her breast. She was still trying to process that sensation when her belt buckle unclasped and the zipper on her jeans slid down. She gasped as the invisible hand pushed its way under her boxers. "Ah! Uh, been getting a lot of practice, have you?"

"Not like this," Ash said, "except in dreams."

"Dreams? When? I had a dream…it was so real…"

But "when" didn't matter. "Now" was everything. She stood, shrugged off her shirt and bra, wriggled out of jeans and boxers, and made it to the bed and onto Ash in one leap. They rolled together, laughing and gasping, until Cleo paused on top. "I like to do things the old-fashioned way." Her fingers got Ash's shirt unbuttoned almost as fast as hers had been, made quick work of the rest, and then her skin moved against every inch of Ash she could manage while her mouth ranged from lips to throat to breast and back again.

"So nice to have a bed," she murmured against Ash's ear.

"Nicer than in Paris?" Ash flipped Cleo over and started nibbling down from her breasts to her belly.

"Nothing could be nicer than Paris, but wherever we are now is always the best," Cleo said, then yipped at a nip in a tender place. "Nothing could be better than now," she went on between gasps, "even twisting around like pretzels in the…in the jeep when that was the only place we had… Oh!" She arched her hips into the pressure of Ash's tongue, infuriatingly fleeting. Ash lifted her head and swung their bodies crossways on the mattress.

"And the bed is wide enough for this," Ash panted, rolling them together from its head to its foot and back again, over and over. The frantic pressure of body on body, hollow on curve on skin slippery with sweat and arousal, felt so good that it was hard to stop, until the hunger for even more intensity where it was needed most grew, and swelled, and couldn't be denied.

"Let me…" Cleo managed to raise up enough to press her face down into Ash's belly, then moved up to her full breasts and went back and forth from one to the other, worshipping them with lips, tongue, even gentle teeth, feeding on the tantalizing swelling of their tips, until Ash moaned and thrashed and tugged Cleo's head down between her thighs.

Hands, tongue, lips, Cleo burrowed her whole face into that demanding heat, where every slick, sensitive inch pulsed with hunger for more, harder, harder, more, please! No drawing the pleasure out, as they used to do in the jeep, in the desert; it had been too long now to wait. Ash arched her hips, moving them to a demanding rhythm, and with Cleo's fingers inside her and Cleo's mouth impelling her clit to a frantic hardness, she screamed out her wordless triumph.

Cleo stroked Ash with increasing gentleness as she floated down from that peak, her kisses light on Ash's skin, keeping the brakes on her own need. But when Ash recovered enough for her breathing to slow, she flipped over and devoted herself to Cleo's pleasure.

The small breasts, so easily concealed, could tighten and swell and fill a lover's mouth as enticingly as any other woman's. Her taut buttocks were a perfect fit for Ash's hands. She raised Cleo's hips, ran her own still-rigid breasts one by one along Cleo's glistening folds, teasing as long as she dared, then responded to her lover's desperate pleas with firm strokes of tongue and fingers and an even tighter hold on her buttocks. Cleo erupted in cries increasingly shrill, all control abandoned in ways she would never have allowed anyone but Ash to hear.

"Shall I stop now, or not?" Ash said when Cleo could focus again.

"Just…just hold me now."

So they held each other, breathing each other's essence, until sweat and the lubrication of their pleasure cooled and they burrowed under the blankets. Cleo could feel the bond they'd had renewed, and strengthened. She could even sense what Ash was thinking while they were this close together, but some things still needed to be spoken out loud.

"Cleo," Ash murmured, "nothing is worth giving you up. Nothing. I was a fool. You, being with you, is the only thing that feels like home. Like being me."

"I know," Cleo said sleepily. In a few minutes she roused, though, and said, "So what have you been up to? Saved any of the world yet?"

Ash hesitated. "Maybe a little. Too damned little. I helped someone get away from the PsyCenter along with me, but I don't know how she got along afterward. And coming into Boston I sort of saved just one sex-trafficked Irish teenager, but I guess I'll never know for sure how things worked out for her. I sent her back to Dublin with enough cash to live on for a while, and felt relieved not to be responsible for her anymore. Some world-saving."

"Gotta start someplace, I guess. Sounds like you found a way to make enough to bankroll your world-saving mission. That's progress."

Ash sighed. "Funny how you were talking about getting lucky. I've been hanging out in casinos a whole lot more than anybody should, and making a bundle without needing any help from luck."

Cleo sat up and stared at her for a second, then caught on. "Roulette! Of course! Some racket! And here I worried about you being too much of a straight arrow to get along in the grubby, gritty world."

Ash sat up too and spread the blanket across both their shoulders. "I've been as gritty as anybody. And as grubby. Not at the casinos run by the tribes, but there are some cruise ships and a riverboat out of New Orleans that feature roulette. Couldn't work any one place for long, of course, so Vegas was the place to go. When I had to get out of there fast, too, I headed for Boston."

"So where did the Irish chick come in?"

Ash told her the whole story, even, after some hesitation, the part about Bridget peeking at her in the shower, seeing the dropped soap rise to her hand, and deciding she must be an angel. "She'd upgraded me in her mind from nun to guardian angel. Way to make me feel like hell!"

Cleo chuckled. "Makes sense that she thought you were a nun when you turned down her offer to put out. And you did, after all, save her from a cruddy life and give her at least a chance at a better one."

Ash was silent for a while. Finally she said, "I got something from all that. Something big. I know now what I'm supposed to do, just not how to do it. At least not alone."

"Saving sex-trafficked girls." Cleo nodded. "Sounds good. And you're not alone now."

A few days later they were on the way to being even less alone.

Cleo had been close friends with Mags in her early days in Boston and had learned a great deal from the older woman. She was more than happy to find that Ash and Mags had found common ground in their northwestern origins, and surprised that Ash hadn't already enlisted Mags in her cause.

"I ran into Mags just now," Cleo told Ash over the coffee she'd brought back. "She wants us to come over to the bar for lunch, before opening, catch up on the last ten years or so. I said we would."

"Sounds okay." Ash sounded less than enthusiastic.

"What's the matter?"

"Nothing. But sometimes I think she's all too perceptive."

Cleo did wonder how much Mags had noticed about Ash's bar bouncer tactics, but didn't say so. "She has to be, in her job. She knows everybody, and hears everything, but she doesn't tell everything she knows or hears. At least she didn't back when I first knew her, and I don't think she's changed. You can trust her."

Ash was still lounging in bed with her coffee. "I know, I know. But how would she handle *this*?" Her nearly-full cup sailed slowly through the air to land on the table in front of Cleo.

"Probably okay. Eventually. But we can take it one step at a time. Just chat her up a little on the subject of sex trafficking. I bet she'll run with it." Cleo picked up Ash's coffee cup, took a good swig, carried it over to the bed, and held it just out of Ash's reach. "Yeah, I know you can take this away from me without touching it, but if I try to hang on to it can you do that without spilling any?"

It turned out that Ash could. Almost. Cleo grabbed the napkins from the bag that had held the coffee, mopped up a few dribbles from the floor, and sat down on the edge of the bed so hard the mattress bounced and a little more coffee was spilled.

"Sorry!" she started to get up for more napkins, but Ash gulped down what was left, sent the empty cup spinning back to the table, and pulled Cleo down beside her with a very firm and altogether human arm.

"You," Ash said sternly, "will just have to lie over the wet spots."

"Yes, ma'am," Cleo said with mock contrition, spread-eagling over that side of the sheets while the buttons of her shirt unfastened themselves and the zipper of her jeans slid down on its own.

Three hours later, they woke for a second time and barely made it to the Galaxy Bar in time for lunch.

Mags had sent out for pizza and served it with icy-cold beer from one of the local breweries. Between bites and sips they talked about their Army adventures, the all-female medical mission, the hardships as well as beauties of the desert, and various other topics that Ash had only referred to briefly in the weeks before Cleo arrived. Then Mags and Cleo reminisced about the "old" days in Boston, how things had changed in in the lesbian and gay communities, and what had become of old friends. By the time they were topping off their meal with coffee and chocolate chip cookies it seemed perfectly natural for Mags to ask what they were thinking of doing next.

"After all your adventures overseas, Ash, you're going to want something more than a job as a bouncer pretty soon, and Cleo is bound to get up to something or other."

Cleo shot Ash a "go for it" look, but Ash's body language practically telegraphed, "careful now!" so Cleo was startled when Ash did, in fact, go for it.

"You're right, Mags. We need to get off our butts and find something worth doing. I'd been wondering for quite a while what that would be, and then on the plane to Boston I ran into a...a sort of situation." She paused, considering, Cleo knew, how much to say.

Mags leaned forward, all attention. "A 'situation'? C'mon, don't leave me hanging!"

"Well, it could have happened to anybody, but the end result was that I managed to get a young sex-trafficked girl away from her nasty keeper and sent her off on a plane back to Ireland. It was the old story, promised a good job here, then trapped into sex slavery."

Mags's jaw had dropped, but she recovered quickly. "What you should do is write a book about this, all the details, in the Army and beyond. Hell, it would make a great movie!"

"No," Ash said firmly. "What I should do is find ways to help more girls like that."

"We," Cleo put in. "What *we* should do."

Mags was right on it, just as Cleo had predicted. "If your team needs a source of local information, the lay of the land, the political situation, stuff like that, I'm here for you. We hear about that stuff going on over there where you were, thousands of women captured and kept as sex slaves, but we have plenty of that kind of thing going on here, too, just without the fighting. All for money.

"I see articles and editorials about it fairly often, and once in a great while there's a police raid, but they're stretched too thin with other kinds of crimes, and the politicians think they have better fish to fry—fish that vote, I guess. Plus there's always some corruption where there's money to be made."

Her enthusiasm was a bit daunting. "It's not that we have any actual plans yet," Cleo cautioned.

Ash nodded. "We're still in the studying stage. I've been reading up on the local situation, too, and it's a tangled mess, knots within knots."

"Well, I'm here if you need me. And I know somebody you ought to meet. Jana's a former Army nurse, with connections to an agency that helps girls who manage to get out of the sex trade on their own. She and her partner Val come into the bar once a month or so. How about I give them a call? You folks would get along fine. Val was in the Army, too."

Cleo felt the tension building in Ash. The more people involved, the more chance of her powers being discovered. Cleo figured that was inevitable anyway, but she'd protect Ash's privacy as long as she could.

"It'd be nice to meet them, have a drink or two in the bar, without saying anything about our interest in sex trafficking right away. How about it, Ash?"

"Sure. That'd be okay."

Ash's tone wasn't exactly genial, which wasn't lost on Mags, who looked at her watch and said, "Hey, time's been flying. My first shift staff will be here any minute to get the bar ready to open. I'll give you a call if I find out when Jana and Val will be around."

Ash was silent on the way home, and almost didn't see an impending squirrel/car collision in time to toss the critter safely to the curb, but Cleo grabbed her arm, pointed, and tragedy was averted.

"Are you thinking I shouldn't have agreed to meet Mags's friends? You've talked about not being sure what to do with girls after you rescued them, and apparently this nurse *does* know, so it seems like too good a chance to pass up."

"Yeah, it does. I've known, in theory, that to accomplish much we need the help of people we can trust. I guess I'm just having trouble getting used to that theory closing in on being a reality."

An hour later, things got even realer. Mags phoned to say that Jana and Val would be at the bar that night. "All I mentioned was your shared military background," she told Ash, with Cleo listening. "Anything else is up to you two to bring up, or not."

Mags was spot-on in thinking they'd all get along. Jana, with her pale freckled face and neat mid-length brown hair showing gray at the temples, had the warmth and competent manner of the best type of nurse. Dark-skinned Val, with her direct gaze, vice-like handshake, and the muscular forearms of the jazz drummer she was, lit up the dim corner table where they sat with her frequent grin.

"How are things in the Army these days?" she asked. "We got to do the Don't Ask, Don't Tell Tango and managed to fly under the radar, but it was a challenge, and not the fun kind."

"It's still a challenge," Ash said. "Depends on who your officers are. Some will get you on one charge or another and claim that being gay or lesbian has nothing to do with it."

"We were lucky in our last posting," Cleo added. "Our colonel knew perfectly well what was going on. But there was always the chance that somebody higher up would get us for illegal fraternization, sergeant and lieutenant, so we still had to be careful."

By the time they'd finished a couple of drinks each and exchanged humorous anecdotes of hiding their relationships—and a few not so humorous—Cleo felt like they'd been friends forever, but it was still a shock when Ash came right out with, "Jana, Mags mentioned that you know something about an organization that shelters sex-trafficked girls when they get away."

Jana set down her drink and gave Ash a searching look before responding. "It's not widely known, but yes, there is such an organization, somewhat like the shelters for women escaping domestic violence. It was set up originally for oppressed sex workers in general, which has come to include sex-trafficked women. I do some occasional work with them when there are medical issues."

"That's good to hear. I had...well, I happened to get involved in a case and was able to send a girl back to the country she'd come from, but I wondered at the time what I could have done with her if she'd had nowhere to go."

"That's got to be some story!" Val raised her glass in a salute. "Anything you can share?"

Ash told the story again, adding a few details she hadn't already told Mags, who had just sat down with them. Cleo kind of hoped she'd include the really startling parts, but it was probably just as well that she didn't.

Jana was clearly impressed. "I can see why you've taken an interest in the sex-trafficking problem. If you'd like to get more involved, I can connect you with a coalition working on getting stronger legislation passed."

"I was thinking of something more immediate," Ash said. "More hands-on."

Cleo choked on her drink, trying not to laugh at the thought of how much more Ash could offer than just her hands. She put her glass down, realizing that she'd had quite enough. Possibly more than enough. Ash's second glass was untouched, so she must know what she was doing.

"Oh, well, the shelter—" Jana began, but Ash shook her head.

"Maybe sometime. But I've been thinking of getting together a small, discrete group to brainstorm other approaches. Mostly information gathering at first."

Val, with three empty glasses in front of her, sat up straight, eyes gleaming. "So would that include us? There's nothing I'd rather do than mess up those sex-slavers!"

Jana, more subdued, considered for a minute or two and then nodded. "Worth considering, anyway."

Cleo, who was facing that way, noticed a slight girl in an MIT sweatshirt hovering outside the nearby restroom, a laptop case hanging from her shoulder, but didn't think much about it until she advanced to stand right behind Val.

"If you guys really want to know what's happening, cutting edge, up-to-the-minute," the girl said casually, "you need somebody wired, like me. If it's those trafficker sludge-slugs you want to take down, I'm your geek."

All this, Cleo thought in a bit of a daze, from a thin, wispy blonde who could have been a grown-up Alice in Wonderland after a few too many years of "eat me" experiments.

Mags stood up, frowning. "Nobody's talking about taking anybody down. Who are you, anyway? I've seen you around before. You go to MIT?"

The girl shrugged. "Off and on. You can call me Twelve. Right, Val?"

Val strained to turn far enough around to see her. "Uh, right, Twelve. How's things?"

"Boring as fuck." She shrugged again, turned away, said over her shoulder, "Think about it and let me know." Then she wandered off out the door.

Jana turned to Val. "You know her? Really? Somebody who calls herself 'Twelve'?"

"Yeah, a little. She's sort of a freelance hacker and a hell of a video producer. A jazz groupie, too. She made those terrific promos for the band when we went on tour last time."

"A jazz groupie?" Jana's expression verged on ominous.

"Not that kind! I only talked with her a few times. She has some interesting theories about the relationship between math and music and the structure of the human brain."

"Okay, but... Twelve?"

"Yeah, it's weird. I think she's obsessed with that Star Trek character with a number for a name, the one that's part cybernetic. Lets her feel smarter than regular people. Which she may be."

Ash looked intently at Val. "Would you trust her?"

"Trust?" Val considered. "Well, I'd trust her once she showed she was on my side. And I'd trust her to do anything she set out to do, legal or not. There was this one time..."

"C'mon," Cleo urged. "You can't stop now." There were murmurs of general agreement.

"Okay. I don't know all the details, but somebody in the band—I won't name names—was being blackmailed, and Twelve worked some kind of hacker magic and got enough dirt on the blackmailer to shut them down. If we need, as she said, a 'geek,' she's the one to have."

"Something to consider." Ash looked thoughtful.

Mags, who'd sat down as soon as Twelve left, got up again. "Let's think things over. Ash and Cleo can meet me tomorrow in my office, if that's okay with them. No more shooting our mouths off in the open bar."

Cleo caught the silent question in Ash's eyes, the way they'd had of understanding each other back in tight spots in the desert, and said, "Jana and Val too, if they can make it." She sent back an unspoken question of her own.

"And if anybody runs across Twelve," Ash said, "you can bring her along."

When they got home—there'd never been any doubt that they'd share the small room with the big bed—Cleo said, "We've got to face the fact that we can't keep everything secret. In fact, if we really pull something off, the more publicity the better. If news gets to girls that somebody might help them escape, they'll be looking for chances, and if the Johns know somebody is focusing on thwarting the business, they may think twice before plunking down their money for half an hour with an underage Bridget."

"I know." Ash gave a deep sigh. "If the Army spooks find me, they find me. And if I get caught doing…what I do, and get called a freak or witch or something, that's just the way it goes. Meanwhile, planning with a team is what we need to do. For starters."

Mags's office just about held the five of them, with a few chairs brought in from the bar. When Twelve came in fifteen minutes late, they began to shuffle the chairs around, but she just plopped herself down on the floor in a corner with scarcely a word and logged on to her ever-present computer.

Ash shared copies of some of the articles she'd found, and Jana had second- or third-hand information from her friends at the shelter, gleaned from girls passing through. One common thread seemed especially worth following up. There was a pattern of traffickers loading unmarked white vans with women who were then warehoused at anonymous motels or well-fenced houses. They'd be transported, heavily guarded, to events like gangbang parties, where men were charged admission and the girls were forced to act like willing guests. The vans had no windows in the back, or if they did they were covered, so the girls had no way of telling where they were or where they went.

"If we could find some of these parties and follow the vans back to their sources," Ash said, "we'd have something to go on, even if it's just information to feed the police."

"We have an old pick-up truck for transportation," Val said, "and I pass a used car lot every day where there's a white van for sale. Something like that could be camouflage, letting us blend in."

"Good idea," Ash agreed. "Find out how much they want for it, and we'll buy it. I can cover the cost."

A sharp exclamation from Twelve in the corner grabbed their attention.

"Got it! I worked on this all night, and now I've cracked it. There's an ad on the local Craigslist site, 'Hot Action after the Big Game.' I replied under one of my dude identities, got a link to a middleman, and hacked the poster's e-mail. The last info just came in. Private party with cover charge near Foxboro after the big football game next weekend. Johns are supposed to meet up with a guy at a certain bar in Mansfield to pay and get directions. I'll bet he looks you over real good first."

"I could pass." Cleo tried to sound more confident than she felt.

Ash shook her head. "Pass as what, a fourteen-year-old boy?"

"Sixteen, at least!" Cleo's fake indignation held a hint of relief.

"Can't we just watch from the parking lot and follow the obvious Johns coming out? Any guys who go in and come right back out looking like randy roosters should lead us right to the spot."

"Mags is right," Ash said. "That's the safest way, and safety is our highest priority this time. We don't just want to get a few girls out;

we want to know where they're kept, follow the vans back so we can keep an eye on those places."

"Can't we get a few girls out before they have to put out?" Cleo was perched on the corner of the desk. "I can fix a magnetic gadget to attach and track the bad guys' vans without following them. Kind of like a bugged GPS."

"I could go inside the party joint," Twelve said. "I'd warn the girls and tell them to get in our van." Five heads began to shake. She was small, and looked about fifteen if you didn't look too closely; then you'd see faint lines around eyes burning with a fierce intensity you had to hope was sane. "Really. I've known guys like the ones that dig these things. There's always some that want a girl to be young and skinny and kind of scared looking. 'Course, sometimes skinny girls have real sharp knees and know how to use 'em." She looked around. "Plus, I'm the only one with hair long enough to blend in." She patted her wispy blonde ponytail.

"No." Ash's take-charge voice made everyone straighten up. "Not this time. We may come to that, but we need to know much more. First comes surveillance at the bar, and following some of the customers to the site. Then we watch for the delivery vans to arrive, if they haven't already, and look for a chance to plant the magnetic bugs on them. If they don't hang around until the end, we wait for them to come back to collect. No risking the troops when we have so little information."

"But what if we see a real good opportunity to snatch a girl or two?" Twelve asked.

"Check with me first. Or Cleo."

Val shook her head. "Sounds mighty chancy. Car chases, girl-snatching, danger every step of the way."

"So you're in," Cleo said with a straight face.

"God, yes! Can't tell you how much I've missed danger!"

CHAPTER 8

THEY FOUND THE PARTY PLACE, a country estate that had seen better days but at least had plenty of parking space along a wide, curving drive. Two white vans and a gray one were at the far end of a narrow uphill driveway, each with a thug leaning against it. Cleo figured she and Ash together could take out at least two of the thugs, but that would raise too much noise and frenzy. So would Ash doing some long-distance takedown.

Ash parked the van they'd bought out of sight behind some shrubbery while Val's truck waited near the highway end of the drive. Mags had reluctantly remained back in Boston, tending bar and staying available in case anything went so wrong they needed help, like ambulances. Or lawyers. Or bail. Or all of the above.

"So much for our planning," Ash griped, looking uphill at the guarded vans. "Maybe we should just call this a trial run."

"We can still get the vans bugged if somebody makes enough of a diversion." Twelve toyed with the case of magnetized tracking gadgets. "I could walk up there crying, saying my sister is in there."

"Forget it. You go back to the truck with Val and Jana. Cleo and I have, ah, Special Forces training. If we can sneak up on the enemy in the desert, doing it here with grass and trees should be a cinch. We'll get those bugs attached."

Twelve looked pissed, but handed Cleo the case and trudged back down the driveway.

"Special Forces?" Cleo's eyebrows lifted.

"I came mighty close to saying 'ninja.' C'mon. We can do this as long as the magnet part hitting the van doesn't make much noise."

"It's a magnetized strip as flexible as plastic, but be careful anyway."

Cleo did feel like a ninja as they made their way through the grounds in the dusk until they had a reasonable view of the rear panel of one of the vans. She held up a bug, Ash focused, and it was gone, landing gently but firmly where nobody was likely to see it at night. A few more maneuverings, and each van had two little extra bits of technology stealing a ride. The occasional conversational exchanges of the guards, mostly dirty jokes followed by their guttural laughter, were undisturbed. Ash and Cleo, however, *were* disturbed when they got back to their van to find Twelve twenty feet in front with a video camera, filming the house and surroundings.

"I need to keep records of all this," Twelve said, as though it were self-evident. "You never know when you might need them, or when something wild might happen."

As if she'd just clicked a link, something did happen. Sounds of screaming and yelling and general uproar erupted.

Twelve pointed toward it with her camera. Cleo vaulted into the driver's seat. The engine leapt to life with a feral roar, and Ash yanked the door open just in time to get in. As their van raced up the drive, a young girl stumbled downhill, screaming, sobbing, weaving, while another girl yelled and punched and kicked at the goon in pursuit. The other punks cheered him on.

"Ash!" Cleo shouted, veering as the crying girl tripped. Before she could fall, Ash's invisible grip steadied her and she staggered onward. Then the other girl, tossed aside by their pursuer, nearly fell but recovered and ran after him, a second goon now coming on fast behind her. Ash focused on one guy and then the other, lifting each a foot or so and heaving them into the thick shrubbery lining the drive.

Cleo slowed, braked hard, and spun the van around so it was side-on to the fleeing girl. "Grab her!"

Ash swung the door open. "Get in!" she called, and girl seemed to leap into her arms, although her legs flailed as though she were still running. "It's okay, you're safe now," Ash insisted, but the struggling only increased.

"She thinks we're just another white van." Cleo spun the vehicle again to point uphill. "I'm going back for the other one."

The second girl stood her ground as though daring Cleo to hit her, springing aside when Cleo slowed, and pounding her fists on the van's side. Ash made the rear side panel slide open, and the girl jumped in under her own power.

"Don't hurt her!" she gasped, then grunted as Ash heaved the still struggling girl over the seatback onto her.

"Tell her it's okay. We're here to help. Just hang on." Another swerve headed them downhill.

"Watch for Val's truck!" Cleo yelled out the window as they passed Twelve, still fervently filming it all. Up the hill, the gray van was revving its motor, ready to follow.

Ash got on the phone to Val. "Move out fast, pick up Twelve by the service driveway, and try to follow us. Block any gray or white vans pursuing us on the highway as best you can without getting in trouble. We have passengers."

"Roger that. We got Twelve already." Val's truck, with Twelve hanging out the window recording, was behind them before the gray van turned onto the main road.

"Get Twelve the hell inside!"

"Roger that in spades!"

Cleo wove deftly through the evening traffic. "Why did they have to build the football stadium twenty miles from Boston? I don't know the side roads around here."

"If they look like catching us I could try—"

"No!" Cleo knew Ash had the power to toss the pursuing van over onto the roadside, but she might have to be in real emergency mode to work up enough adrenaline, or whatever it was that fueled her. This wasn't an emergency. Yet. "Think of the unintended consequences of a car crash on the highway!"

"Right." Ash turned to check on their passengers. Cleo dared a quick rearview glance as well. The hysterical girl was quiet now, held tight in her friend's arms. The friend looked back at Ash with challenge in her eyes.

"Who the fuck are you guys? What do you want from us?"

"We're just getting you away from those scumbags. If you have someplace safe to go, fine, we'll make sure you get there. If you don't, we'll find someplace for you. Is she hurt? Does she need medical treatment?"

"Just a first aid kit. Scrapes and bruises and a nasty cut, but not bad enough for stitches." Her tone had moderated, but she was still wary.

"How about you? That's quite a bruise on your cheek."

"We get those all the time, and worse. Nobody cares as long as our faces don't get too marked up for too long. This time I'd be in for a beating, though, for fighting and getting myself bruised."

Cleo, in fleeting glances, knew by Ash's clenched fists that she was itching for some target to attack.

"Tell Val to veer off at this next exit and meet us at the bar," she shouted. Ash managed to phone those directions before Cleo yelled again, even louder, "Hang on, everybody!"

The gray van was passing them, threatening to shove them off the road. Cleo slowed just enough to let it by. It edged in front, angled to cut them off, and Cleo braked abruptly, swung into a controlled skid, crossed the highway and the median strip with huge thumps as their wheels went up and over the low curbing, and sped down the road in the opposite direction.

An exit onto a country road, a series of turns onto smaller roads, and they were safe from pursuit. Cleo pulled off in the lot of a closed gas station. "Everybody all right?" She could see in the rearview mirror that the girls were huddled together as low as they could get.

"I guess nobody broke anything, anyway," Ash said. "But is our van all right?"

"I'm about to check." Cleo got out and circled the vehicle, inspecting the axles and suspension, and then the wheels and tires, though she already knew by the feel. "She's fine. I wouldn't ask anything of her I wasn't sure she could handle."

Half an hour later, they reached the familiar streets of Boston. Val and Jana's truck was parked in the alley behind the bar, next to the back entrance to the office.

Once inside, Jana examined the girls with a nurse's expertise and an extra dose of gentleness. She shooed Cleo and Ash out of the room when the girl who'd first run began to tremble. Twenty minutes later she beckoned them back in.

"I've arranged to take them to the shelter tonight, and tomorrow I'll be notified if they need any more help from us. Lida here," she motioned toward the fiercely protective girl, "says she knows somewhere she and Annie can go, but it's a long way away."

"You'll be okay?" Ash went closer and took the hand Lida held out to her.

"Physically," Jana confirmed. "But…there's no telling."

Cleo, both tense and exhausted, tuned out their conversation. Her hands felt like they were still clutching the steering wheel, interpreting every jolt and vibration of the van. She would have paced if there'd been room in the office, but there wasn't, so she headed for Mags and the coffee machine set next to a microwave oven in a corner, and after a few gulps of the hot brew she asked, "Where's Twelve?"

Mags jerked her head toward the back of her desk. Twelve sat cross-legged on the floor behind it with her camera plugged into her computer. Cleo couldn't see much from that angle, but she could tell that Twelve was viewing her videos, tapping out a quick rhythm on the keyboard and nodding from time to time.

Suddenly, as Cleo watched, Twelve stiffened. Her tapping abruptly ceased. She looked up, saw Cleo, stared at her intently, looked back at the computer screen, then surveyed Ash across the room with the same searching look. In less than a minute she had the computer shut down and was up and away out the back door.

Next morning, the six crusaders met again in Mags's office.

"Well, they found out at the shelter what was going on, what made them run." Jana paused. "This isn't easy to hear, but we need to. The younger one, Annie, would disassociate from herself, from her mind, when she was forced to service customers. In fact, she's been kind of drifting full time lately. The other one, Lida, looked out for her as much as she could. Last night, Annie was taken by three guys together, all drunk, in a room with a mirror on the ceiling. What they were doing to her…well, Lida wouldn't say, but the boiling point came when one of them threw up on Annie. She suddenly woke up, in a sense, saw herself and the scumbags in the mirror, and snapped. She made a commotion and ran for it. Lida shoved her own John into a full bathtub—he was fucking her in the bathroom—and ran after her." Jana paused, rubbing her eyes. "The rest you saw."

"We got them out totally by accident," Cleo said. "But maybe, if word gets around, other girls will be watching for us."

Twelve had been uncharacteristically silent. Now she declared, emphatically, "We need to advertise. And we need a logo. A brand. And a catchy name." She looked defiantly at Ash. "I thought maybe something like 'The Avenging Angels,' and we could have a big decal of angel wings on the side of the van, covered over when we don't want to be recognized, and then we could whisk off the cover dramatically, and…"

"Not angels." Ash said.

Cleo was relieved that Ash wasn't quashing the whole idea. Yet. "We can think of something else," she said soothingly. "Maybe just words, like 'Here to Help,' or 'Freedom from Sex Traffickers,' or, I don't know, something shorter." She met Ash's eyes, took a deep breath, and felt like she was diving off a ledge. "Something like 'The Shadow Hand,' with a silhouette of a dark hand. I dunno. Something like that."

Ash was silent for a long minute. Then she turned to Twelve. "Come by our place around two o'clock and you and I and Cleo can discuss this." Then, to the others, "We'll all get together here tomorrow night, if that's okay with you, Mags."

Twelve arrived just past two o'clock. She seemed excited and nervous and didn't look Ash directly in the eye. Cleo's skin tingled. She guessed what Twelve was going to say next.

"Guys. I've been going through the videos from last night, and... well, I guess you know what—"

Ash cut her off. "Does anyone else know?"

Twelve took a deep breath. "We all do. It's pretty clear. Annie was lifted into the air by an invisible force and flung into the van. The tracker devices suddenly appeared on the vans when you guys were nowhere near close enough to them. What the whole gang wants to know is...what exactly do you two mean when you talk about 'Special Forces'?"

Cleo held her breath, waiting for Ash's reaction.

When it came, Ash's tone was remarkably mild. "You saw something like...a shadow hand? Is that what you mean?"

"You got it! I won't tell anybody outside the group, but we really need to trust each other and know what we have to work with." Twelve seemed unfazed by the revelation of supernatural powers in her friends. She saw how Cleo was looking at her, and recited, "'There are more things in heaven and earth, Horatio, than are dreamt of in your philosophy.'"

She saw their blank faces. "That's Shakespeare. From *Hamlet*. Talking mostly about ghosts, but it fits. For instance, I can do things with computers and other tech that go beyond anything that can be explained. I don't complain, don't get a tech superhero complex, I just go with the flow. So one of you—I'm betting Ash, 'cause Cleo was driving—can pick up a running girl and haul her into a van without reaching out and physically grabbing her. Not to mention sticking magnetic bugs on vans while much too far away."

Cleo, still tense, watched Ash's face. Denying Twelve's discovery, making a big deal of it, would just encourage more snooping. But Ash had apparently decided to go with the flow, too. "Speaking of magnetic bugs," she said mildly, "let's see what they can tell us."

Twelve took the hint and suddenly it was back to business. Maps were unrolled and marked. Three different locations. Twelve tapped the map with her fingertip. "This is a rundown motel. I ran past it this morning. 'No Vacancy,' back lot parking with a six-foot-high wire fence." She ran her finger along the highway to another marker. "Motel number two, on the south shore. I looked it up on Google Street View. Also 'No Vacancy,' and gate fencing again." At the last marker she hesitated. "Val checked this one out earlier today. She says it's an abandoned warehouse near the airport. She saw two white vans parked out back."

That evening, the meeting in Mags's office centered more around these new locations than on Ash's talents. Her curt explanation about a mysterious virus she'd caught in the desert was accepted, if not exactly believed. She did a few no-hands tricks to show a little of what she could do, tossing around barstools, juggling beer steins, untying Jana's shoelaces and drawing them out of her shoes to twist and twirl in a spiraling dance in the air. Their friends laughed and applauded and did their best to show this was cool with them.

For her part, Cleo was as impressed as anybody. Ash really had been getting in some practice while they'd been apart.

"Some weird shit over there in the desert," Val said with a wink. "I always hoped to stumble across Ali Baba's cave, but no such luck." And then, turning serious, "Anything you want to throw at me, Ash, I'll catch."

Jana nodded and put her arm around Val's substantial shoulders. They had Ash's back.

Mags didn't say much until the others had gone. After shifting and straightening the papers on her desk, she finally, in an uncharacteristically low tone, said what was on her mind.

"Back in Idaho, west of the Bitterroots—" she looked briefly up at Ash, who knew that country. "A long, long time ago, my Gran used to take me to visit an old Nez Percé woman, a friend from back when they were the only kids for miles. Gran's folks were about the only ones farming that stretch. Anyway, that woman could do things— not exactly like you, Ash, or not that I know of. Mostly things with water. She could make it go uphill, or jump up in a cloud of droplets that made rainbows in the sun, and she always knew where to dig to find a well. There were other folks who claimed to be able to do that last one, but her way was different, more like calling the water to where it hadn't been before."

Mags paused, shrugged, and looked from Ash to Cleo and back. "'Course, when I got too old to believe in such things I chalked them up to tricks, or maybe hypnotism. Gran told me never to tell anybody about it, and I never did." She paused, seemed about to say something more, then came out with it. "Gran was the only one who ever believed in me. I just want to thank you for letting me believe in her again, and her friend. I don't think they'd mind me telling you. Just one thing, though." The square jaw lifted, and the ice-blue eyes raked them. "Don't even think about leaving me back here every time! Next time I go along, too, and get my fair share of the fun."

CHAPTER 9

Twelve had been busy with her "creative" online work, putting together a video with a few shots of the party house and the vans and the running girls, from enough of a distance that nobody could be identified.

There was a long shot of the front door, though, showing the street number, fuzzy but not impossible to read if you really tried. There was also a shot of the street sign down the road. She gave it an enticing clickbait tag, "Sex Slaves Freed by Mysterious Strangers," and added text emphasizing the proliferation of sex traffickers in the Boston area.

"No telling how many guys who see this will go looking to get some for themselves," she admitted, "but you still need to raise awareness. Folks might start to speak up if they see something suspicious, and trapped girls could be watching now for a chance to escape." She'd photoshopped an image of a black, open hand on the side of their van, with the words "The Shadow Hand" curving beneath it. Then, in a comment, she'd tagged a couple of local newspapers and the state police.

She showed it to Ash before posting, pseudonymously, and Ash, to Cleo's amazement, let her do it. "We need to use everything we have, as long as we can. This is like cheating the casinos, only worse. We'll have to move along one of these days, or be gunned down."

Their next target was the motel on the south shore. They chose a day when Twelve had info on another party and got there a little before sunset. The location had once been a main road near the coast, now bypassed by the superhighway, but even in its best days, the motel had been strictly low budget. From the sad remnants of a fake windmill and bridge, Cleo judged that the miniature golf course out front must have been pretty cheesy.

Mags, who'd gone so far as to close the bar for the night so she could come along, insisted on being the scout on this mission. The others waited with the van and Val's truck and Mags's jeep around the corner of a boarded-up former carwash. Between that cinder-block building and the motel, a stretch of scrubby pine saplings had grown up, too sparse to hide a vehicle but enough to provide some cover for Mags, who went ahead on foot.

Twelve got antsy waiting. "Ash, put me on top of the van! I want a better view for recording."

Ash's look would have made a presumptuous Army recruit shake in her boots. Cleo almost felt sorry for Twelve.

Ash was silent for a moment or two, and only Twelve's muted squeak alerted Cleo and the others that the girl was very slowly rising through the air, up, up, just past the top of the van, then horizontally onto the flat roof of the carwash. Twelve stumbled to her knees and quickly stood, her mouth twisting in disgust. "This place is covered with seagull shit!"

"Now you have a seagull's view. Sit down and deal with it. And be quiet." To Val, Ash murmured, "You folks get her down when we've got what we came for."

Mags signaled just then that vans were being loaded with girls. Ash went to join her, and Cleo followed with the rifle she'd brought along just in case.

One van was backed up close to a service entrance and girls were being hustled quickly into it by a pair of guards. It was hard to tell, but Cleo thought at least six were loaded by the time the van's doors closed. Another backed up, and when the process had been repeated both headed for the gate, which swung open by remote control. A third van was parked outside the fence by the motel's front entrance.

"Go get our van and truck up closer," Ash told Cleo. "Make sure that coil of rope Val has in the truck is accessible."

Cleo brought their van up to the edge of the pines just as the second transport vehicle cleared the gate. All at once, the sound of grinding metal sliced through the air, and the leader's front left wheel twisted ninety degrees sideways. Then the second van spun sideways too, and the gate clanged shut behind them. When both drivers got out, they were shoved hard together by an invisible force, and before they could recover a heavy rope came at them through the air like a great flying serpent, trussing them together and knocking them to the ground, where all they could do was roll around on the gritty pavement.

Val ran for the first van, sliding open the side panel and yelling for everybody inside to get the hell out. Mags did the same for the second van.

Some girls moved quickly, seizing the opportunity for escape. Others were sluggish, as if in shock, or, Cleo supposed, already drugged up for the night's activities. One was being more or less carried by another, and not as many came out of the first van as had gone in. Cleo realized for the first time that this rescue business was more complicated than she'd thought. What if somebody didn't want to be rescued? Sex work as a choice was a woman's own business, wasn't it? As long as it really *was* a choice?

That thought was ripped away by the tingling of Cleo's scalp, a warning of incoming fire.

"Get down!" she called even as gunshots sounded from the motel windows. She crouched with her rifle behind the cover of the van's front tires, returning fire.

Ash began to mentally lift the girls sprawled on the ground and hurl them unceremoniously into the rescue van while Cleo kept firing sporadically, pinning down the shooter in the motel until Val hollered the all clear and she sprang back into the driver's seat.

The remaining van outside the front entrance had started to move in pursuit. Ash called out to the rescued girls, "Any more of you in that one? Any others we can get out?"

"No!" came the response, so Ash flipped the pursuing van on its side, leapt up into the front passenger's seat, and they were off. A quick stop to transfer the girls to Val's pick-up and Mags's jeep, and Cleo drove Ash in a different direction in case of further pursuit. "How many laws have we broken tonight?" Cleo called to Val as they parted. Val just shrugged and grinned.

Cleo took the long way back, along the meandering scenic route, where once in a while the bay could be glimpsed between run-down vacation homes through the gathering dusk. She could sense the tension that still gripped Ash, and didn't think it was just worry about the ethics of the nonconsensual rescuing of people. She waited, with one hand on Ash's thigh, and felt the moment when Ash took a deep breath and came out with the truth.

"I wanted to smash more things back there! It's scary how much I wanted to throw those vans around, bang them together, flip them upside down. I couldn't do it with some girls still inside. But when they started with the guns... I wanted so hard to smash them into tiny shards I could barely see straight. The sound of clanging metal, the surge of power, the rush of it all."

Cleo felt her way cautiously. The last time—well, the only time— she'd seen Ash hurl a heavy vehicle high in the air, the effort had drained her so badly that she'd almost passed out. Granted, tipping the vans had been far less dramatic, but Ash's strength hadn't seemed to be affected at all. More like enhanced. She'd changed since the desert. "Do you still wish you'd gone that far?"

"Yes. In my gut, at least, I do. It's like...like getting almost to orgasm, so close, sooo close. And then, suddenly...not coming."

Cleo couldn't resist. "And you'd know so much about that, of course."

Ash dug Cleo so hard in the ribs it was a good thing she had an iron grip on the steering wheel. "No. And no. In my mind, I'm proud of not giving in all the way to impulse. The punks in that van deserved to die, and I hope they got bruises and a broken bone or two, but things would get too complicated for us if murder entered into it. I stayed in control. The thing I've needed most to learn, according to the major."

Cleo pulled off the road onto a farm lane and stopped. "Sounds like there's a story there."

"Oh yeah. A story about how god-damned dangerous I am." Ash couldn't quite conceal a shiver. "Something you'd better know."

"You think I don't? But tell me about it anyway."

Ash hesitated for a moment. "That day I left the base, in the Black Hawk, I was…I don't know. Keyed up, tense, thinking of you standing down there watching me go." She paused. Cleo's hand found hers this time, squeezed it, and she went on. "The last thing I thought I would do was fall asleep, with all that noise from the rotors on top of everything else. But I got used to the rhythm, and I did sleep, for quite a while. When we began to descend, the rhythm changed. I woke up groggy, annoyed at the new sound and vibrations, about to reach up to stop them—and if the major hadn't stopped me just in time, I'd have made us crash."

Cleo was shivering now too, inside, but she kept her voice steady. "Good for the major. I'll bet she reamed you out, and not in a fun way."

"She was mad. But she was disappointed in me, too. That hurt almost as much as knowing what an idiot I'd been. 'For God's sake, learn some control before you kill yourself and everyone around you!' she said. And later, she said, 'I'd hoped….' I got the idea that she'd had some other plan for me but changed her mind."

To fill the sudden silence, Cleo said, "Never fly anywhere without me along. I'll keep you awake. But maybe McAllister just didn't happen to feel like flying with you anymore right then. Who could blame her?" At which Ash, of course, pinched her leg, hard.

Or did she? Cleo noticed that she was still holding Ash's left hand, the only one that could have reached her. Cleo began to consider some other kinds of scenes that might be very interesting indeed. No-hands spanking, for instance.

This was not the time to bring that up. Not even when Ash said firmly, "Now *that* impulse was very much controlled."

"Yes, ma'am!" Cleo pulled her hand free and started the engine. "Anyway, now we'd better go see how our latest crew are getting along. Jana will have had time to settle them down a bit, so maybe we can even get some useful info."

Jana was waiting with the new girls back at the Galaxy Bar. Val and Mags were decompressing in the office with something strong from the bar. Twelve sat at Mags's desk, oblivious to anything besides her laptop.

The main room looked more like a Girl Scout sleepover than a rescue scene. Most of the girls were sitting with mugs of hot drinks, coffee and cocoa. The girl who'd had to be carried out lay slumped on the bench of a booth with Jana's coat as a cushion. The others seemed pretty much okay, although one kept her head bent and stroked the front of her shirt over and over as though it were a pet kitten, so it was hard to tell what condition she was in.

Jana introduced Cleo and Ash to the group, mentioned each girl by name, and asked calmly what the two would like to drink. Cleo opted for cocoa, Ash for coffee. Jana waved Ash into her own chair and went to the office kitchenette. Many of the chairs had been stacked against the wall, as usual for ease of sweeping up when the bar was closed, so the girl named Edie got up to offer Cleo her seat, but Cleo just grabbed one from the stack.

"Is everybody okay?" she asked, genuinely concerned.

Edie seemed to be taking on the role of spokesperson. "Yes ma'am," she said, "we're all right, except for Huan." She jerked her head toward the booth. "She'll sleep it off, but still not be exactly okay."

Ash had smiled at Cleo's uneasy reaction to being called "ma'am," but now she turned serious. "What's Huan on? How bad? Should we take her to the hospital?"

Heads around the room shook energetically. "No, not the hospital," Edie said quickly. "She mostly only gets that bad when they're taking us to a big affair. She knows they'll beat her for not putting out well enough, but she can't face any of it without being high."

"Addicted?"

"Yes'm, but not as bad as some."

"As most," somebody muttered.

"Is that why some stayed in the vans when they could have escaped? Couldn't leave their drug suppliers?" Ash's question was more of a statement.

"Yes'm," Edie said. "That, and being afraid you were the police."

"So," Ash mused, "if word got around that we aren't police, maybe we could get more out."

"Maybe." Edie sounded doubtful. She shot a quick glance at another girl. Cleo looked closer and noticed her distinctly Asian features, with smudges where she'd tried to rub off the obligatory make-up. Without it, her face had strong lines and a grim, determined look. Right. She was the one who'd carried the girl now dozing on the couch, whose face looked Asian as well, what could be seen of it.

"You look like cops." Her blunt statement fell just short of antagonism.

"You still came with us," Cleo observed.

"Yeah, well, I figured our chances of getting away were better with you than with those fuckers."

This was getting interesting. Cleo prodded her a little more. "You mean your chances of getting away from us were better?"

"What else? But that was before I saw some strange shit. If cops can do what one of you did..." She looked directly at Ash, who held her gaze for a long moment before responding.

"We're not cops," Ash said at last. "What's your name?"

"Chiu."

"Chiu, we were in the Army until recently, so I guess we might look like law enforcement, but trust me, I have at least as much reason to avoid the law as you do. If, in fact, you do." She looked over at the girl in the booth. "Or if she does."

Cleo had been putting together those same pieces of the puzzle. This scene was worthy of a movie. Chiu was clearly American-born, or as close as made no difference, with just a slight trace of Boston accent. And she'd noticed at least some of Ash's more interesting contributions to the escape. They already knew that most of the Asian girls trafficked through the massage parlors were illegal in more ways than one, and often didn't speak much, if any, English, so they had nowhere to escape to, and feared the law even more than their captors. Chiu was an outlier.

Ash pushed on. "I'm not convinced that you were forced into sex slavery. But she was. Is that why you got involved?"

"What, you think you're the only ones interested in getting girls out of all that?" Chiu tried to stare Ash down, but finally shrugged. "Yeah, this was personal."

Once she got started, the words kept coming. "Huan is a distant cousin on my mother's side, scammed into being smuggled in for a nonexistent job. I met her, briefly, when we traveled to China for a family funeral two years ago, and recently we heard that she'd left for the Boston area but hadn't been heard from since. We thought…a friend and I thought… Well, my friend paid to go to one of those big orgy deals, and recognized Huan from a photo I had. Lucky, in a way. If she'd been trapped into the massage parlor trade I'd probably never have found her. There's just too much of that going on, shipping girls back and forth between states, bringing them up here mostly from New York.

"So anyway, we figured she'd be at the next one, too. Our plan was for my friend to attend, and for me to infiltrate, pretend not to speak much English, get dolled up and mingle. Between us we might be able to sneak her out. If I couldn't get her away then, I could play stupid and confused, say I was Huan's cousin, and get into the van that would take her back to, well, wherever." She shook her head like a dog coming out of a lake and scrubbed reflexively at her face. "Plan A didn't work, but Plan B did. Sort of. I've been cooped up in that place for three days. It's a good thing you got to us before I cracked and did major damage to at least one of those goons, never mind the guns."

Ash had visibly reverted to the stern Army officer faced with a terminally stupid soldier. "And your so-called *friend*," she barked, "let you get away with all this?"

Chiu's chin went up. "Okay, Plan B was all mine. I did it on the spur of the moment, without telling my—oh, what the fuck, telling *her*—what I was going to do. I'm in more trouble now than you could ever imagine."

Cleo could imagine it, all right. "This friend could pass for a John going to a gang bang?"

Chiu nodded and hung her head, not quite hiding the ghost of a smile. "Oh yeah. She can pass, all right. But I need to use somebody's phone to let her know I'm okay."

Cleo dug her old flip phone out of her pocket, with an apologetic shrug at not having anything more hi-tech. Chiu took it with muttered thanks and disappeared into the restroom.

Jana returned just then with a tray of hot drinks and plates of food she'd heated in the microwave. Cleo's stomach growled.

Jana's aura of everyday casual hospitality came over as completely natural, but Cleo could see that it was also expert nursing. These brutalized victims needed a good, warm dose of the ordinary just now. Even the compulsive fabric stroker looked up long enough to grab something to eat.

Later, though, they'd need something more than a brief interlude of normality. Cleo knew that from personal experience, although her long-ago abuse had been briefer and less dramatic than theirs, and she'd managed to leave some significant scars on her tormentor. She just had to hope that between Jana's connections and Mags's knowledge of activist organizations, these girls could be helped.

She could see that Ash was trying hard to wait a little longer now, let them have a bit more peace, but there were things that needed to be asked, information they had to have.

When Ash did speak, her tone was mild. "I'm hoping you folks can help us out so we can rescue some more. Do any of you know where more girls are being held?"

Edie shrugged. "They drag us around from place to rundown place, but we don't know where we're going or where we've been, and we don't stay together long. I was in one place, a motel, where girls got their own rooms and the Johns came to us, ten or a dozen a night. That was mostly for the youngest girls, jailbait. We each had 'owners,' and some of them had several girls, like a herd. Once you don't look so young you get sold, and maybe moved along to wherever there are party scenes." Her voice had been steady, but now it wavered. "And if you don't bring in enough cash that way, you… you get sold for the truck stop trade."

"Edie…" Cleo could hardly speak for the rage building inside her. She saw the same reaction on Ash's face. "How long…"

"Maybe two years. I couldn't tell." Edie had control of herself again. "I was drunk most of the time, but now I'm not. Not for months. I never did the drugs, and when Chiu came along I was ready to try to escape, no matter what."

Chiu, looking shaken by her call, returned in time to hear most of that. She put an arm around Edie's shoulder, and glared at first Cleo and then Ash. "Ease up, will you? She's been through enough. They've all been through enough."

"They," not "we." That confirmed that Chiu *had* been an infiltrator, as she'd said. How would she have coped if she'd been dragged all the way to a gangbang? Had she been already? Cleo sure as hell wasn't going to ask.

Jana stepped in then and started sending the girls one by one to the restroom to clean up before she drove them to the shelter. Cleo and Ash moved into the office to start planning the next campaign with Mags and Val, and Twelve, if she wasn't too immersed in the depths of the digital universe.

Chiu followed them as though she belonged with the rescuers rather than the rescued, which seemed only natural. "There's something else, too," she said, moving into the doorway, where she suddenly stopped. She was staring at the back of Twelve's blonde head. Twelve swung around in her chair, stared back, and recovered first.

"Hey, Chiu," she said coolly.

"Hey, T. You involved in all this?"

Twelve just nodded and turned back to her computer.

"You know each other?" Mags looked from one to the other with interest. "You do look kind of familiar... Chiu, is it? Maybe you've been in my bar. Do you and Twelve know each other from MIT?"

"Yeah," Chiu said, and seemed to be searching for what to say next.

Twelve swung around again. "Last I heard, you were doing a master's in social work at BU. How's that working out?"

"Um, fine. Okay. One more year to go." She looked around to see the others gaping at her. "You might as well know. I'm doing my thesis on sex trafficking, so I have more than one motive for being mixed up in all this."

Val set down her foaming glass and stared. "Tiger? I mean, Chiu? That was you under all that makeup? I thought you looked familiar!"

"Hey, Drummer," Chiu said. "Still doing that body percussion scene?"

"Um, not so much. Once in a while."

Mags began to grin. "Small world, isn't it? Every lesbian in Boston gets to the same parties sooner or later."

"Sounds like the parties have gone up a few notches while I've been away," Cleo said. "Getting beat on by a jazz drummer! Cool!"

Ash's face was unreadable, even to Cleo, until she felt a tapping along her back in a rhythm that could easily be from a classic jazz piece. Ash was still so expressionless that no one but Cleo would have noticed the faint ghost of a smile.

Jana was listening from the doorway by then. "Not to interrupt this party, but we have strategies to discuss. At least one of these girls needs psychological intervention, and I think I can arrange for that privately. But Huan doesn't speak much English, and isn't in the country legally. We'll be running up against the same problems again and again, especially if we try to take on the massage parlors."

Chiu had found a stool to sit on, but now she stood up. "I've been working on that with some friends, building up a support network before we try any actual liberation actions. It's...kind of nebulous, still, and dangerous in its way—getting involved in anything illegal, going to jail, could kill our plans for careers—but some of us, even law and medical students, are willing to take that risk."

Val asked, "Including Jian? You're still together?"

"Yes, and yes." Chiu's response was abrupt. "You know Jian. She'd like to just steal a bus, crash through some fences, load up all the captive Asian girls even if they had to be picked up and carried—*especially* if they had to be picked up and carried—and roar off into the sunset. The problem is getting someplace set up beyond the sunset to take them. We've got a committee set up for fundraising, and a liaison with an organization being set up for helping sex-trafficked Asians, but that's as far as we've got."

"We haven't come anywhere near that far." Val shook her head. "We can help get 'em out, though, if you can take them in afterward."

Jana moved on into the room. "We can't do everything on our own, Ash. We'll have to outsource some of it."

Ash nodded, somewhat to Cleo's surprise. "Chiu, if we can make a successful raid on someplace where the massage parlor girls are held, can your group take charge of them afterward?"

"Whatever it takes," Chiu said grimly, then flashed a wide grin. "As long as we get in on the action! Maybe it'll distract Jian from wanting to tear me limb from limb."

"You're on." Ash was in full lieutenant mode now. Cleo inwardly cheered. "As soon as we identify a location, we'll strike, so let's get going."

"Oh," Chiu said. "I got distracted. Huan told me that most of the Chinese immigrant women in the business around here are stowed in a cold, rat-infested warehouse kind of place. They can hear airplanes coming low overhead. Must be out near Logan Airport."

Cleo caught Ash's eye. Bingo. *That* warehouse.

CHAPTER 10

ASH AND CLEO MET WITH Chiu's friends in an empty classroom at MIT. Ash could see that some, especially Jian, weren't happy about working with non-Asian strangers. She didn't blame them. Most were what Chiu had termed ABCs, American Born Chinese, and college students or young professionals. They'd been planning their own heroic crusade as a kind of tribute to their roots.

Jian was clearly their leader, not the damn-the-torpedoes hothead Chiu had claimed, but certainly forceful. According to Chiu, she'd been on the women's basketball team as an undergrad at MIT, and with that tall, athletic build and fierce, don't-fuck-with-me face, Ash was sure Jian could pass as a man if she wanted to, even with her long black hair. Ash was also sure Jian was antagonistic to what she considered to be intruders.

Chiu introduced Ash and Cleo, but didn't name any of the dozen or so others beside Jian. Ash understood the need for discretion. As Chiu had said, any of them working toward careers in law, medicine, or pretty much any profession risked a great deal if they got involved in anything legally questionable.

Jian, not even trying to suppress a scowl, started off with, "Let's get to the point here. What's your pitch?"

Ash ignored the condescending tone. "We rescue sex-trafficked women," she said bluntly. "I've been told that you have an interest in doing that, but if we're not all on the same page, there's no point in this discussion." She looked coolly around the room, meeting each pair of eyes. There were a few nods in response.

"That," Jian said, "depends on what you can do for us. And what you want from us."

"A fair question. We've managed already to free almost a dozen girls. Not all that much progress, but a start. With remote tracking devices, we've located several places where more are imprisoned. Our next target is a much bigger project, possibly more than we can handle without help. We've identified a warehouse where we believe women trafficked from Asia are being held, but we're faced with a language barrier."

"So that's where we come in?" Jian's gaze swept the room. "How many of us were made to learn some Mandarin as kids?" Most hands were raised. "How many of us remember much?" Many hands went down, amid ripples of laughter. "More to the point," Jian went on, "How many of us besides Chiu know any Cantonese?"

Half a dozen hands twitched uncertainly upward and slowly lowered.

"C'mon," Chiu said. "You bunch from the classes I've been giving know enough by now to get by in a case like this. And any of the rest of you wanting to help sex-trafficked women from China had better join my classes, too, even if you don't have any intention of working in social services for immigrants." The half-dozen hands moved upward again with more confidence.

Ash let her stern expression soften. "Any of that is more than we have going for us, and we have plenty going against us already." She searched for a diplomatic way to approach her next point.

Cleo stepped up and did it for her. "Let's face it, what we look like, who we are, won't inspire confidence in these women. They won't trust us. I mean, look at me!" She ran a hand over her red hair and skin already fading from lack of desert sun. "Would you trust this face if you were new to the country and had been treated like hell ever since you got here?" In a quick shift of mood she flashed a wide grin, and quite a few women smiled in response.

"Yes, exactly," Ash said. "But what we do have going for us is experience, and some special tactics we've found to be very successful."

Jian opened her mouth, but another woman spoke first. She looked more likely to play football than basketball. "About those tactics." Her expression was frankly suspicious. "Care to elaborate on those?" There were scattered mutterings of agreement around the room.

"No." Ash was firm. "Not at this stage of negotiations." Chiu must have told them a thing or two. Or maybe Twelve had posted the video of their most recent escapade already. Let them wonder.

Jian took back control of the discussion. "Why not just give us the location of this warehouse and let us handle it all?"

For an instant Ash felt the heat of Jian's glare, and responded with steely composure. "If you can guarantee that you'll succeed, we'll consider that. Let's keep in mind that freeing and then supporting these women is what matters, not who gets the credit for it."

Suddenly Jian laughed. "All right then, we're all on the same page." She scanned her group. "Anybody else have questions? No? How about we discuss this privately for a few minutes, if you two don't mind." She nodded toward Ash and Cleo. "There's a nice courtyard outside where you can wait. We won't be long."

In the small courtyard, Cleo paced back and forth while Ash looked thoughtfully up at the window of the room they'd left.

Cleo stopped beside her. "What's your impression? What do you think they'll do?"

"I think," Ash said, still looking toward the window, "they'll go along with whatever Jian decides."

It was Chiu who came to deliver the message. "Jian won't commit to anything yet, but six of us will agree to meet with your group tomorrow at your headquarters—the Galaxy Bar, isn't it? —for further discussion, and all the others will go along with whatever's decided."

Ash and Cleo walked back across the Charles River on the Massachusetts Avenue bridge. At the midpoint, Ash slowed and said, "What did you think?"

"I think we're in luck, if they'll sign on. That they're smart goes without saying, coming from MIT, and there were even a couple of them toting Harvard bags. I used to think all MIT girls were head-in-the-clouds rocket scientist types, but this bunch looks athletic, too. With them on our side we could work wonders. I mean, even more wonders."

"Just don't forget that they're on their own side, above all," Ash warned.

"That's just what we need, though. We don't know how to handle the massage parlor deals, don't speak the right languages, don't know how to cope with the legal aspects of undocumented sex slaves. These guys may not have everything figured out yet, but they've got a head start on it, while we've got a head start on the action front. We join together for one or two escapades, and then they take over their mission and we keep on with ours." She shook her head. "But who knew MIT had a women's basketball team?"

Jian joined Ash in the "war room" well before the others arrived. Ash took advantage of the time to make it clear that the two of them would be consulting on tactics and strategy on an equal footing if they decided to work together.

Jian had questions, though. "What's all this crap Chiu says about you and some crazy tricks?"

"Like tipping over vans? Lifting girls when I'm nowhere near them? Don't ask me to explain how it works, because I can't. But it does work." She did the bar stool flipping thing, and then made the heavy desk hover two feet in the air. Pens and papers slid off. She had to set the desk down before she could pick them up. "Drat, I keep trying to figure out how to multitask, but so far, no luck."

Jian's eyes narrowed. "I could maybe believe somebody invented an anti-grav device, or some kind of ray that could exert invisible force. I'm no physicist, just a mathematician. But what you seem to be doing…"

Ash shrugged. "Like I said, I don't understand it either. Something happened to me over in the desert, and now I can do these things.

Maybe it won't last, but while it does, if you want my help, you've got it."

Jian looked the desk over closely, then tried lifting it from one end, her muscles bunching, her face contorted into a fierce grimace. She got that end several inches off the floor—which was a good deal farther than Ash could have without extra power—and managed to set it back down gently. "Oo-kay then," Jian said. "Whatever works."

Chiu and the others from their group arrived, as well as Mags and Jana and Val. The room was so crowded that Ash and Cleo perched on the desk. Twelve, coming last, hunched on the floor in a corner with her open laptop.

After first-name-only introductions, Ash laid out a tentative plan. "We're pretty sure we know where a lot of the massage parlor girls are kept, and Jian and Chiu have friends who've already been planning ways to help those girls, so we're thinking of combining forces for at least one attack. We hope to be able to rescue more than we have before, and we'll have several vans, trucks, whatever—" she looked over at Jian, who nodded, "—to make room for them. Cleo's drawn a rough map of the warehouse we'll be attacking and the neighborhood around it. Everybody should look it over."

Chiu had gleaned more information about the warehouse from Huan, so Cleo knew roughly what it was like inside, where the girls were kept, and where any guards and keepers were likely to be. Everyone who could fit leaned over the map spread on the desk. Then Jana, who had stayed close to the door, said, "This sounds like a great idea. I've said before that at some point we'd need to outsource some of the work. I was thinking more of getting the police involved, if we could do it anonymously, but having Jian and Chiu's group take on the most legally complicated part would be a big relief."

"The police?" Two or three voices were raised at once.

"Yes." Ash was emphatic. "It has to come to that, eventually. I've known it all along. It's their job, after all. For that matter, stopping us from what we're doing is their job, too. We can accomplish things outside the law better than they can inside it, but public awareness and legal crackdowns are the only things that can have a widespread effect."

Some muted grumbling began, but then Twelve piped up. "The cops saw the video I posted this morning and are already getting involved." She turned her laptop so the others could see the screen. The motel they'd raided was shown, with several police cars and two ambulances, and three scruffy-looking men in handcuffs.

Twelve shifted from the news clip to her own video showing the place while they'd been there, with the men tied together on the ground, the vans in skewed positions or tipped over, and even the running girls, but no shots of the rescuers except one bit where Mags's elbow showed at the edge of the frame. Twelve's clickbait line this time was, "The Shadow Hand Strikes Again! More Sex Slaves Freed!" A white flag showing an outspread black hand had been photoshopped into the picture.

The map was abandoned while everyone had a good look at the video. Meanwhile, Cleo backed Ash into a corner. "You let her do this, too?"

"We can't hide forever. And we can't accomplish much with just a few rescues at a time. Like Chiu, I'm willing to take the risk. But…" she looked up at Jian, who had come charging over to them, "Twelve won't be doing any filming of the warehouse raid. Too many lives involved to risk identification."

"You think you can stop her?" Jian barely suppressed her rage.

"I can take her cameras away. Even from a distance. But I think she'll give them up voluntarily."

Twelve appeared suddenly at Ash's side. "I know, I know, I won't film it. We really need to get our brand out there in the world, though, make our cause go viral. More viral, that is. What's already out there is being shared and reshared all over the place. It's great! But I understand why we can't film things this time." She looked up at Jian, her stance as challenging as it could be while she was clutching her laptop to her chest. "Look, Jian, I know what you think. I *am* a little crazy, but not *that* crazy!" She turned away, took a determined step or two, then turned back. "Ash, I forgot to tell you, but the cops raided that house down by Foxboro, too, after I posted that video. Of course there was nothing much there by then, but at least there won't be anymore parties in that area for a while. We're good-guy terrorists, scaring the bad guys by our acts of disruption! Social Justice Terrorists…I might use that line." Then she was gone, out the door, taking her laptop with her.

"She's right, though, about spreading the word," Cleo admitted. "Maybe we should wear disguises. Costumes. Or at least cover our faces, so we could be seen but not seen."

Chiu came up in time to hear that. "What, are we making a movie or rescuing trafficked girls?" But Jian looked thoughtful.

Ash stepped behind the desk and looked around for something to use to get attention. Val moved in beside her, cleared a swath of desktop, and pounded out a military drum tattoo with her big fists.

"Whoa!" Cleo muttered when the general uproar subsided. "Wish I hadn't missed all those parties, Drummer!"

"That makes two of us," Ash said, then turned to the now-attentive group and ratcheted up her Army officer voice.

"We'll take two days to reconnoiter, be sure we all know what we're doing, and make our move the following day. Jian and I will work out a plan of action and let you all know in time for discussion and fine-tuning. In general, Jian's group will take charge of rounding up the girls, bringing them out, and taking them away, while our group will break into the warehouse, disarm guards or whoever, and keep the others from being followed."

One of Jian's friends who could have been a basketball player, too, offered a last bit of advice before the meeting broke up. "Most of those massage dens are run by women as dangerous as any hired thugs, so watch out for them. There may be some men, too, but it will be the older women keeping the girls in line, and none too gently. They may well have guns or knives."

"Maybe we're making a movie after all," Cleo muttered, and followed Ash out into the chilly autumn air.

"I just need to smash something!" Ash flexed her shoulders and arms. The leafless branches of a nearby tree thrashed, while everything else remained still. "Something big. Like that warehouse." Too much talking, planning, staying calm, she knew. Too much damned impulse control.

"C'mon, Godzilla." Cleo put her arm across Ash's twitching back. "Let's see how much smashing our bed can take."

The bed, being flexible, survived, but the springs might never be the same. It was a good thing nobody lived beneath them on the ground floor—or above them, for that matter—because Ash had a vague notion that she'd lifted the roof a time or two while Cleo was making sure that however long she held Ash so close to orgasm that she wanted to scream, the pleasure that finally pounded through her body was worth every second.

A heavy mist rose from the harbor while their convoy of cars and vans crept through narrow streets toward the warehouse. Low-flying planes landing or just taking off loomed like ghostly whales in a gray overhead sea, then disappeared into its depths. Even the roar of their engines seemed muted.

Ash was both on edge and invigorated. No more waiting for girls to be loaded for transport to wherever men would pay to use their bodies. This would be an all-out attack on the prison itself, no one left behind. According to some of the girls already rescued, the hour or two just after dawn was the likeliest time for everyone to be inside, and in this rundown area there didn't seem to be much chance of passersby as witnesses.

"Is Jian's crew all in place yet?" Ash knew by the set of Cleo's head that she was listening for engines, and with her uncanny ability to hear and differentiate them, she'd know to the last car when their allies were in position.

"All present now. Some were here ahead of us. Just a sec." Cleo tapped out a text on her muted phone, watched for a response, and nodded. "Ready to move in."

Ash edged the van forward. Mags and Val followed in their vehicles, all their engines super-muffled by Cleo so that only the tires on the rough pavement made any appreciable noise, and not much at that. They stopped behind the abandoned building closest to the warehouse, got out without making any noise closing their doors, and looked around the corner at their target.

"Wait... there's something moving..." Ash squinted, not quite sure the gray forms she saw weren't just denser patches of mist.

"Of course. Jian's crew are supposed to be moving into place. I wish we could have staged a rehearsal, but we went over the plan so many times there shouldn't be any surprises." She peered around Ash, caught her breath, and then released it. "Oh, cool! Ghost ninjas!"

Now Ash could see a dozen figures hovering between nearby buildings, all in gray sweatpants and hoodies with scarves wrapped around the lower halves of their faces. Jian could be identified by her height. "Ninjas are Japanese," Ash muttered. "Maybe they're supposed to be Wuxia heroes."

"Or maybe they'll burst forth from those gray cocoons and turn out to be butterflies." Cleo grinned. "Whatever, as long as it works. C'mon, we're up now!"

Back into the van, newly equipped with a bullet-proof windshield. Cleo drove while Ash half-stood inside, bracing against the bumpy ride. Cleo gunned the engine, racing toward the side of the warehouse where a loading dock extended from the building. Ash focused with all her mental strength on the great metal doors, which shuddered, began to inch apart, then slid faster and faster behind the walls until the dark entrance was completely open, an ominous, gaping mouth.

The gray guerillas swarmed up over the loading dock and ducked inside. Cleo followed, her rifle ready to spew terror but not, if possible, actual death. Two gray-clad latecomers sprang up behind her, one so close they nearly collided, and Ash heard Cleo growl, "Damnit, Chiu, you could have warned me about today's dress code!" Then they all stepped through the open door, Cleo turned with a brief thumbs-up signal, and they disappeared inside. The girls, they'd been told, were kept on the third floor.

Ash slid into the driver's seat and steered the van toward what appeared to be the conventional office entrance around the corner. Mags and Val were already there with the jeep and truck. Somebody inside knew it, and had turned on a light.

The three of them got out, Mags first, and moved cautiously toward the door, backs to the splintery wooden wall, while the shrill, angry shouts of a woman inside alternated with the rumble of a deeper masculine voice.

"Go out there!" the woman yelled. "Do your job!" Then she rattled off a stream of Chinese that Ash suspected was the same orders augmented with colorful profanity.

The man gave a sharp cry, opened the door, and stumbled through it, carrying a pistol in one hand and bleeding from a stab wound in the other arm. When Ash sent his gun spinning away and into Val's grasp, he took one more step, looking dazed, put a hand up to his wound, and slumped down onto the gritty pavement. Through the open door, they saw an older Chinese woman brandishing a dagger and glaring at them with venom. She raised the blade, lunged toward Mags, and just in time Ash twisted the dagger from her grip and sent it spiraling up, up, to imbed itself in the high wooden ceiling. The woman still took two steps toward them, then saw how many they were, and how large, turned back, and dashed down the hall and up a staircase.

Shouts and thumps were already coming from upstairs. Another female voice yelled, "You would not spend on real guards!" followed by a string of rapid Chinese.

"Get set," Ash called to Val, and ran back around to the loading dock while Mags was tying the unconscious guard's hands and feet.

"Six coming down," Cleo called from above, and within two minutes six Asian girls clutching clothes or thin blankets around themselves emerged uncertainly from the darkness.

Ash texted Val to alert her, and almost at once the atmosphere pulsed with deep, low vibrations. Val's bass drum was muted in some mysterious way that let the sound spread far without creating enough noise to be noticed if you weren't waiting for it. In a strange way it could have been whale song, as if those ghostly overhead illusions *had* been whales instead of planes.

Jian's backups had been waiting for it. From between the surrounding buildings, along the rutted road and out of alleys, four cars, two vans, and a vintage minibus approached the loading dock and lined up.

A gray-clad passenger stepped out of the first vehicle, spoke to the shivering girls on the dock, helped them down and into the car, and they sped off. By then, two of the rescuers who'd gone inside had appeared leading six more girls, and helped them into a waiting van. Two more of the crew emerged, each carrying a figure so slight neither could be much more than a child, and passed them down to the van as well before darting back inside for more.

The next group brought five girls, and a hurried message from Cleo: "Trouble on the fourth floor. Two armed hellcats barricaded in a room with a very young girl. Stay down there and watch the windows."

Ash backed away from the building and looked up toward the top floor. She could see sporadic movement behind a middle window. "Keep loading," she called to the workers on the dock and in the cars.

The window opened. A woman leaned out. "All come back!" she screamed. "Bring all back!" She turned away, then back with a slight figure struggling in her arms. "Bring back or else!" She thrust the girl so far out the window that only her grip kept her victim from falling.

A tall figure hurtled through the gaping door and leapt from the loading dock. "Jian!" Ash called, but Jian, racing toward a spot beneath the window, didn't seem to hear. Staring up, face twisted in a snarl of rage both more and less than human, she shouted a stream of words that Ash couldn't understand, but the grim harridan above, screaming back, clearly could. She shook the girl, leaned farther out, shook her again, grabbed one side of the window to keep from falling out herself, and lost her grip on the girl.

Jian leapt, wild black hair flying, arms reaching up, trying to catch the girl in time to cushion the impact of the ground even if it meant crushing injury to herself. Ash, who had already slowed the falling body, switched impulsively to lifting Jian higher than any basketball hoop, impossibly higher, until her upraised arms closed around the girl. Then, in full view of the rescuers and rescued around the loading dock, both figures descended gradually to a safe landing. No one but Ash saw the startled look that Jian shot her on the way down, or the huge smile that flashed for just a second across her face.

The woman in the window still screamed, with fear now instead of anger, a fear that turned to shrill panic when Ash plucked her out, raised her, and set her down on the flat roof of the warehouse. Another older woman leaned out the window to see what had happened, so Ash set her on the roof as well.

It was Cleo's turn to come dashing out the gaping door and leaping from the loading dock, with Chiu close behind. "What…" She looked around, saw Jian still holding the girl, and ran to Ash, who pointed up at the roof where the two women slumped near the edge. "I missed all the fun! And there won't even be photos this time!"

"There had better be," Chiu said, close behind her. "I gave Twelve a camera on my way. That's why I was almost late. Once we decided to go in disguise, Jian thought we might as well let her film us." She strode over to Jian, who looked almost as much in shock as the girl she was still holding. "The poor child's shivering! Here, Jian, wrap her in this." She wriggled out of her hoodie and offered it. "The sooner we get her to Jana, the better."

"Where?" Ash looked around at the closest buildings to see where Twelve was filming from.

"Hey! Get me down from here!" Twelve, in a gray hoodie, waved at them from the roof. "The trap door doesn't work from this side, and I don't care for the company."

An hour later and several miles away Ash alternated between slumping in the car seat and sitting up so rigidly her body quivered. "I should have been upstairs with you!"

"We all knew that you should be guarding the loading end," Cleo pointed out, "and positioned where you could see the wider picture. *I* should have been able to keep that witch from dragging the child upstairs, but everything was so confused and chaotic that I couldn't see well, or risk firing for fear of hitting somebody else. You were where you could disable the guard and get that bitch's dagger away from her. Mags told me about that. If she'd still had it..."

Ash couldn't stand to think about what might have happened. She slid back into the slumped position and covered her face with her hands.

"The woman on guard up there just had a kind of short nasty whip for keeping order," Cleo went on, "so I got that away with no trouble. I think their whole idea was to keep the girls in, without giving any thought to keeping rescuers out."

Ash straightened enough to lean her head back against the headrest. "Once more of Twelve's videos get around, the traffickers will know enough to up their defenses."

"I thought you approved of what she's been doing."

Ash shrugged. "The upside is that trafficked girls will know that escape is possible, and thousands of people will have a notion of what's going on."

"Including certain people who've been searching for us?"

Ash didn't answer, just stared out the window. Finally Cleo said, in a lighter tone, "You're grumpy now because you still haven't had a chance to smash whole buildings." She sighed dramatically. "I guess we'll just have to resort to sex again until something better comes along."

The sex came along within hours. The building smashing took a day longer.

Twelve's newest video showed the building, the neighborhood, the grey guerillas inside on the stairs coming and going with groups of confused rescued girls, and then aerial views from the rooftop that included the cars and trucks being loaded and rushing away (carefully angled so no license plate numbers were visible). The climactic shots were of the girl being held half out the window, Jian's miraculous leap to catch and save her, and the screaming Chinese women being lifted by an invisible force onto the roof. She had even captured from above the fierce, unearthly look on Jian's face as she leapt for the girl.

The banner Twelve added showed the Shadow Hand logo with a calligraphy-style dragon's head beside it, and the line, "Teaming Up to Terrorize Traffickers."

"It's all going viral now," Twelve said complacently. "Just think how much I could do if I had a rich backer and the right gear!" She looked hopefully at Ash, with no response, so she shrugged and went on. "Each of the videos is linked to the others, and millions of people all over the world are sharing them. And the comments! Plenty of trolls being nasty, of course, but far more positives. But look at this one!" She brought up a couple of lines from an anonymous poster with just a street name and number and the word, "Help!"

"That street's in South Boston," Twelve said. "I looked up the address. It's an old motel that's supposedly closed now, but a Google Earth scan shows cars there at night inside the fenced parking lot. The cops are sure to see this, and maybe even do something about it."

"We're going to get there first." Ash's tone allowed no dissent. "Can you contact whoever posted that comment?"

"Nobody can hide from me behind 'Anonymous.' When shall I say we'll be there?"

"Tonight. 7 pm. It'll be dark by then, but not likely to be many customers yet. Tell Anonymous to get ready."

It was too short notice to organize with Jian's entire crew, but Jian and Chiu wouldn't be left out, and brought three cars with allies.

They pulled up outside the gated fence, shining their headlights on the building. Ash tore open the gate, then peeled back sections of fence and rolled them into one huge coil. Several men ran out of the office, one holding a cell phone to his ear, but when Ash lifted the phone from his hand, smashed it against a post, and made the sharp fragments attack whatever heads came close like giant hornets, they all ran back inside.

Anonymous was ready for them. Ash could see a figure moving along the third-floor outside walkway, pounding on each door. Wherever she passed, a door opened and a girl came out, ran to the stairs, and dashed down to the parking lot. Chiu was there by then, motioning them toward the waiting cars. A few times a man stumbled out behind a girl, fumbling to get his trousers back on. Ash, with grim enjoyment, would pluck him off the walkway and fling him through the air to land in the dumpsters out back.

"Anybody left inside?" Cleo snapped after the last girls came stumbling down the stairwell.

"Not unless some John is hiding under a bed." Their Anonymous friend looked them over. "You're from the Shadow Hand?" She looked about sixteen, but close up her eyes were much older than that.

Cleo nodded, while Ash scanned the area, focused on the two-story-tall metal lamppost outside the office, and uprooted it. Dozens of eyes watched as the post shot through the air to embed itself in the middle unit on the third level so hard the whole wall caved in, windows spewing shards of glass. The pole backed off, rose high, and, like a cudgel, smashed down on the roof, caving that in as well. Over and over, up and down the length of the building, the battering continued, with special attention to the area over the office, where the guards still cowered until the assault had them running in panic. The walls on the second level began to crack, and the whole building seemed to slump.

Anonymous watched with as much satisfaction as awe, until a distant sound of sirens sent them all—including Ash, who finally allowed herself to be dragged away by Cleo—scurrying into the cars and trucks and racing off.

"So," Cleo said, after they had escorted their passengers to the agreed safe house set up by Jian's gang. "Was it good for you?"

Ash was still energized, but mellowing by the minute. "Oh yeah. Just fine." She grinned over at Cleo. "Not the *very* best, but fine just the same. You?"

"Well, it sure was fun to watch, but I do prefer more hands-on fun from time to time."

They drove on in perfect understanding, each with a firm hand on the other's thigh.

Twelve's videos of the girl-snatchings had been avidly shared online even before this last one. Now comments came from all over the world, and stories circulated that were far wilder than anything they'd actually done. T-shirts printed with "The Shadow Hand" appeared for sale like mushrooms after a rain. There were even reports of girls inspired to get away on their own initiative, and police departments cracking down on traffickers. Twelve had been right that the local police had been monitoring the videos, and they'd begun taking action. Awareness had definitely been raised.

"It's time," Ash told Cleo a week or so later as they lounged on their backs in the big bed. "We need to move on. Val and Jana have contacts in New York inviting them to come and help set up some new rescue crews. The others can handle things around here without us."

"You sure set Jian up with an impressive reputation," Cleo said lazily. "Have they decided what to call their crew?"

"Still haggling over it. Chiu favors Dragon Tongue, but Jian says that's too clichèd." Ash could predict Cleo's reaction.

"Really?" Cleo sat up. "Tongue? Almost makes me wish we were sticking around."

"You would. One of these days, though, either the traffickers or the Army spooks will get us. Twelve says most folks think the superpower aspects of our videos are faked, but they don't mind. And then there are those who believe because they want to believe. But Major McAllister can certainly connect the dots."

"Yeah, it's time." Cleo flopped over and began to trace the seams in Ash's denim jeans with her fingertips.

Ash wriggled, but kept on with her train of thought. "We'll make plans tomorrow and pack up. Maybe we could go someplace with mountains. Stop by New Hampshire, and then on to Montana." Then, as Cleo's fingers got more insistent, "But okay, let's see how much advantage we can take of this roomy bed tonight."

It was just as well they did, Ash realized in the morning, when the spooks caught up with them. Or, more precisely, one ex-spook.

Major Margaret McAllister knocked on their door just as they were getting ready to go out to grab some breakfast. "Nice to see you two," she said. "Great work you've been doing."

Ash's fingers twitched. It took considerable effort, but she didn't try anything. "How long have you known?"

"Quite a while. Let's just say those remarkable videos came as no surprise. I ferreted out a good deal of information about you from those, and about their creator as well. Food for thought. I didn't want to interrupt your campaign, though. May I come in?"

"Might as well." Ash backed away from the door.

"I'll get right to the point. I need your help. No, not on official Army business; I retired two months ago."

Ash sat down on the bed, willing to hear more out of curiosity, but still feeling a grudge.

Cleo leaned against the door, arms crossed firmly over her chest, jaw raised at a challenging angle. "That 'you' had better include me! Where Ash goes, I go."

"It definitely includes you. And your 'instincts.' Your skill at detecting explosives is as rare and valuable as the lieutenant's abilities. I suspect your automotive skills go beyond rational explanation as well. I have quite a file on you, and would have tracked you even if you hadn't been linked to Ash."

Cleo, looking half-stunned, slid down to sit on the floor. McAllister turned her attention to Ash.

"Before I retired I took care of your records. Listed you as not a candidate for further study, even deleted your AWOL status." At Ash's frown of disbelief, she added, "I have my ways. And friends in the right places."

"Blackmail," Cleo muttered.

"No, just…persuasion. And now I need to persuade you two to undertake an undercover, unofficial, and quite possibly deadly mission. In case my powers of persuasion aren't enough, I've brought someone else I'd like you to meet." Her gaze swept the small room, the rumpled bed still musky with their lovemaking, the half-packed duffle bags, the teakettle on the single electric hotplate perched on the shelf next to the sink, the cereal boxes on top of the tiny refrigerator. "Is there somewhere convenient we can go?"

"If it's privacy you want, Major, what you see is what you get." Ash had no patience with condescension.

"Oh, just call me Mac, will you? I'm no longer officially in the Army." The words were spoken with confidence, but her stance and tone revealed a trace of anxiety. Whatever she wanted from them, Ash thought, it was personal, and mattered so much that she was shaken.

"All right, Mac." Ash couldn't help feeling some sympathy for the woman. "Go ahead and invite your friend up here. We'll listen to what you have to say."

Cleo stood up. "I'll go out and bring back some coffee and muffins or something. We haven't had breakfast yet. Coffee okay, or would you like tea?"

Mac shot her a look of deep gratitude. "Coffee's fine. Two, please. Large. Black. We've already eaten, though, so no need for food." She scooped a phone out of a jacket pocket and texted a few words. "She's parked a few streets away."

"I'll be back with coffee pronto," Cleo said. "No fair doing anything exciting until I get back." She dashed out the door, and they could hear her bolting down the stairs two at a time.

In just under ten minutes they heard voices, and two sets of feet on the stairs. Cleo came in, juggling a take-out tray and bracing the door open with one elbow to let a fit, mature woman with short dark hair and khaki pants and jacket enter past her.

Mac introduced the newcomer all around. "Colonel Razhan Khider."

"Pleased to meet you, Colonel." Ash felt a grudging respect for Khider's firm handshake, direct gaze, and lean face, all the stronger for being lined by weather and hardship.

Cleo slid her tray onto the table and offered a steaming cup of coffee instead of a handshake.

"Thank you." Khider took a sip. "I'll get right to business, if I may." Her slight accent left no doubt that she served in the women's branch of the Kurdish Peshmerga.

"There are thousands of women, Kurds and Yazidis, kept in slavery by my country's enemies. I was one of them, but not for long." She raised her chin, ostensibly to look around her, but enough to reveal deep scars on her throat and jaw. "Some have escaped, with aid, and often with lives lost. Some have been purchased out of slavery by their families, but our funds ran out some time ago. Most, especially the youngest, are offered for sale, sometimes in encrypted posts on social media." She paused to drink more coffee, and to let what she'd said sink in. "Some are my...our...friends." Her gaze flicked very briefly to Mac, now perched on the bed beside Ash. Mac's tension was so pronounced that Ash had a fleeting impulse to put an arm around her.

"My sister Nisreen, also a colonel in the women's division of our army and a good friend to Mac, is one of those, captured in battle, now imprisoned in an ancient walled city along with hundreds of others." She paused, the lines on her face appearing to deepen. "There seemed to be no hope... We have been battling the enemy on so many other fronts, and the city is impregnable without endangering the captives. Our army will give what little aid they can, but it did not seem possible until..." She paused. "In honesty, it still does not seem possible, but I have known Mac for two years, and if she says that you may help to do the impossible, I must bow to her powers of persuasion."

Ash caught Cleo's eye, and Cleo nodded almost imperceptibly.

They had known, of course, about the women's troops in the minority resistance effort, and about the enslavement of women, but suddenly it was personal, no longer something far away and impossible to affect. Now they were being asked to join a campaign more than likely to fail, and quite possibly to cost their lives.

Ash straightened. "Colonel, just tell us what we can do to help."

Cleo nodded. For better or worse, they were in.

Colonel Khider smiled. "My forces would welcome the Shadow Hand. Yes, your fame has spread even that far. We will discuss in time whether revealing your identity would be more useful than keeping it under cover, but that is just one small point on the list of what must be discussed. Before we can mount any attack, there must be planning, and training in the mountains, and gathering of troops and weapons."

Ash dipped her head in agreement. "Mac, was this what you had in mind when you hinted at some other plan for me, then decided I needed to learn more control?" She didn't try to hide a trace of bitterness.

Mac sighed. "Yes. I know it was harsh, dumping you at that place. I realized then how badly it was being run, but I'd just received word that Nisreen had gone on a rescue mission so daring, so dangerous..." She paused, drew a deep breath, and pulled herself together. "I had to go, and I had to leave you there for Mona's sake. I knew you'd take care of yourself, and of her. I did return as soon as I could, when Nisreen succeeded against all odds. But by then you were gone. Good work getting both of you out of there!"

Cleo started throwing more gear into her duffle bag. "And now," she said, "Colonel Nisreen Khider has been captured? Another mission for Shadow Hand!"

Ash stood up and sent her own gear floating toward her bag. "How soon do we leave?"

PART THREE

CHAPTER 11

"Place your bets, Mesdames, Messieurs."

The casino in Geneva was heavy on slot machines, light on table games, only two for roulette. It would have been suspicious for Ash to win every time, so Cleo took several turns, intentionally losing at first, then winning as much as seemed wise while Ash watched from just close enough to be able to work her will on the wheel. It was a relief when Cleo could give up her seat and retreat to the impersonal rows of slot machines. Most of those were computerized, but a few mechanical ones remained, for the sake of tradition, Cleo guessed. She watched the machines play for a while. The garish colors, glaring lights, set her on edge. Given long enough, she was pretty sure she could figure out their patterns and quirks and win a fair amount of the time—machines held few secrets from her—but she didn't think she could stand being in the casino atmosphere that long.

Fair was fair, though, and they'd already taken a two-day trip to Chamonix and Mont Blanc as she'd wanted, although she had to admit that the grandeur of the mountain had been nearly canceled out by the glossy commercialization of the ski resort.

Now she'd put up with the casino for a while, people-watching from a corner to pass the time, observing Ash from a distance. The dress code here was casual, so ski clothes like those they wore, bought for the wintry mountains where they'd be going, were common, but there were also folks dressed as formally as extras in some James Bond movie. When she caught a glimpse of intense blue silk from the corner of one eye, she didn't bother to turn and look until a familiar voice right next to her ear cut through the general buzz.

"What that girl needs is a big enough challenge to make her stretch."

Cleo's head jerked around. Mac, stylish and composed in a form-skimming blue silk dress, gold jewelry, and glossy, upswept hair, was observing Ash as well.

"And challenge is exactly what she's going to get," she went on. "You too. And you'll both meet that challenge."

Cleo nearly blurted out, "Who're you calling a girl?" But dazzled by Mac's elegance, she stammered, instead, "You're...you're two days early!" They had arranged this rendezvous in Boston.

"I concluded my last piece of business sooner than I'd expected, just half an hour ago, in fact, so we'll be leaving early tomorrow morning. Very early."

Half an hour? Had she been dressed like *that* for whatever her business had been? Cleo's question must have shown on her face, because Mac gave a short, sharp laugh.

"I have enough irons in the fire to build a fence around the Pentagon, but now nothing matters more than our mission. I'm off to the hotel to get some sleep. Can you get her to the airport by 6 AM, Aegean Airlines, or do I need to come pounding on your door?"

"We'll be there. She can sleep on the plane, but I won't. Don't worry."

"You heard about that 'copter incident, I gather."

"Won't happen now. She's been teaching herself to control her impulses. Besides, it's got so that I can feel when she's about to let loose before she knows herself. Kind of like when a mine's about to go off, or a gun about to be fired. It's like the prickle on your skin just before the lightning flashes."

"Yes," Mac said. "Like lightning. Just like that." She turned and walked away, perfectly balanced on spike-heeled shoes the exact color of her dress.

Cleo stared after her. Ash appeared beside her just in time to follow the direction of her gaze. "Who...?"

"Mac."

"You're kidding."

"Nope. We have to fly out early. 6 AM at the airport. And it's now," she checked her watch, "1:30."

Ash looked back toward the roulette table, rubbed the back of her neck, and sighed. "Okay. Let's cash in our chips and be on our way."

At the hotel, in bed but not yet wound down enough to sleep, Cleo gave Ash a back massage. The repetitive motions, the flexing of her hands, the familiar feel of Ash's body, worked together to center her on the bond they shared. Ash, face down, mouth half pressed into the pillow, seemed to relax, but after a while Cleo felt tension again in her muscles.

"It's not about the gambling," Ash muttered out of the corner of her mouth. "I need to DO something. Something that matters. Something big. I know I can't win enough gambling to buy back all those women from their captors, but even if I could, once they were safe I'd still go after those bastards and bring the wrath of Ishtar down on them."

"I know." Cleo dug deeper into the tense back. "That's what we're heading out to do."

"The thing is," Ash went on, "what I want to do is so huge, so immense, that...that I don't know if I can do it."

"Mac said you need a challenge that will make you stretch. And she says you'll meet the challenge."

"Yeah, well, I could do without Mac being right so often. But she is." Ash yawned, sighed, and snuggled down into the bed, finally relaxing now that she'd shared her inner turmoil.

Was Mac right? About Ash, yes. Cleo was sure of it. About what she was leading them into? They had to take that chance. The hardest part was taking Mac's hints about Cleo herself seriously. Were her own instincts, skills, occasional dumb luck—were they powers in the same way Ash's were? Well, this mission would prove something, one way or another. She was suddenly drowsy. None of that mattered, as long as she and Ash were together, doing whatever they did, in the best way they could.

She slumped down beside Ash, an arm across her back, head nestled into the curve of her shoulder. She breathed Ash's scent, felt Ash's dark hair brushing her face, and slept pressed against her for what remained of the night.

Ash didn't fall asleep on the plane. She sat by a window with Cleo leaning across her while they both looked down on the white peaks of the Alps.

Mac said, from across the aisle, "Impressive, aren't they? But so small when viewed from way up here. Are you considering trying to move mountains?"

Cleo sat up straight. "Don't give her ideas!"

"No," Ash said bluntly. "I have too much respect for mountains. They do their own moving without any help. One tectonic plate shoving under the edge of another."

Mac nodded. "No place shows that better than the Zagros Mountains. Row upon row of layered limestone folded into steep ridges with narrow valleys between."

"Sounds interesting. Kind of like the Rockies."

"A different climate, but yes." Mac gave her sharp laugh. "Except that thousands of years of human predation have stripped away almost all of the lush forests of cedars that were renowned even in Biblical times. And now some areas are being raped by giant oil rigs." She shook her head, leaned back, and closed her eyes, sinking into her own grim thoughts. After a while, she slept. Cleo noticed lines of stress on her face, of pain and sorrow, emotions that she managed to conceal when awake. Ash saw them too. She and Cleo exchanged glances, then turned back to looking at the world below, giving Mac privacy in the vulnerability of sleep.

They flew over Italy, and then the deep blue of the Adriatic. "Too bad there aren't any clouds for you to mess with," Cleo murmured, remembering what Ash had told her about making the clouds move apart.

"I'm making waves down there in the sea move in different directions, and redirecting currents. Can't you tell?"

"Sure you are. And I'm scanning for submerged mines in the water." How long had it been since they could be playful like this, the way they used to be traveling across the desert? Too long. Except for sex, of course, where there was usually a playful element.

"Find anything?"

"Not yet. Oh, wait, now I have. There's an ancient galleon a hundred fathoms deep over there, still fully armed with Greek Fire."

"Sure there is."

They snuggled as close together as their seats permitted, each with an arm around the other. A flight attendant came by, gave them a professionally neutral smile and nod, and went on. Cleo saw a genuinely amused smile tease at the corner of her mouth before she was more than a couple of feet past them.

"This is nice," Ash said. "Peaceful." But in a few minutes she straightened and checked her watch. "When did you say we land in Athens?"

So much for those moments of peace. "In about an hour," Cleo said. "Just a three-hour layover. No time to leave the airport."

"Then we should be flying over Greece soon." Ash stared intently ahead through the small window. "If that wing weren't in the way, we might be able to see the coast already."

Cleo reached automatically for her arm, then pulled her hand back.

Ash grabbed the hand and squeezed it. "Ha. You were afraid I was going to move the wing."

"Just a reflex. If you'd really been about to try that I'd have felt it." Cleo bent across Ash's lap to stare out the window herself. "Look! An island, and a hazy coastline." She leaned back and reached for the in-flight magazine in the pocket of the seatback in front. "There's a map in here…"

"Greece?"

"Just about, or the southern tip of Albania. Nearly Greece now." Cleo riffled through the pages. "Says here there's a small museum upstairs at the Athens airport with a few statues and things they dug up when they built the place."

Interest flashed briefly across Ash's face, then faded. "Dug up?"

"Good point." Cleo shivered even though the air was warm. "I guess we'd better focus on one goddess at a time."

The land seemed to flow toward and then beneath them. Ash sat upright, absorbed in the panorama. It was only natural for Ash to feel some bond with the country, Cleo figured, even though she'd never said much about her Greek heritage, and disliked her given name of Athena. Cleo would like to explore Greece sometime, too—who wouldn't?—but she sat back in her seat and didn't interrupt Ash's concentration.

After a while, Cleo looked over at Mac, Ash turning from the window to follow her gaze. Mac still slept, her face now more set than sorrowful. She didn't have the luxury of any peace at all, Cleo thought. Her Nisreen had attempted another daring mission, too daring, and now she was a prisoner who could not be ransomed, only kept alive for possible high-profile exchange.

As if she'd caught them thinking about her, Mac woke suddenly. She saw them looking at her, blinked, and arched her eyebrows. "Well, what? Did you have a question?"

"We just wondered," Ash said quickly, "how long we'll have in Lebanon."

"Not long at all. Certainly not long enough to explore the delights of the famous casino there."

"I wasn't thinking of that," Ash said, so defensively that it was clear that she had been.

"Just as well. The Casino du Liban has a strict dress code. Formal dress for women, suits for men." Mac smiled wickedly. "Too bad I left my blue dress behind. You wouldn't have filled it out quite the way the designer intended, but you'd have got by." Her smile widened. "See, Cleo's imagining you in that dress already."

"Let's just say," Cleo retorted, "that I'm imagining someone in that dress, and let it go at that."

Mac laughed out loud. Ash looked from Mac to Cleo and shrugged. "Well, since there won't be time anyway, I'm spared the painful decision as to whether it would be worth wearing a dress for the sake of twiddling yet another roulette ball."

"Seriously," Mac said, "we'll be doing well to meet Colonel Khider in Beirut in time to catch the flight to Erbil. Very few airlines fly to Kurdistan, and there are only six flights a week from Lebanon." She checked her watch. "Looks like we'll be on time in Athens, anyway, so we should get to Beirut with enough time to spare for a Turkish coffee with baklava while she updates us on plans, but not much else."

The colonel was there to meet and greet them, and steer them through customs. In a café a cut above most airport food vendors, they revived on pita, tabbouleh, and lamb kebab.

"You must all call me Razhan," she said over Mac's promised thick dark coffee and sweet, sticky baklava. "You are all on first-name terms, and so should I be. Our forces do not pay so much attention to titles; in fact, they tend to refer to whoever is leading them in action as 'Commander,' and simply by name in informal situations. Also, it would be better that we do not appear to travel together on military business."

"I was about to suggest that," Mac said, and Cleo and Ash agreed. It was a relief not to have to bother with titles.

Before their next flight, Razhan had papers for them, with new identities. "You, Ash, will be a journalist for a women's magazine in the States. Our female soldiers get quite a bit of attention from journalists. Cleo, are you willing to be the photographer accompanying her? Or would you two like to switch roles?"

Cleo suppressed a smart-ass reply but couldn't resist a sly grin. She answered sedately enough, "I'm fine with being the photographer. I don't have much experience with cameras, but I'm good at figuring things out."

Mac had grinned, too. Now she nodded. "Good. At first, as we go high into the mountains, it will make more sense to say you're from a travel magazine, or something like *National Geographic*, but with luck, up there we won't have to say anything to anyone."

CHAPTER 12

THE SECOND PLANE'S ROUTE TOOK them over terrain so much like the desert they'd known that Ash had an odd sense of coming home. From the way Cleo squeezed her hand she knew the feeling was shared. Much as they'd often been desperate to get away from not just the war but also those arid expanses, that same land was part of them now, part of who they were together. The mountains, though, as they came nearer and nearer—line after line of abrupt ridges with shadowed canyons between—drew them with the promise of new sights, and possibilities, and challenges. And new dangers.

The Zagros range rose from plains made fertile by the rivers running down from its rocky heights, Razhan told them. "The plains that lie between the Tigris and Euphrates are known as the cradle of civilization," she said. "But the mountains are the source of all irrigation water, so really they are the lifeblood of humanity."

The international airfield was in the district capital city of Erbil. Razhan had arranged for them to be met by a truck driven by a very young woman in army fatigues, with a traditional keffiyeh scarf around her head and a square, determined chin still softened by youth. Razhan introduced Ariya, who responded with a grin that reminded Ash of Cleo. The Sisterhood of the Motor Pool, she thought.

Their luggage was stowed in the back among sacks and supplies for their mountain trek. Cleo was provided with a padded case containing a high-tech camera so she could study the instructions along the way. Razhan warned that they had hours of travel ahead before their first stop, so they'd better make use of the airport restrooms and grab lunch to carry along.

In spite of her apparent hurry, Ash noticed that Razhan had Ariya drive them in a wide circle around the central city, where streets of centuries-old structures were interrupted by stark modern buildings, some with petroleum company logos on their facades. There was also a wide, elegant park, its expanses of grass still green in early winter. Fountains rose and fell over reflecting pools and along the sides of the park walls, which were made up of graceful open arches echoing those of the ruins of El Ukhaidir, where this journey had begun.

Razhan spoke proudly of a great elevated plateau of ancient buildings called The Citadel, thought to be the oldest continually inhabited settlement in the history of humanity.

Cleo, squeezed close to Ash in the middle of the truck's back seat with Mac on the other side, leaned across to take her first photo. She murmured in Ash's ear, "Such a great tour guide! We should tip her well."

Ash, who had been on the verge of making the same teasing comment, dug Cleo in the ribs with her elbow. Mac, always able to hear anything meant to be private, elbowed Cleo's other side and muttered, "If you haven't already figured it out, in times of peace Razhan is a professor of Kurdish history at the University of Salahaddin in Erbil."

She really was a natural tour guide. Her love of the land shone through her fierce determination to defend it. Ariya, too, pointed out things of interest, her English less fluent than Razhan's, but adequate. She soon pulled off her keffiyeh and shook loose her short brown hair. "Always cover to visit my grandmother in the city. You know how it goes!"

Outside the city, the road wound through towns also mixing present and past, with the past predominating. They were often centered around one or more religious shrines of great beauty and antiquity. Farther along there were smaller villages surrounded by farms and orchards. Fertile land, well-watered. Cleo photographed farmhouses with fruit trees and trellised vines growing flat against their warm stone walls, and pastures where cattle and horses grazed.

"Here," Razhan said, "you would not think that war could reach, but we fight to hold it back. So far our enemies have little interest in farming, only in harvesting our young men for their armies and our women to be sold as slaves. They raid the villages farther south and southeast, and that is where we stand against them. Soon enough you will stand there with us."

Soon enough? Ash chafed at moving away from the war zone rather than toward it. She'd been aware for some time of pressure from Ishtar, goading her toward battle, but much of the impatience was her own. Soon enough for Razhan's captive sister? For Mac's… close friend? She understood, from a military viewpoint, that those who knew the terrain and the people and the ways of the enemy had to be the leaders, even as it was getting harder and harder for her to tolerate anyone else being in charge. At least she recognized the dangers of that influence and that attitude, and had managed to keep them suppressed. So far.

By late afternoon they began to climb into the foothills. Plateaus and wide valleys there were still farmed, and there were hollows with stands of oak whose copper leaves still clung to their branches. Gradually, the slopes became more suited for grazing than for tilling.

After dark, they stopped for the night in a town on the banks of a river rushing down through a chain of valleys to join the mighty Tigris. They were welcomed into the home of Ariya's aunt, whose daughter was away fighting with the troops. Ash and Cleo slept on separate pallets in a tiny upstairs room overlooking the river, and next morning Ash watched at first in amusement and then with a twinge of envy as Cleo roamed about shooting photos of the river, the distant line of snow-topped mountains, the flocks of sheep and goats brought down from higher pastures for the winter, and details of the village and people right down to a cat snoozing on a window sill. When the cat's owner, a young girl on the verge of adolescence, spoke to her shyly, she took her picture and then called Ash over.

"Here's someone interesting to interview, Ash, for that magazine article."

Ash managed to string together some human-interest questions for the girl, with Ariya to translate. How did she like living in a village with such a lovely view? What animals had she besides the cat? Would she like them to mail her photographs of the cat and herself after they got back to America?

"Oh yes, please." She gave her mother's address, but went on to say, "in five more years I will not be here, but with the soldiers, like Ariya, fighting our enemies."

Ash had understood most of what had been said without translation, although it seemed wiser not to say so. Her years in the Army had given her a bare-bones familiarity with everyday Arabic, and the people here spoke a mixture of that and their regional Kurdish dialect. But she could scarcely keep from blurting out, "Oh, no, the fighting must stop long before that!" before Ariya finished translating.

"Don't you wish you really could write a magazine article about that girl?" Cleo sat beside Ash on a rough stone bench beside the river, eating a late breakfast of pita, tabbouleh, fruit, and strong coffee.

Ash didn't want to think about that child going to war. "You're having way too much fun with that camera," she said, evading the question.

There was a momentary distraction when a motorcycle pulled noisily up in front of the house, and several voices were raised, but they were in no hurry to give up their relative peace.

"It turns out that shooting with a camera is pretty much like shooting with a gun," Cleo said, "except that nothing gets destroyed and something gets preserved. Focus is everything. Who knows? Maybe I'll get a real *National Geographic* gig someday. How about a photo spread of you making boulders float in midair?"

Ash glanced around to make sure no one was watching, stood, moved back a step, and suddenly one end of the heavy bench tilted high enough to make Cleo slide off, struggling to hold onto both camera and coffee mug.

Just as the bench settled back into its customary position, Mac appeared around the corner of the house. The look on her face stripped away any trace of their playful mood.

"Bad news?" Cleo asked, taking a step toward Mac.

Mac strode on toward the riverbank without replying, then swung suddenly back to face them. She jerked her chin toward the bench. "How far could you throw that damned thing instead of just fooling around with it?"

"I can't tell until I try." Ash tested the bench just enough to make it shift an inch. "Across the river, at least, farther with enough adrenalin." She stood tensed and ready for whatever Mac wanted her to do.

"Not now. That's what we're going into the mountains to figure out. Soon. Sooner than we'd thought." She slumped down onto the bench in a most un-Mac-like manner. Ash and Cleo perched precariously in the scant space at either end, ready for whatever support they could give.

Almost at once Mac straightened. "Yes, bad news. Not that the news is ever good. Worse than usual this time. A captive just ransomed with funds from American kinfolk reports that Nisreen is being kept bound and drugged and accused of witchcraft. We've seen this sort of thing. A woman who manages to escape and yet returns to fight is often accused of some type of demonic possession, and there's no limit to what they'll do to her, short of killing her. They know Nisreen's military history and value for exchange too well for that. I thought…she hadn't contacted me…"

"She's alive, though." Ash was sure even before she spoke that Mac would know that. Just as she was sure she would know whether Cleo were alive, no matter where she was, and Cleo would know the same of her. They had even communicated mind-to-mind in a few times of extreme danger, mostly Cleo warning, *"Guns! Down!"*

"Yes." Mac looked from one to the other. "What I said about not being exactly a mind reader is true, but in this one case, I come close. Nisreen speaks to me, however far away she may be. I'm not much good at it, but I can at least let her know when I've heard her. When I didn't hear, I thought that there might be someone among the enemy who could sense it if she spoke to me mind-to-mind, so she didn't dare to do it at all. We've discussed that possibility before. But drugging her... Why? So she can't use their imagined witchcraft against them? Or to escape?"

That rhetorical question had no answer, so Cleo steered in a different direction. "How did you two meet?"

Ash glowered at Cleo—this didn't seem like a good time to invade any more of Mac's privacy—but Mac didn't seem to mind.

"I wasn't kidding when I told you, Cleo, that I had plenty of irons in the fire. One was as Army liaison with the women's forces of the Kurdish and Yazidi Peshmerga. Still is, in fact—one of those under-the-radar, 'these are your orders but we've never heard of you' deals. A year and a half ago I was already doing the bird-dogging bit for the PsyCorps, also nominally under the radar, but not so much so that I couldn't reveal it in a pinch. People anywhere enjoy a good laugh at the US Army looking for psychics."

"So you bird-dogged Nisreen."

"I was absolutely flattened the minute I met Colonel Nisreen Khider. For a while I couldn't be sure the power I sensed wasn't an illusion, ignited by infatuation. I still don't know—even she doesn't know—how much of her strategy and leadership in battle is due to supernormal abilities. Some of her feats are legendary among the soldiers." She sighed and rubbed the back of her neck. "Who knows whether Julius Caesar, George Washington, hell, maybe even Rommel, had powers beyond what's considered normal? But I do know that Nisreen can communicate at any distance with me. Except that now, she can't."

Suddenly Cleo stood, looking past the house as though she heard something, and seconds later the others heard the truck's engine start. "Grab your gear," Mac said. "We're hitting the road again."

They'd already packed what little had been unpacked. They went through the house, picked up their things, and once outside, with a glance around to see that they weren't watched, Ash made their bags blink out of their hands and appear sedately nestled among the other bundles in the truck bed.

"Can't resist, can you?" Cleo teased.

"Gotta flex those non-muscles every once in a while." Ash climbed into the truck and claimed a window seat. It went without saying that Mac would get the other, Cleo between them. Razhan would sit up front with Ariya.

Cleo made a face, but Ash knew perfectly well that being squeezed in between her and Mac wouldn't be much of a hardship. Their last stop was at the town's only gas station, where they filled several big gas cans and cushioned them with their bundles.

Yesterday Razhan hadn't talked much except about the country they passed through, and its history. Now everything was more urgent. She pressed Ariya to drive faster even though the road got rougher, and twisted around in her seat to talk with those in back.

"We won't go as far as I'd planned, and there is not much time for training. You know already that our target is a walled city, though to call it a city is not entirely accurate. It was utter rubble for hundreds of years, and only recently partially rebuilt as a fortress by the enemy. But the walls of stone are strong enough for their purpose, and land mines have been planted for a kilometer or more in every direction, leaving a narrow route, changed often, for vehicles to pass through only if they have a guide to show the way. Escape by individuals is impossible. A direct attack is also impossible because of the mines, and launching rockets into the city would endanger the women inside. Those about to be taken away to be sold are kept nearest the inside of the walls, so bombing those would also endanger them." She turned away to ease her back and shoulders from the unnatural position. The tension in her whole body was apparent.

"Tell us what you want done," Ash said, "and we'll figure out how to do it." Much as she hated to face it, the minefield would clearly be Cleo's department one way or another. Would hers be to hurl huge boulders at the city walls? That seemed likely to endanger the women inside, too, though not as much as rockets would.

"So there is a route through the mine fields," Cleo said thoughtfully, "wide enough for a truck, and wide enough for escaping captives."

Mac took over. "I asked this morning how far you could throw things, Ash, but it may be more a matter of moving distant stones. Not an entire city wall, but the supports of a massive gate. A gate that has stood for more than a thousand years."

"How will the women know to be ready to escape through this gate when it falls? Are there guards on the walls with guns?" Ash shook her head, wondering what she'd gotten herself—and Cleo—into.

"Some of our troops…" Razhan paused and took a deep breath. "Some will allow themselves to be captured and spread the word inside."

"And someone will lead them out through the mine fields," Cleo said. "That will be my job."

Ash tensed and turned on Mac. "You had that in mind from the first, didn't you!"

"So did I," Cleo said emphatically. "I wouldn't miss it."

They glared at each other until Ash looked away. She had known it, too, without admitting it to herself. She still wasn't prepared to accept it.

Razhan said, her voice close to unsteady, "I wish to go myself, but Mac has persuaded me to remain free so that if Nisreen becomes too ill…if they fear she will…will die, and be of no use to them, they may accept me in exchange, as I have offered several times already."

A moment of silence was broken by Mac. "There are certainly more plans to be discussed, but first let's see what is and isn't possible when it comes to Ash breaching the Lion Gate."

The Lion Gate. Ash felt Mac watching to assess her reaction. Lions were symbols of Ishtar. Babylon's famous Ishtar Gate, now in a museum in Berlin, had great lions portrayed in mosaic tiles, but that sort of thing was unlikely to have survived unlooted so long in the desert.

"An Ishtar Gate, then," she said. Beside her, Cleo tensed.

"Probably," Mac agreed. "This one has stone lion heads at the top of the supporting pillars on each side. Eroded by time and wind, but still lions."

What might happen if she destroyed the sacred stone lions? But freeing these women could be the very task Ishtar wished her to carry out, no matter how much destruction it took.

Cleo must have been thinking along the same lines. "Maybe Ishtar sent you here." Then, with a glance at Mac, she added, "Sent both of us."

"Ishtar, was it? I thought as much. Does it matter what she thinks?" Mac's voice, for once, was dead serious.

"No." Ash was serious, too. "We do as we choose, and we choose to do this."

Razhan, in the front seat, had been holding herself rigidly erect. Now she let her face slump into her hands.

CHAPTER 13

THEY STOPPED BESIDE A THUNDERING waterfall to eat a cold lunch and stretch their cramped joints. The rocky gorge of the river, spray rising from turbulent white water, was breathtaking. Ariya, sitting beside Cleo and Ash as they ate, waved a hand at the torrent. "This is small next to the flow in spring, when mountain snows melt. You should see it. Many hike here to view the waterfalls."

Cleo stifled the urge to say that there were such sights in the mountains where she came from, too. It would have been impolite, and not quite true. Few, if any, of the waterfalls she'd known, and climbed beside, and fished beneath, could compare to this. She did go so far as to ask whether there was good fishing here.

"Oh yes, when the spring flow slows. But a favorite fishing rock may be overturned and moved year by year, and tumbled about." She shot Ash an oblique look. Cleo was amused. Ariya must already know something about Ash's powers, or Mac wouldn't have talked so openly on the drive.

Ash strolled to the edge of the gorge. Cleo followed, glad to see that the drop-off wasn't quite sheer, just a steep, rock-strewn slope. Ariya was right beside her.

Ash pointed at a boulder halfway down, then pointed again at a spot in the river and put her hands in her pockets. As they watched, the boulder twitched, tilted, rose an inch or two, heaved itself slowly into the air, and lurched suddenly out over the gorge to plummet with a great splash, soaking the ground far up the slope.

Ariya clapped and beamed. "Ah! So there truly is a Shadow Hand!"

Ash still stared intently into the gorge. Not quite satisfied with her feat, Cleo thought. Ash pointed again, to a bigger boulder on the far side and then a flat rock in midstream, then hid her hands once more in her pockets. This time the rise was quicker, the flight higher, and when the boulder smashed into the flat rock, both split into pieces. Shards of stone rose with the leaping water and fell back in a storm of splashes and clattering as they struck rocks below.

Mac and Razhan had joined them. "Not bad," Mac said. "Got a touch of Babe Ruth showmanship."

The younger women stared at her blankly. "Babe Ruth!" Mac repeated. "Baseball legend! He liked to point to where he intended to hit a home run." She sighed. "Kids these days. No sense of history."

Razhan, who had looked as puzzled as the others, got serious. "Very good, Ash. Mac is right about your potential."

"Right? Of course I'm right. Good God, Razhan, she held up a helicopter about to crash and eased it to the ground! I've never seen anything like it. Okay, so that was an automatic, adrenaline-fueled reaction." Mac turned to Ash. "I have to admit, I hadn't realized until now how much control you've learned." Then, in a less congratulatory tone, "Physical control, at any rate."

"An impressive display, Ash," Razhan said. "But you will be much farther from the city walls than you are from these rocks. A very great deal farther." It wasn't exactly a question as to whether Ash's power was strong enough, but almost.

Cleo held her breath. She knew how a burst of pride, an emotional high, surged in Ash when she'd done something this dramatic. Those other times, though, had been genuine accomplishments, freeing people, saving them. This had been entirely a show of power. Cleo herself might get away with calling it "showing off," but nobody else would. She'd been wondering whether being closer to where all this had begun, to the influence of the goddess, was having an effect on Ash. How would she react now?

"Right," Ash said after moment's pause. "We'll need to experiment."

Cleo breathed again. She had a fleeting impression that Mac did the same.

"So far, I've had to be within visual range of my target, or to have seen it before and know exactly where it is. There's plenty yet to know about what I can or can't do."

"Perhaps with field glasses? But we must have more privacy to try such things. Even in winter hikers come this way to view the waterfalls and mountains, though fortunately there seem to be none today."

It wasn't quite a rebuke, just a warning. Ash nodded curtly, acknowledging the reminder for necessary caution.

They left one gas can behind some bushes to refill the truck's tank on the way back, and piled in after Ariya and Cleo had inspected the tires and undercarriage to be sure the rocky road, hardly more than a trail, hadn't yet done serious damage. The less they had to carry over such treacherous terrain, the better.

The snow-covered mountain peaks to the north claimed more and more of the sky as the truck climbed up over the hills. By the time they reached the empty herdsman's hut, their shelter for the night, clouds had gathered in the west, and as sunset approached, they took on intensifying tones from pink to salmon to vermilion, while the highest snowy peaks, still in sunlight, were touched with gold.

"Is there such beauty where you live?" Ariya asked.

Cleo, taking photo after photo and pausing in between to just breathe in the grandeur of the view, told her that there were mountains and brilliant sunsets where she came from, too, but none more beautiful than this.

"It's different here," Ash said. "Not just the mountains themselves; all mountain ranges have their own character. It's the way the light strikes them. Back home in Montana, the spruce forests climb far up the mountainsides, though not to the very tops. And something else…it must be the direction. For me the mountains were always to the west, so the sun set squarely behind them, or nearly, depending on the season. These get more of the sun slanting along them from the west."

Just random conversation, Cleo thought, but it felt good to share aspects of life as similar as sunsets, and as diverse. It felt good as well to work together unloading what they'd need from the truck, making a game of it. Ariya tossed a bundle to Cleo. Cleo threw it toward Ash, who kept them guessing whether she'd catch it or make it float slowly through the doorway of the hut. It was a good game until Razhan ordered them to treat the gear with more care.

A small fire inside in a circle of stones was enough to boil water for tea and cook sausages on sticks. Then Razhan and Mac claimed the front and back seats of the truck, while the others slept, or tried to, wrapped in woolen blankets on the earthen floor inside the hut.

In the morning, they gathered fallen branches and twigs from a thicket of stunted pine trees, enough to heat breakfast coffee and leave a little kindling behind for the herdsman who would return in the spring with his flocks.

"I had hoped to travel through the mountains to a wilder area on the Armenian side," Razhan told them over breakfast. "But we haven't time for that now."

Mac stared into the little fire, expressionless, but Cleo, beside her, knew she was thinking of Nisreen lying drugged in the enemy stronghold.

"What's your Plan B, then, Razhan?" Cleo asked.

Razhan shook her head as though clearing her mind. "Ariya, you've traveled often in this area. Is the small valley where Nisreen trained with recruits still isolated? You were there, I think. No drilling for oil yet?"

"Not yet," Ariya said. "And no roads big enough for the oil company machinery."

Mac got straight to the essentials. "How is it for our truck?"

Ariya shrugged. "It's an old goat herder's trail. It worked well enough two years ago, though we had to climb on foot up the last ridge and even further down into the valley. It was bad up here last winter, so the way may be blocked."

Mac stood. The others followed her lead. "Let's get going."

As Ariya predicted, the way was blocked, but she and Cleo took turns maneuvering the truck and scouting ahead. Ash sent any larger obstructions sliding over the edge, and slowly, they made a zig-zagging, bone-jarring ascent.

When Ariya stopped driving at last, Ash surveyed the terrain with a practiced eye. "The truck won't get any farther. I used to climb in the Rockies. You guys up for a hike?" Cleo suspected that climbing wasn't all she had in mind.

"This is the bundle with the food, right?" Before anyone could answer, Ash sent the big canvas sack up the ridge to the first sharp turn.

"That's one way to motivate us to climb," Mac grumbled, but looked amused. Ariya grinned and clapped her hands. Razhan shook her head, not so amused, though she said nothing.

Two more sacks went up the trail that way, and soon, stage by stage, bedrolls, more food, and cooking utensils followed. Nobody asked whether Ash could move people too.

The day was cool, but the climb heated them. Ash and Cleo shed their parkas and tied them around their waists. Ariya had stuffed her gray wool jacket into her pack at the start. Near the crest of the ridge, an inch or so of granular snow coated the winter-browned grass and sparse, thorny bushes, making their first view of the valley all the more striking.

Cleo paused with Ash and Ariya, not, she hoped, making it too obvious that they were waiting for Mac and Razhan to catch up. The view below them was well worth stopping to see. She reached for her camera, but paused to be in the moment, absorbing the wild beauty of the scene.

The tapering valley, sheltered from winds by curving ridges, caught the late afternoon sun for most of its length. Clusters of oak, pine, and cedar were interspersed with outcroppings of rock, all taking on a mellow glow. At the very bottom, along a river flowing from a high waterfall at the head of the valley, were swaths of still-green grass that would be flooded at high water in the spring. The far side of the valley was higher and steeper than this one, a series of cliffs soaring skywards, and beyond were much higher peaks already blanketed in snow. A golden eagle circled overhead on an updraft. Cleo finally remembered the camera in her hands and shot several panoramic photos, hoping the eagle would show in some.

Ash seemed as awed by the view as Cleo at first, but soon her mood changed to an edgy impatience, shifting from one foot to the other. More of Ishtar's influence?

"That's where we're heading," Ariya said, pointing down into the valley. "In summer, the flowers are like a carpet, but more bright and beautiful than any weaving could show." She spoke to them all, but looked sidelong at Ash. "You should come back to see how beautiful they are." She ducked her head in shyness, or embarrassment, and suddenly set off downhill like a young mountain goat as the steep trail wound between boulders.

The rest picked their way more slowly, with Ash moving the gear along bit by bit to wherever she could see a reasonably safe landing spot. Cleo amused herself with her camera, snapping pictures of Ash with her parka hanging down over her rump, planning to compliment her on the casual version of a superhero's cape. They could both use some lightening up,

At a ledge just before the trail wound into underbrush and small trees, Ash paused, looking down the valley and then up. Cleo took advantage of the chance to shoot features of the valley from this perspective. Where they stood was much closer to the upstream end—with the high waterfall—than to the lower.

When Razhan caught up with them, Ash asked, without turning, "What would you say this valley measures from end to end?"

Razhan studied the land. "Perhaps four kilometers."

"How close will I be able to approach the walls of the city?"

"We can get you safely to within two kilometers."

"Then I assume we have plenty of room for whatever training you have in mind." Her tone was just short of a challenge. "Now we'd better find a place to camp before it gets dark."

Ash set off down the trail again. Ariya, who had stopped, picked up two of the three bundles of supplies Ash had deposited, slung them over her strong young shoulders, and looked back with her firm jaw tilted upward.

Mac came up beside Cleo and paused while Razhan went ahead. Then, as they saw Ash raise the remaining bundle and make it follow along beside her above the ground like a weightless dog on a leash, Mac said, "Does she do that for show, or for the exercise?"

"Both." Cleo watched until the others were out of sight around a turn, Ariya forging ahead again. "Sometimes she just has to let off some of the pressure." She turned to face Mac. "You tell me, with all your talent for reading people; what's up with Ariya? I though she was beginning to crush on Ash, but that looked like a challenge."

"Both." Mac shrugged. "Crush and challenge. Why not? You know that better than anyone."

Cleo gave a short laugh. "Fair enough." Not that she challenged Ash, not much, but maybe she should.

Close to the floor of the valley, they crossed a spring-fed stream flowing across a slanting ledge of bare rock and tumbling in a series of cascades in its rush toward the river. On the far side, as the stream veered one way, the trail proceeded in the other direction over step-like shelves of stone down to a grassy plateau. They could hear Ash and Ariya not far away, but out of sight. Once on the level they noticed a well-built fire circle on bare ground, surrounded by suitable stones for seats. A camping spot.

"Cleo? Mac? In here!" Ash's voice seemed to come from the steep slope itself. Just a few more steps around to the side and they could see where time and the river had carved a wide cave with a roof of solid rock and a level floor of sand. Here there were signs of use—a stack of firewood, two tin water buckets with other assorted tools and containers, and a smaller circle of fire-blackened stones just far enough inside the entrance to be sheltered from any moderate rainstorm. Ash and Ariya were already burrowing into the supply bundles while Razhan took the individual packets from them and set them into some sort of order.

"Make yourselves at home," Ash said. "Cozy, right?"

"What's this?" Mac shrugged out of her pack straps and sat down hard. "A roof over our heads? And I thought we were roughing it!"

A cave. Another cave. Cleo hesitated just outside the entrance. Funny how she could stay calm when Ash needed her, but with Ash apparently at ease it was harder to suppress memories of near-suffocation.

Ash came to meet her, holding her gaze. "Bring your pack over here next to mine. I'm staking out our own little corner of this palatial hostelry. Solid roof, firm walls, plenty of open air."

Our own corner. No privacy here, of course, but the declaration of their bond warmed Cleo. She glanced obliquely at Ariya—who stared intently at nothing in particular on the ground—and let herself be drawn inside. After a deep breath or two she heaved off her pack and set it upright against Ash's in a kind of surrogate hug. "Nice! Recommended by former travelers, I see." She looked along the stretch of rock wall where words, probably names, had been chipped with tools or scrawled with charred sticks in the time-honored tradition of "Kilroy was here."

Mac, also surveying the marks, spoke Cleo's thought aloud in her own inimitable style. "Ah yes, 'I write my name, therefore I am.'"

The sun was so low now that its rays slanted deep into the cave. "I am happy to see that there are no very recent names here," Razhan said. Her stern look at Ariya, who had been there two years ago, said clearly that there had better not be. Ariya's response was a smile of exaggerated innocence.

"Kurdish...Turkish...Armenian...hmm, could be Italian." Razhan turned back to them. "There are caves in the more travelled parts of these mountains, passes that were trade routes for thousands of years, where Romans trapping our bears and lions for their gladiator arenas left their marks in Latin."

"Bears and lions?" Cleo managed to sound merely curious, which, on the whole, she was. Bears were familiar from her New Hampshire home; you just had to keep your food where they couldn't possibly reach it, hang it in bags on high ropes between trees when you were camping. But lions? The fire pit in front of the cave might have more significance than she'd thought.

"All gone, long ago. They say a few bears are left, in the farthest reaches, and we have leopards that may not be quite extinct, but no lions. Gone. Just as the great cedar forests were ravaged to build the palaces of sultans and caesars."

Ariya nodded agreement as Razhan spoke. This was the history taught in Kurdish universities, Cleo guessed. How strange it must be to belong to a land where mankind had lived and died, come and gone, and ravaged more often than not, for so many millennia. Not that her own country's history had been all that different, but the ravaging by Europeans of the indigenous cultures there had happened a few hundred years ago instead of thousands.

The sun dipped below a high ridge, leaving the cave dim, and colder, though the sky outside was not yet dark. Ariya began to build a fire in the outer circle, and Cleo helped by carrying wood and scrounging kindling-sized twigs and branches from the low bushes along the trail leading to the river.

Much to Cleo's surprise, Ash carried two buckets of water from the spring-fed stream, just like any ordinary person. Ash saw her expression. "Hey, I'd probably slosh the water if I tried any funny business. Plus I do have to flex my original-equipment muscles now and then."

Cleo dumped her armload of kindling and gave Ash's right bicep a playful squeeze. "Feels like you're doing okay. Any more original equipment you feel like flexing?" Her arms slipped around Ash's waist. Water did, in fact, slosh from the buckets onto her legs as Ash let go and sent them floating a foot off the ground toward the fire circle. She wrapped her freed arms around Cleo. Who cared if Ariya was watching?

They did care, though, when Mac came out of the cave with a metal tripod to hold a kettle over the flames. "What? Not ready for coffee? It'll be a tough meal without a hot drink to wash it down."

That was true. Their remaining supply of pita bread was getting on the stiff side, and the rest of the meal consisted of goat cheese and dried apricots. There were sacks of rice and lentils in the food supplies, and zip-locked packets of herbs and sun-dried vegetables, but Cleo at least was too tired and hungry to wait for anything that needed long cooking. With coffee, what they had now was just fine.

When the eating slowed and their mouths could be used for something besides chewing, Mac drew Ariya into a lively conversation about the time she'd been here training with Nisreen. "What was it like? She wouldn't have brought your group all this way just for target practice."

"Oh no, although we did shoot at some moving targets. Not each other, of course!" Ariya's spirits had visibly risen at this attention. "Some of our training was for wilderness survival, in case of being driven into hiding, so we were permitted to do a little hunting for game like the...the..." she looked helplessly at Razhan and spoke a word unfamiliar to the rest.

"Rock partridges," Razhan supplied.

"Oh, yes," Ariya went on. "Not very much meat to them, and anyway I preferred the nuts and berries we found at that time of year, but I liked showing that I could shoot one in the air. As none of the others could!" Her proud smile, flashing in the firelight, was contagious.

"Valuable training," Mac said.

"Agreed," Ash said, "but our current mission must involve some different training." She looked across the firepit to Razhan. "Let's go back over the plans we discussed on the way. You've told us that hundreds of women are captives in an ancient walled city that can't be bombed or attacked by rockets for fear of injuring the captives. Mine fields all around prevent a direct attack. As I understand it, your soldiers and...and Cleo... will let themselves be captured and imprisoned, then prepare the captives to escape once I've taken down the gates."

"Even now my troops are training for the mission," Razhan said. "Our time here is only possible because other arrangements are also being made, and need time. Our allies must be contacted. A field hospital will be set up in secured territory. Enough trucks and private cars and refitted buses and even motorcycles with sidecars are being gathered to transport the prisoners once they are past the mine fields."

"Like the small boats rescuing the stranded soldiers at Dunkirk," Mac said.

Ash nodded. "So what will the training here involve?"

Razhan hesitated. "We must plan that as we go. You, Ash, are uncharted territory. The valley itself will provide natural targets, trees taller than others, rock formations, loose boulders for projectiles, so we can discover what you can do."

"So we're talking about testing, rather than training," Ash said. "Fair enough. I need to find out myself how much I can do, and stretch to do more. This is uncharted territory for me as much as for anyone else. But since it happens to be *my* uncharted territory, tomorrow morning, with Cleo's help, I want to set up a target. I noticed some likely loose rocks and boulders upslope on the way yesterday that could make a rough tower. After they've had a chance to settle in for a few hours so I can be sure the structure is stable, I'll climb much farther downstream and see what I can do from a distance."

She gazed around at the others. It was hard to read their expressions in the flickering light from the dwindling fire. "Suggestions, of course, are welcome." She stood and flexed her shoulders. "For now, though, what I need most is sleep. I imagine we all do."

There was a general murmur of agreement. Ariya set about banking the fire so there would still be embers in the morning, and only glanced once or twice toward the corner where Cleo and Ash cocooned in their separate bedrolls close to each other.

The sand of the cave floor was firm though not unyielding, and a faint glow and hint of heat came from the fire pit. They could have combined their blankets and lain together, skin to skin, not caring what Razhan or Ariya thought, but in wordless agreement they both looked toward Mac in her solitary corner and Ash shook her head. Beneath all of Mac's self-control and sharp wit, her fear for Nisreen showed through.

Razhan, too, feared for her sister, but it was Mac's sorrow that kept them from flaunting a closeness that she couldn't have now, and might never have again.

They were still close enough for their hands to meet, and for Cleo to whisper, "We're still us."

"Always," Ash whispered back. As she drifted off to sleep, dreams, memories, or maybe something else, washed over her like the touch of Cleo's fingers.

CHAPTER 14

A LIGHT COATING OF FROST glittered on the bushes and sparse grass between the cave and the river, but dissipated quickly in the morning sunshine.

They divvied up the chores. Ash took on water-bearing, while Cleo searched for kindling. Ariya rebuilt the fire for Mac to make coffee and stir up a pot of bulgur wheat sweetened with chopped dates.

When the food was ready, Ash tried briefly to resist temptation, but she was getting the hang of using her power to transport liquids in containers, and soon a tin cup of coffee floated from her hand to hover in front of Razhan, who sat deep in study.

"Oh!" Razhan set aside her maps. "Thank you, Ash." She grasped the cup's handle and looked around. "Thank you, everyone. I'll do my part after breakfast by washing up."

Ariya started to object, but Ash shot her a silencing look. Rank couldn't be entirely ignored, but a commander's honest efforts at equality should be accepted graciously.

Mac nodded, giving Ash that all-too-familiar feeling that on some level she had read her mind. "Good, Razhan. I'll do my best not to burn the cereal on the bottom of the pot. If I do, though, scrubbing with sand is the best way to clean it."

"If you burn it, I will be glad to watch you demonstrate the method," Razhan said with a straight face, while Ariya giggled.

The meal was tasty, and the mood remained remarkably congenial. When Ash made each filled bowl float from Mac's ladle over to someone's eager hands, it wasn't showing off, just good-natured fun.

Even more so when Cleo teased by moving her hands back and forth as her bowl approached. The persistent bowl followed each of her movements, until suddenly it began retreating. Cleo lunged for her breakfast, and managed to spill some cereal in her lap.

Amid the general laughter, Razhan said lightly, "Ash, is there anything you can't do?"

Ash wasn't deceived by the playful tone. "That," she responded, "is exactly what we all want to know. What we're here for. I can't promise we'll find out much. Most of the time I don't know what I can do until I've done it."

She looked around the group, avoiding Ariya's worshipful gaze. "I think this mission will be within my power. I've committed to it, with everything I possess, even my life, but there's no way to be sure until crunch time comes."

Razhan's slight frown eased when Ash met her eyes. Mac's face was so devoid of expression that it had to be intentional, although Ash thought she detected a smile trying to break through.

Cleo set her empty bowl aside. "After all that inspiration, it must be time we went looking for some rocks to crunch."

"Right back up the trail we came down, for starters." Ash headed for the cave's opening.

"Wait a minute." Mac reached into the capacious pockets of her camo jacket and came up with several energy bars. Another example of her versatility. "Here's something better than rocks to crunch on."

They'd climbed almost to the halfway point of the trail when Ash paused, looking upward. The scrub pines and thorn bushes had become shorter and shorter, and above them a mound of rubble could be seen where a long-ago rockslide had stopped, slowed by a great rock ledge.

"This is far enough." The prickles of irritation she associated with Ishtar's influence had begun to return. The valley itself seemed to shelter her from the goddess's ever-simmering savagery beaming from the desert far away, but the higher they went the less sheltered she felt. Cleo, right behind her, wore a worried, pinched look.

"You feel it too?"

"Maybe," Cleo said, "Or it could be I'm just feeling you feeling it."

"Some action ought to help." Ash focused on a boulder and made it roll to the center of the ledge. Another, flatter slab rose and moved to balance on the first. Then two smaller rocks, side by side, with another large one perching on top of them. Ash had to move closer to choose her next couple of layers.

"How high are those damned gateposts I'm supposed to topple?"

"No idea," Cleo said, "but if you get the lower parts moving, gravity will take care of the rest.

"Good point!" Ash managed a genuine smile. "Just one more, then." A thinner slice of stone, rounded on one side by erosion, rose toward the top of the tower.

"Hey, can you make it hover there?"

"Sure, but why?"

Cleo snapped a photo. "We could make flying saucer videos with stuff like that!"

Ash gave that comment the disdain it deserved by letting the stone drop onto the tower hard enough to shatter into numerous pieces. All the rest, though, remained steady.

"Let's move along and let it settle." She took off back down the trail with Cleo close at her heels. They slowed, though, well before reaching the campsite.

"What shall we do now?" Ash asked. "No need to get back this soon."

"Explore," Cleo said right away. "Let's go upriver, toward the falls."

A narrow trail along the river showed old animal tracks. Cleo led the way upstream for some distance until they found a place where a couple of good-sized rocks stood at the edge of clear, shallow water. Perched on one, she scooped up a mixture of wet sand and gravel, and let it trickle through her fingers.

"So," Cleo said after a while, "this mountain air seems to agree with you. With both of us. I had a hard time this morning resisting an impulse to salute your little speech, and you know how easily I can usually resist that."

Ash, on the other rock, dipped her fingers into the cold water and swished them slowly back and forth. "Nope, it's the valley air. Even more, it's the cave. Up high on the ridge, I felt her like the buzz of a wasp's nest. She was angry when we went northwest, happier the few times we went east or south. And the fortress we have to breach is to the southeast, as far as I can tell."

Cleo nodded. "She must be impatient for us to get there."

"Seems that way. In the valley, the farther down we come, the less I feel her. She hardly gets through to me at all here. Inside the cave, there's total peace, the first I've felt in a long time. No fighting the urge to lash out at any annoyance. Makes it easier to be myself, take control in my own way, do what I know must be done. I'll use what she gave me, but I won't be just her tool."

"That's the spirit!" Cleo did, briefly, salute her. Ash shifted to Cleo's rock, where there was just barely room enough for two sitting very close together, each with an arm around the other. Their perch was too precarious for anything beyond a kiss or two, but being close together, truly together, was enough.

"Nice here," Ash said after a while. "Look, there's the eagle again."

Cleo raised her head from Ash's shoulder. "Looks like he's got a partridge."

"Probably she. Females are the best hunters."

"You sure about that?" Cleo stared harder at the eagle. "I've heard it about lions, but not hawks."

"Hawks, lions, close enough."

Cleo chuckled. "Don't dis lions like that."

"I'm not dissing them. Eagles are noble, too. Anyway, the best part of being here is that she can't hear me." Ash sighed. "I wish we could just stay," she said dreamily, drifting in the smooth current of being able to say anything, however foolish, however impossible, and still be unconditionally loved. "What do you think? If I couldn't do well enough, if I failed the distance tests, would they just go away and leave us alone here? We could compete with the eagle for partridges to roast." Above them, the eagle's prize dropped suddenly from its talons, but at Cleo's sharp nudge, Ash made it rise again and return to the grasp of the rightful (and no doubt confused) hunter.

"We could fish in this river," Cleo said, riding the same current. "Right here. This pool is a likely spot."

"Did you bring a fishing pole?"

"I could improvise something. But couldn't you just lift a fish out of the water if you saw one?"

"Hmm. I don't know. There's something about refraction of the light that makes things under water look like they're not where they really are." Ash stared into the amber-green depths of the pool. A submerged rock seemed to shift back and forth as ripples flowed over it. The sun reflecting on the water dazzled her eyes, and she shook her head. This time her sigh was deep, and resigned. "If I'm going to focus that much on anything, it had better be on what I know I have to do. Find my limits, and then get past them." She slid off the rock. Cleo came too, still with an arm around her waist.

"Yeah, I know. Deep winter here would probably be a bitch, anyway. Not that I couldn't keep you warm." Cleo's arm slipped down so that her fingers could grip Ash's thigh. Then she stepped aside to dip her hand in the water and rinse off the remaining sand.

She caught up with Ash where a tangle of branches arched into the river from a small uprooted tree.

"Look!" Cleo pointed over Ash's shoulder. "There's a real treasure!" She started tugging at the nearest branch, raising it partway out of the water.

Ash couldn't tell what Cleo saw, but she helped anyway, until one particular mass of twigs and dead leaves bound together was within Cleo's reach. What bound them together was some sort of fiber, or...spider web? Ash almost let the whole mass drop into the river.

"Fishing line!" Cleo crowed. "And a hook! No lure, but that's no problem. There probably isn't a prime fishing spot on earth where somebody hasn't got their line tangled in a tree and had to abandon it." She worked at the knots and crimps, and Ash made twigs and leaves break away until what was left was more line than wood. "I'll work on that later, and maybe go fishing. We'd better get back now, before they come looking for us."

"Somebody's coming already." Ash listened for a moment. "Mac, whistling and tramping along to make sure we'll hear her coming in time to stop doing anything too embarrassing. How did she know we were here?"

"Quick, let's do something embarrassing! Don't disappoint her!" But Mac was already visible coming around the next curve. Cleo waved. "Look!" she said, holding up her tangle of line. "I'll go fishing, and maybe get something to add to the pot of whatever gets cooked tonight."

"That would be nice," Mac said. "A while back I thought we might be having partridge to roast." She gestured to the golden eagle, barely visible over the far end of the valley. "Just as well to keep on good terms with our avian neighbor, though." She lifted the field glasses on a cord around her neck and focused on the bird. "Still has her dinner, and heading for home on that cliff above the waterfall."

Was there anything the woman missed? But Ash was more amused than annoyed, and impressed at how well Mac could keep going in spite of the stress lines around her eyes and mouth. For the first time, Ash felt Mac's sorrow almost as though it were her own. It might well be her own, sometime soon.

Mac's jacket hung open, and she let the field glasses fall to her chest. "Razhan is working on maps, and I need something to occupy me. Yes," at Cleo's quizzical look, "not enough irons in the fire to keep me busy." Her wry smile faded. "Just one iron now, and if I can't find something to do about that one, I'll... Well, let's just say if there's any way I can help with your plans, your testing, I'd be more than happy to pitch in."

Ash hesitated. If Mac bore witness to whatever she did or didn't accomplish this afternoon, Cleo could have some time to herself to go fishing.

Cleo echoed her thought out loud. "Sounds good. I could do some fishing and exploring while you two go fool around with boulders and destruction."

Ash didn't want help. If she was going to push herself deliberately to the point of failure, she'd rather do it in privacy. But Cleo's stance and direct gaze affirmed that she didn't want Ash to attempt any extreme feats alone. Ridiculous. How long had it been since she'd come close to collapsing? There was that thing with the burning jeep—and then the helicopter—and other times when she'd needed support after pushing herself past old limits—but that was all in the past. She was in full command of her powers now.

But she surprised herself by nodding agreement. The tranquility of the valley was making her altogether too mellow. Or maybe it was just that putting up with Cleo's overprotective impulses was a small price to pay for being loved by someone whose wiry body and fierce determination could hold her up if she ever did need it.

"Fine. My plan is to get far away from the tower I built earlier and see what I can do at a distance. Knock it down, try to stack it up again, and then get even farther away. I might also pick some naturally occurring targets." She glanced down at the binoculars hanging on Mac's well-padded chest. "Those might come in handy, if you'll let me use them." Then, simultaneously with Cleo's spurt of laughter, added, "The field glasses, I mean." She gave Cleo a stern a look. "I should have brought some myself."

Mac's response was to lift the lanyard over her head, slide it ever so slowly over Ash's, and arrange the binoculars very carefully on Ash's chest. They hung down a bit lower, but still had ample support.

"Hey," Cleo said, "maybe I should—"

Ash cut her off. "Go along and work your wiles on the fish. We'll be fine." She moved off quickly downstream with Mac following right behind.

CHAPTER 15

Ash and Mac followed the trail downstream. "One thing I haven't yet managed," Ash said, "is to move just part of something large and solid, like a ledge or a cliff, unless it has existing cracks in it. I need to see...or to feel... where the edges are, where one thing ends and another begins."

"Does that apply to the human body?"

Ash stopped and turned to her. "You mean, can I tear someone's arm off? Or their head?"

Mac shrugged. "Just curious. You never know what will come in handy."

"I've never tried to...to take somebody apart, but I know where the joints are. All it would take to dislocate an arm would be to lift someone by it and thrash them around. Or by the head, to break the neck." She started walking again, speaking over her shoulder. "As far as separating parts from the body, I don't know. Castration might be a challenge." She darted a look back, hoping to catch Mac looking shocked, but not surprised to see only amusement.

"Good to know. I'll notify you if I come across any candidates to practice on." Mac paused and gestured uphill. "Speaking of practice, there's a good view from here of your tower."

Time to get serious. Ash leaned her head back and surveyed the target far above them. The top stone slowly rose, then sank back, rocking a little. Ash tensed as she willed it into equilibrium, her neck and shoulders tightening with the effort. Then she lifted the top three stones together and set them back very slowly. When she tried to set them down, though, the highest one toppled off and rolled away out of sight. Weight and distance didn't seem to be a problem, yet, but control and balance weren't easy. Would that even matter to what she was expected to do?

She rubbed the nape of her neck and twitched her shoulders. "I think it would be better if I were on the same level."

After a strenuous climb, they sat for a bit in companionable silence, chewing the dense, sticky energy bars Mac had brought. When they'd finished, Mac said, "You and Cleo have the same bond I have with Nisreen, don't you? A connection of mind and spirit."

"You mean the not-quite-mind-reading thing? Not often, and not usually without being actively tuned in to each other, but there have been times…" She hesitated. Some of those times were nobody else's business. "When we were on that medical mission together, we were in several tough spots, facing folks who were dead set against us being there. Cleo has this thing. She knows when guns are about to be fired, and at least once yelled at me, *Drop! Gun!* Except she yelled it in my mind, she didn't use her voice. She saved my life that day."

"Was that the only time?"

"No." This was getting intrusive. It was likely to be important to their mission, though, to have two people who could communicate telepathically, especially since Nisreen couldn't contact Mac the same way anymore.

Ash reluctantly continued. "We've been in other hazardous situations. But it only happens in extreme conditions, emergencies. Other than that, we've got to the point where we can tell where each other is, and know when the other one needs us, but we don't invade each other's minds."

Mac nodded. "But you can communicate if it's important enough."

"You sound surer of that than I am."

"It's my business to know."

Enough of that. Ash stood, squinted at the distant target, and blasted it apart so hard its rocks started a minor landslide. "How much farther will I be from that gate I'm supposed to take down? Razhan mentioned two kilometers."

Mac shook her head. "I haven't seen the gates. But I'm sure it would be farther than we've been working on today."

Ash looked westward to where the lowering winter sun glinted on the waterfall. "That should be far enough." She squinted through the field glasses, concentrated on a high rocky ledge extending above the falls, and a ripple of anger built. What was the point in randomly rearranging features of the natural landscape? If she knocked that ledge down into the river, the flow of water would be altered. Cleo could be down there fishing. Besides, hadn't these mountains and valleys been ravaged enough by humanity, worst of all now that oil companies were tearing into them?

Her voice sharpened. "How can I work without knowing exactly what I have to deal with?"

"Good point," Mac said. "Just the same, you did some very impressive work without knowing exactly what you were dealing with back in Boston. From what I've seen, a crisis brings out the best in you. That, and how much you care."

"Then why are we wasting time here?"

"Because we care so much. We'll only get one chance before… well, one chance." Mac didn't try to conceal her emotions. "Are we wasting time? Is distance no problem?"

Ash wasn't absolutely sure of this yet. "I'll try longer distances tomorrow. We'll start at the waterfall end of the valley and aim at the cliff toward the other end." She shrugged, and said what she'd been thinking for a while. "If it even matters. I work best in a crisis, like you said. When disaster is screaming down on me there's no time for thought, just burning rage, and reaction. Maybe we should have skipped all this 'training' routine and gone straight to the attack."

"I would go to save Nisreen in a flash!" Mac's frustration broke through. She repressed it with obvious effort. "But we're only part of the mission. Preparations are going on elsewhere that take time, discussion, and planning among the volunteers who will be captured, contacting our sources of information, assembling enough transports for the freed prisoners. It will be a few days before we can put our plan in motion."

Ash wished she'd kept her mouth shut. Mac had enough to cope with. "That's armies for you," she said, forcing a light tone, "hurry up and wait."

"You've got that right," Mac agreed. "For now, let's make our way to where we might find some dinner. Armies also travel on their stomachs."

The glow of the outdoor cookfire and the beckoning aroma of fish curry welcomed them back to the campsite.

"Cleo, you caught fish! Where did you find them?" Mac's enthusiasm was a shade overdone.

"Upstream. Give me a line, a hook, and a willow-branch pole, and if they're there, I'll catch 'em," she said with a cheeky grin. "Made me feel like a kid again."

Ariya, continually stirring the pot, raised a spoonful to test it. "Good timing," she said cheerily. "If you will take your rice still chewy, all is ready. Fresh trout stew with rice, dried onion flakes and herbs for savor, apricots for sweetness."

"Nice," Ash said, after dipping a spoon in her bowl. "What did you use for bait, Cleo?"

"Sure you want to know?"

Ash's spoon stopped midway to her mouth. "When you put it that way, yeah, I definitely want to know."

"Strips of dried apricot."

Everyone was listening by now.

"So," Ash said, "Why wouldn't I want to know? Unless you put those same strips in the stew after you used them."

Mac dangled a piece of limp apricot on the edge of her spoon and made it wiggle. "I'm just envisioning what this would look like to a hungry fish."

Ariya gave up on trying to stifle her giggles and burst out laughing. Razhan smiled tolerantly.

After the dishes had been cleaned up, they sat by the smaller inside fire.

"Mac can tell you that I've got the distance factor practically under control," Ash said. "One more day to experiment, and I'll be as set as I'll ever be, although I'll need better field glasses than we have here."

Mac nodded. "I've tried to arrange for some special equipment for that purpose, but I won't know if it will work out until we're back in communication with the rest of the world. In communication…" She stood, her face drawn and weary. "You two," she said, "will be our only hope for communication between those inside and those outside. We need your connection." She stopped to let that sink in. "Ash, I have total confidence in your power to take down the gate to the city. Cleo, I know beyond the shadow of a doubt that you have the power to detect landmines better than anyone I've ever heard of. And the grit to do anything else that needs to be done."

"Then they must practice communication—"

But Mac cut Razhan off. "No. The bond is not something to be learned, or forced, or commanded. It happens when it happens. When it needs to happen. I know." She sat down abruptly, changed her mind, and left the cave to sit by the now-darkened fire pit outdoors, alone with her thoughts.

In the ensuing silence, Ariya looked from one face to another, then said hesitantly to Cleo, "I could make you a drawing of the city, a map, if you would like to study it. The inside is a jumble of rough walls, most not head-high. Only a few rooms have roofs. Many of us would be gathered into a large space where once there had been dividing walls that had fallen down.

Cleo stood. "You were there." It wasn't a question. "Yes, show me. Please."

Ariya smoothed a sandy section of the floor near the fire, took a broken walking stick some previous traveler had left leaning against the cave wall, and began to draw. Razhan shone a flashlight on the drawing.

"The gate. What is it like?" Ash, concentrating only on the city wall, could see by two short lines crossing it where the gate must be.

"I did not see it clearly—I was not...not conscious when I was taken in, and when I went out I was hidden in a truck filled with refuse. Garbage."

"Since then, we have heard," Razhan muttered to Ash, "that they shoot into those trucks as they are leaving to be sure no one else escapes in that way. I have a photograph of the gate for you, taken before the ruins were rebuilt, but they have strengthened it since then with steel bands. There are also accounts from some of our ransomed women."

"Guard towers?" Cleo asked.

"Those we have seen through field glasses." Razhan pointed at the two front corners of the wall.

"There are patrols along the walls," Ariya said, "but not often, and not many at night. I think they put much faith in their minefields. I did not see the whole city, but here," she tapped a central section with the stick, "are the best rooms, for the most important men, and here," she tapped a space next to that block, "is where the most important prisoners are kept. The ones not for sale, but for exchange. Or for information. Or for...for vengeance. Here is where she will be. The commander. Colonel Khider. Our leader." She paused to wipe her eyes with the back of her free hand, but when she looked up her face was set.

Mac had silently returned. "I have satellite photos of the area, but I didn't bring them along. In any case, it's too dark to be straining our eyes over maps." She gestured around the cave, where the fire, dwindling to more ember than flame, sent only faint wisps of light among shadows that moved along the walls. "I don't know about the rest of you, but I intend to lie down before I fall down."

That seemed suddenly like an excellent idea.

Cleo, curled up with her back as close against Ash as their separate bedrolls allowed, rolled over and stretched out her hand to grip Ash's. Then she rolled back, wriggled once against Ash's side, and was still.

CHAPTER 16

Ash listened to Cleo's even breathing for so long that she thought she herself would never fall asleep, but suddenly she woke to find Cleo slipping out of her bedroll and the faint light of dawn creeping into the cave.

"Shush." Cleo laid a hand over her mouth. Ash reflexively kissed her fingers. "I'm going up by the falls. The early worm catches the fish."

Ash felt chilly along the side where Cleo had been, but she must have slept again, because the scent of hot coffee woke her next, and bright sunlight shone into the cave.

Mac stood right next to her, holding a cup. "Last call if you want it hot. What there is left of it."

Ash scanned the cave. Everyone else was gone. She sat up, reached for the coffee, and gulped down half at once. "Thanks for saving me some." She drank more. "What have I missed?"

"Well, Cleo's gone fishing, and Ariya is showing Razhan some smaller caves she discovered when she was here before. Oh, and your breakfast bulgur has congealed into something less than appetizing, but I figured you needed the sleep."

Ash figured she probably needed the bulgur, too, however unappealing. It turned out to not be too bad, augmented by some dried berries and almonds, and still lukewarm.

Mac stuffed her pockets with pouches of some kind of nut and fruit trail mix. "Now let's get on with our day, okay? If it's still all right for me to tag along with you."

"How could I turn down someone with lunch in her pockets? I'll carry the water." The canteen rose from its perch on one of the supply bundles and came to her like a homing pigeon.

They climbed more than halfway up the trail they'd come down the first day, then veered off horizontally on a rough track that would put them on a level above and across from the ledges rising over the waterfall. It was slow going in places, having to test each foothold to be sure the soil wouldn't slide, and eventually the easier course was to climb even higher.

Ash's muscles were sore and tired by the time they reached the place she'd planned on stopping, hot from the effort in spite of a chilly breeze, edgy for more reasons than she bothered to analyze. She'd slowed down a bit in case Mac had trouble keeping up—which she was pretty sure was the case, although Mac never complained—but hurried faster for the last few hundred feet. Whether some outside force drove her, or she just wanted to get to her goal, she didn't know or care, but she did know, and care, that Cleo was down there fishing a little downstream from the falls.

At that thought, Ash saw Cleo emerge from behind a willow thicket far below on the river's bank, look upward, and shade her eyes. She waved, then turned back to her fishing. The roar of the falls was muted by distance, but still impressive. Ash grinned to herself, raised the field glasses, and focused them on the bulge in the cliff at the other end of the valley. Yes, two huge boulders. Or one boulder and a protrusion from the cliff itself. She gripped the one she was sure of with her mind, her hands twitching. If only she could feel the actual hard, rough surface, how deeply its base was imbedded, its center of balance! It was too far away to be sure of anything. She focused intently, tried to lift it, and somewhere deep in her mind she did feel it, feel how to tilt it one way and then another to maintain the balance as it rose into the air.

Keeping it hovering there required more effort than lifting the great weight, but she managed. Setting it down on top of the other one required even more focus, and the boulder, not quite balanced, hit, bounced, and toppled down the cliff. Large chunks of the remaining stone went with it. Handling such large things was very different from making a cup of coffee float across a room, so maybe size and weight did matter after all. Well, at least she had managed the distance part. Good enough.

She swung the field glasses back and saw Cleo turn toward the falls, standing straight, head up. A movement on the high ledge caught the corner of Ash's eye. There was something there, hidden behind the pine saplings.

"DROP! GUN!" Cleo's warning blasted into her mind.

Ash didn't drop. She focused, and tore loose the ledge—stone, soil, saplings, and all. A shot rang out and a rifle fell from the heights to the river below. There came a cry, and a desperate scrabbling. Ash sailed the slab of rock away so as not to block the falls, landed it, then returned her attention to the clinging figure, intending to dash it to the ground.

"NO!" Cleo's command echoed in her head. *"It's Ariya! Just a blank!"* Cleo was tearing through thorny shrubs and weeds toward Ariya.

Ariya? Treachery! Ash focused again, about to raise Ariya and smash her into the earth, but Mac gripped her from behind, pinning her arms to her side. "Wait! Let Cleo handle this. Those blasted idiots. There was no need!"

Ash tuned Mac out, seeing only Cleo reaching the girl, turning to stand in front of her, arms spread. Shielding her.

"MOVE!" Ash shouted with both mind and voice. She turned her power on Cleo and tried to lift her, to set her out of the way. But Cleo didn't rise, didn't move, resisting Ash's power and glaring her defiance.

How could she dare! Ash strained to move her—or, no, she was straining to make herself force Cleo. Not knowing for sure whether she could, or what that would mean between them. Just knowing she couldn't ever hurt Cleo. Or lose her.

"It's a freakin' test, Ash. A blank cartridge." Cleo turned her head to listen to Ariya, then turned back. *"She says she didn't fire. You jolted her and it went off."*

Ash turned to face Mac. "A test? A freakin' test?"

Mac's outburst was as fierce as Ash's. "Damnit, why couldn't they just trust me! I guaranteed Razhan that Cleo could sense when a gun was about to fire. But no, she couldn't leave it at that. I didn't know what she was planning." Mac stopped for breath. "I guess we're lucky she couldn't get hold of a landmine to test that skill, too."

An incongruous urge to laugh struck Ash. She felt dizzy at the sudden shift of mood, and Mac looked like she felt the same. "How fast can we get down from here?"

Mac tried a downward step, and Ash held her from sliding without being too obvious about it. Mac took another step. "A lot faster than we came up."

Halfway down, they paused. Ash stared out over the peaceful valley, drinking from the canteen and then offering it to Mac without facing her. "I came too close to blowing everything apart back there. And it's just going to get worse in the desert. You know that."

"Yes." Mac took several gulps of water. "You'll need every bit of strength. Your own plus whatever edge your savage goddess gives you. Control is going to be a bitch." She handed the canteen back. "You can do it. I got you into this because I need your help, and you agreed even though it's my problem, not yours. Maybe I should apologize. But I know that you can do it."

"Well, let's get on with it." Ash took a few steps down the trail, then said over her shoulder, "It's my problem now, too, with Cleo on the prison team." She looked back. Mac's face was so drawn that Ash regretted her brusqueness. "No need to apologize. We knew pretty much what we were getting into, and we jumped at the chance to do something worthwhile."

By the time they reached the valley floor, Cleo and Ariya were already waiting at the cave with Razhan, who looked both apprehensive and obstinate.

"So." Mac's voice was icy. "What did we find out that we didn't know already?"

Razhan hesitated. Ariya, still shaken, burst out, "Cleo knew I was there! Even before I raised the gun, she knew. I was quiet, and the waterfall makes much noise, but as I climbed through the trees up to the ledge she raised her head like she was listening. And when I aimed the gun, she stiffened, though she couldn't have seen it. Then all was…was rock cracking, and falling, and fear…" She stopped for breath, gulped, and gazed at Cleo with as much awe as she'd ever shown for Ash. "Cleo saved me! She stood strong and would not let Ash move her from in front of me, would not let her kill me." When she looked at Ash it was with dread.

"Fair enough." Mac nodded. "One new thing discovered. Now we know that Ash can't move Cleo against her will."

To Ash, still shaken at how close she'd come to murder, it was also a revelation. Cleo had saved her as well as Ariya. She wondered whether she could have tried harder to move Cleo, whether it was as much a matter of "won't" as "can't," and hoped she'd never be forced to find out.

"We already knew," Mac went on, "because *I* knew, that Cleo can detect firearms before they fire. And that she can communicate that knowledge to Ash. I saw it in Ash's face. Knowing almost immediately that the shot was a blank cartridge is a plus. I know from many eyewitness sources that she can also detect landmines in ways that seem impossible."

"Oh, there are dogs that can do it almost as well," Cleo said with fake modesty.

Trying to lighten things up, Ash thought. *That's Cleo for you. Thank God…or goddess…Cleo's for me.*

Mac smiled slightly, but her tone was still hard. "We also knew already that Ash can move almost anything she chooses at great distances. I witnessed her reach the far end of this valley today, which happened just before your *test*," she spit out the word, "interrupted us."

Razhan's jaw was set, but she managed an even tone. "Mac, of course I believe you, but with so many other lives at stake…not just the prisoners, but those who will become prisoners to get inside the city, and the hundreds of others who bring their cars and trucks as transport—family members, volunteers, troops—I must be sure."

"Well, you'd better be sure now, after what Ariya's been through." Mac gave a deep sigh. "How fast can we get out of here? I have plans to work out, too, and with no cell service I feel bound hand and foot." She looked severely at Cleo. "Don't think I can't tell what's on your mind. Get it out of the gutter."

"Can't go to jail for what you're thinking," Cleo quipped, and the tense atmosphere was pretty much defused.

"We'll leave first thing tomorrow morning," Razhan said.

CHAPTER 17

THEY BROKE CAMP AT THE first pale light of dawn, well before sunrise. Heading out provided a sense of urgency that brought them to the crest of the ridge faster than they'd gone down that same slope, and the glory of full sunrise hadn't entirely faded away. Cleo lingered to shoot pictures of the glowing colors reflected on distant snowy peaks, then raced downhill to meet the others at the truck, not quite as surefooted as a mountain goat but without any serious slipups.

Once the beauty of the sunrise receded in her mind, she found herself tensing at each jarring bump on the dirt track, which meant tensing most of the time.

When they stopped to move rocks that had slid across the track in the few days since they'd passed, she claimed her turn to drive, and Ariya conceded the driver's seat with such deference that Cleo was embarrassed. Ariya crushing on Ash had been amusing, but Cleo wasn't comfortable being on the receiving end of that kind of thing. Saving young girls turned out to have its perils.

In control behind the wheel, each message of engine, suspension, and gears vibrating through her hands and into her ears, she began to feel better, organizing her thoughts and emotions.

Sure, the chances of failure were high, and failure could well be catastrophic, but all you could do was go at it with everything you had. She'd been in tight places before, and knew how much she had to give. Instincts, experience. Mac hadn't totally convinced her that she had superpowers, but so what? Mac might be wrong, deluding herself out of a desperate desire to rescue her lover. It didn't matter.

Cleo trusted Ash and her powers absolutely, and would back Ash with all her skill, strength, and, well, level-headedness. Even to the point of challenging her. It did Ash good to be challenged.

They stopped to grab a bite of lunch and pour in the gas from the reclaimed can at the herdsman's hut. Then they pushed on, Ariya back at the wheel. It was late afternoon when they halted briefly at the rocky falls where they'd stopped before. Mac and Razhan checked their cell phones, as they'd been doing compulsively all during the trip, but still with no luck.

Cleo refilled the tank from the last can and checked the headlights. Not the brightest, but they'd have to do. "It's pretty much downhill from here. We can make it back to town by midnight if we hustle. Let's go."

Well before midnight, Ash and Mac and Ariya were asleep in the back seat, jumbled together in various positions that fit like pieces of a jigsaw puzzle. Cleo enjoyed night driving. The truck was its own dimly lit world, moving through a universe invisible past the beams of the headlights.

She liked to be alone with her thoughts, but Razhan was awake beside her, and after a while she felt that a little conversation was in order. "Say, Razhan, I guess I'll need to dye my hair for this mission. Any ideas on how to do it?"

Razhan's face was just perceptible in the faint glow from the dashboard. "We'll darken it a bit with nut juice, to keep you from attracting too much attention, but red hair is not unknown here. Those Roman and Greek and even Nordic travelers who took so much from these mountains left traces behind them as well. A girl in town has red tints to her hair, as have her mother and grandmothers through many generations. We also have fair-haired people. Prick a Kurd and you see the blood of the world."

They talked for some time in muted voices about the mission, how Cleo would fit into it. "The team that you will be with plans even now where and when they will allow themselves to be captured. Ariya will be among them, and several others who were imprisoned previously and escaped before the minefields were quite so dangerous." Razhan paused to check her cell phone and shook her head.

They arrived as predicted, around midnight. Razhan knocked on their safe house door and they were welcomed by their drowsy host. Hot, sweet tea was prepared, and they rested in a semi stupor. Cleo and Ash sprawled shoulder to shoulder on the floor. Mac was propped in the corner, her cup at a perilous angle.

Cleo must have drifted off, for she was dreaming of motorcycles when Ariya gently squeezed her shoulder. She startled awake to find Mac and Ash already up and heading through the door to the kitchen.

"Razhan has news and asks you to come quickly," Ariya said in hushed tones.

The news had arrived in person rather than by phone. A woman looking as though she'd been on the road all night—Cleo could sympathize with that—sat by the kitchen stove drinking coffee and eating toasted pita with cheese. Razhan was barking out questions in Kurdish with occasional pauses for the messenger's responses.

Mac translated quietly. "We've had word that there will be a raid in two days on a village farther into the hills than usual. Not for military purposes but solely to capture women as slaves." At Ash's questioning look she added, "We have sources, in this case a young man converted by the enemy and serving with them, but still with family ties to that village."

The newcomer swiveled to look them over, first Cleo, then Ash, and back to Cleo. Her leather jacket, weathered face and windblown tangle of graying hair reminded Cleo of something... "Hey, did I really hear a Triumph Thunderbird out there, or was it a dream?"

The woman's face remained as impassive as a face could be while chewing on toast, but her eyes flickered. She looked toward Ariya, whose puzzled look switched quickly into translator mode. She addressed the woman in Kurdish, but "Triumph Thunderbird" clearly needed no translation. After a brief exchange, Ariya turned to Cleo. "Ilham asks what you know of motorcycles, and what model do you think you heard."

This was a familiar game, one Cleo played well. She tilted her head, pulling up the memory of her dream. "Triumph 6T Thunderbird, 1952, Brando's 'Blackbird' in *The Wild One*. Or maybe," so as not to sound too cocksure, "a year or two later."

Ariya began to translate, but the older woman waved her words away and spoke again. Ariya turned back to Cleo. "She wishes to know what experience you have of motorcycles."

"I learned to repair classic models when I was ten years old, helping in my uncle's garage. Rode them whenever I could, but never had a chance at a Thunderbird. The one out there sounds a bit overheated, but otherwise in good shape."

Ilham shrugged when Ariya translated, stood and zipped up her jacket, then held out one hand tilted sharply downward.

Cleo nodded, not needing any translation. "Yeah, sure, it'll be okay going downhill. Mind if I have a look before you go?"

"Sure thing. Go right ahead." Ilham grinned at Cleo's surprise that she spoke English. She gestured expansively and headed for the door. Cleo followed, and so did Ash, with Ariya hurrying after carrying the parkas they'd left in the hall. The morning was cold and cloudy and felt like there'd be snow soon.

The motorcycle was still warm. Cleo stroked the front fender as if it were a horse's muzzle. "Beautiful. It's great that you've kept her going all this time." No need to mention that not all the parts were originals, or even from the same model. It was still a Thunderbird.

Ilham grinned, nodded, and then waved a hand toward Ash. "You're Shadow Hand." It wasn't a question. She swung her hand toward Cleo. "You're Shadow Hand's right hand."

"Um, left hand, maybe. Just call me Cleo. But how—"

"YouTube. That stuff real?"

Ariya giggled. No wonder she'd hesitated before beginning to translate. Ilham needed no translator, and Ariya knew it. In fact, Ilham's accent had a trace of New Jersey about it. Ilham had travelled.

"Yeah, the action is totally real, but made to look its best by our filmmaker."

Razhan and Mac had come out by then. "How about a demonstration?" Mac looked at Ash and then at Ilham, who nodded, but took half a step forward as the Thunderbird's front tire lifted from the ground, higher and higher. For a moment the motorcycle looked like a rearing horse, then settled gently back down.

"So," Ilham said, regaining her composure, "Shadow Hand will tear down the great gate, and you, Cleo, will lead the prisoners across the sea of landmines."

"That's the plan." Mac looked relieved. She also looked like she was suppressing some secret excitement.

Ilham gave a thumbs-up, then patted the bike's long seat and looked at Cleo. "Going my way?"

"Sure, just let me grab my pack." Cleo looked to Razhan for approval.

"Good idea," Razhan agreed hurriedly. "Ilham can take you to the mission camp, and we'll meet you there after I check in with my transportation fleet commander."

Mac followed Cleo inside. "Good going. That's a load off my mind. If Ilham says you're okay, there'll be no problem with the others. They'll follow you when the time comes. Ash and I have other business to attend to, but she doesn't know that yet."

"She does now," Ash said, just coming in to give Cleo a goodbye squeeze. "But Cleo and I will get together again before the major push begins. That's non-negotiable."

Ilham was a magnificent driver over the rough territory she clearly knew well. Still, even though Cleo had had only five or six hours of sleep, she knew Ilham hadn't had any, riding all night to get to them.

When they made a brief pit stop a few hours later, Cleo didn't suggest switching drivers. She just looked the bike over admiringly, asking with a glance if it was okay to straddle the saddle. Ilham waved her permission, and then, while Cleo sat there enjoying the feel, climbed on behind. "Wanna see how she handles?"

Half an hour later, Ilham shouted into her ear, "Wake me up in two hours at the big crossroad," and leaned her head against Cleo's back. When they stopped at the crossroad, Ilham gave muttered instructions for the rest of the way and went back to sleep, and on arrival at the mission camp late in the day, the faces of the observers wore uniform expressions of shocked amazement.

One came forward, a pretty girl about Ariya's age, sure enough of herself to give Cleo a dirty look, but when she reached out to touch the Thunderbird, Ilham growled, "Hands off!" and slapped her fingers away. Mutters interspersed with laughter swept through the gathered troops.

An older, more seasoned soldier asked in English, following Ilham's example. "Who is this you allow on your precious machine, Ilham? And even to drive?"

Ilham swung herself off the passenger seat. "This is Cleo, who's gonna lead you through the minefield. She drives because she's a skilled driver." She said a few words in Kurdish, grinned, and thumped Cleo on the shoulder. Cleo dismounted to take her place in this staged scene. Whatever her place was. From the looks she got from some of the onlookers, they weren't at all sure about that, either, but at least they knew now that she had Ilham's approval and, if it came to that, protection.

There were about two dozen women in makeshift uniforms. Several tents stood at one end of a field, along with a battered metal trailer. The woman standing in its door gave the impression of being in charge without any noticeable difference in uniform. Cleo went right up to the cinder block steps, considered saluting, and settled for standing more or less at attention. "Cleo Brown, ma'am." She'd learned quite a bit of Arabic during her time in the desert, and knew Kurdish-speakers were likely to know Arabic as well, but it seemed best to stick with English.

"Yes, I understand that you will be detecting landmines." The woman came down the steps, her expression carefully neutral. "We have been wondering just how that works, what it is that you do."

"I served in the US Army for many years, sometimes with mine clearing units, so I've had a good deal of experience in the field, and developed an instinct for detecting mines and IEDs." She looked around at the circle of faces. Of course they had some doubts; their lives would depend on how well she did her job. "Based on my record, Colonel Razhan Khider has asked me to join this mission, and I've committed to putting my own life at risk carrying it out."

"Experience and instinct only? Nothing more?" The voice came from behind Cleo. The older soldier who had questioned Ilham.

Cleo didn't bother to turn. "Those are my claims, and those must be enough." So much for anonymity. Had somebody, maybe Ariya, leaked their identity? More likely, Razhan had decided that this elite team needed to know everything about them.

Ilham was suddenly beside her, facing the others. "Think! If she steps wrong, she's the first to go. I would follow her."

Cleo, still facing the trailer, bellowed abruptly, "Drop that gun! You, behind the middle tent!"

Ilham laughed and clapped. "See? Good instincts, just like she said."

Cleo turned in time to see the pretty young girl shuffle out from behind the tent, rifle lowered.

No point in alienating the people who would be her comrades and risk their lives with her. "Okay, *one* test is reasonable. We need to know what to expect from each other. Someone must have told you that I can also detect threatening guns." Cleo's tone was stern. "But if anyone else tries that damned trick, they can expect to discover how much experience I have in hand-to-hand combat." She turned in a slow arc, meeting the eyes of every woman there. A few were translating for companions who looked bemused, but most nodded in agreement, and possibly respect.

The woman from the trailer offered her hand to Cleo. "Welcome to our camp. I am Captain Kizilhan, temporary commander here, but informally you may call me Shifra. Come in and have tea with me."

A strong mint tea was already brewed. Cleo sat across a small desk from Shifra, looking over photos and maps of the territory they'd be working in.

"The irony of our plan," Shifra said, "is that our best fighters go on this mission, but to succeed we must not fight, at least until near the end. We must not reveal that we are soldiers. Soldiers would be treated even more harshly, maimed and tortured with no regard for their market value." She watched for Cleo's reaction. Cleo nodded, so Shifra went on, "I'm sure that you are an outstanding fighter, but can you show convincing fear, even panic? Can you be timid and submissive? When you are captured, can you play the village woman or farmer's wife whose terror surpasses even her outrage? It might be best to appear somewhat weak-minded, and say as little as possible. Do you speak any Arabic?"

"I hung around Arab truck drivers and laborers working for the Army, and I drove for a medical team treating nomadic women, so I can manage the language."

"Can you manage to show fear? Most of all, can you be beaten without striking back in anger?"

"I can do what I have to do." Cleo hesitated, debating how much of her inner demons to share. Something about Shifra made it seem safe. Or maybe it was the calming effect of the tea. She took a deep breath, but still didn't say more than, "I have known gut-deep fear, felt blows and worse when I was young, and weak. I can tap into that fear when the time comes, but I won't open the closed door until I have to." Another deep breath. "As to not resisting brutality, I never did learn that well, but I've learned to resist my own impulses when needed, so I think I can manage." Then she grinned and veered away from dangerous memories. "I'll bet you have this same conversation with all the girls. Nice ice-breaker."

Shifra's answering smile was fleeting. "Yes, I do. And with myself, over and over again."

CHAPTER 18

Ariya drove the truck while Mac and Razhan grew more and more obsessive about checking their phones. Ash witnessed the exact moment when Mac finally connected, her face shifting suddenly from frustration to intense alertness. The few words she barked into the phone didn't reveal much; "Yes…you're sure? How soon? Can't you find out?" interspersed with long intervals of listening.

Razhan twisted around in the front seat to stare at Mac. Ash had debated asking what was going on, but was glad to leave it to Razhan, who blurted out as soon as Mac set down the phone, "Who have you reached? What is happening?"

"Just some news about a scheme of mine. It was a long shot, but looks like it may work out after all."

Ash and Razhan kept on looking at her expectantly.

"All right, all right," Mac said. "It's still not a sure thing, but I guess it's likely enough now that I can say something about it. Turn back around, Razhan, before you get a permanent twist in your neck. And Ariya, you keep your eyes on the road. You'll all hear what I have to say, but keep it to yourselves."

"This is the 'business' you said you had with me?" Ash asked.

"This is it, if everything aligns just right. Here's the deal. I've commissioned a special kind of drone."

"*Drones*?" Ash was aghast. "You're going to bomb the walls after all? In spite of all the potential casualties? We can't—"

"Not that kind of drone." Mac looked like she was enjoying their consternation. "Not weaponized. This is a new optics development of standard spy drones, a device that doubles as high-tech field glasses. So top-secret that even the military doesn't know about it, developed by an independent entrepreneur."

"But you, Mac, of course, know all about it." Razhan sounded both exasperated and impressed.

Ash expected a response like, "It's my business to know about things," but those words didn't come.

"Not all. Not enough." Mac's brief elation faded. "And the gear may not come in time. It'll be a close thing."

"Gear?" Ash probed, determined to get some solid information.

"Yes. For you. As I understand it, you'll have a helmet programmed to let you view what the drone sees, and you'll have controls to make the image brighter, or magnify it, and steer the drone wherever you want it to go by movements of your head. It can even follow your eye movements."

"As *you* understand it?" Ash struggled to keep from sounding as skeptical as she felt. "When will *I* get a chance to understand it?"

"That," Mac said, the stress showing briefly on her face, "is the big question." Her customary façade of confidence returned. "But with this gadgetry or without it, you'll succeed. It's my job to know things like that."

Ash and the others didn't arrive at the camp until well past noon the next day. As they neared, she looked eagerly for Cleo, but couldn't see her at first in the turmoil of people and tents and piles of gear and munitions.

Then, abruptly, she felt her. Cleo was under great strain. Ash herself, as she came closer to the desert, had felt the pervasive anger of the goddess grow and grow, but that had become familiar enough that she could handle it and stay in control. What Cleo was feeling was far different.

But where was she? *"You okay?"* she called voicelessly. So many figures milling about, so many curious eyes on the new arrivals and especially on Ash herself, but no sight of the one figure in all the world she would know in an instant. Then, as her gaze crossed a beat-up old metal trailer, she saw Cleo slowly emerging from behind it. By her expression, Ash knew that the thought she'd sent had been received.

While Razhan and Mac conferred with Shifra in the trailer, and Ariya hung out with friends in the camp, Ash drew Cleo into the truck, where they could speak privately.

"What's wrong?" It wasn't just that Cleo looked different, with her red hair toned down to auburn. Something was bothering her.

"Nothing's wrong, now that you're here." Cleo leaned in for a long kiss and then bent her head against Ash's shoulder, hiding her eyes.

Ash tilted Cleo's face back up. "Something's been going on."

"Isn't it always? We're about to storm a walled city to save hundreds of women from slavery. So what else is new?"

Ash didn't let her get away with that. "Plenty, from my perspective, but you won't get my news until I know what's eating you. Or who."

"Nothing's eating me."

"Look, when I hand you a straight line like that and get nothing, there's definitely something wrong."

That got a smile. A very small one. "I'm just getting myself into gear for being captured. I need to will myself to show weakness, helplessness, fear—the bone-deep kind of fear that comes from tapping into memories from when I was a kid." She shifted gears and shrugged. "Those are my orders. I'll carry them out, no matter what. How about you?"

Ash's answer had to wait until she'd hugged Cleo hard, and Cleo hugged her back. At first it was for comfort. Then one thing led to another until they were in danger of rocking the truck so hard folks would notice, so they had to pull apart. But that wasn't the main reason, Ash knew; however compelling it would be to make love when it might be the last time, refusing to admit that it might be the last time was the better mindset. Plus, the truck had too many windows, and there were plenty of curious eyes around trying to look not so curious.

"So what's your news?" Cleo was still breathing hard.

"It's really Mac's news. She may or may not have scored a major coup, involving drones." Ash knew Cleo's first reaction would be like her own, and she wasn't disappointed.

"*Drones?* They can't bomb—"

"No, not a weaponized drone. It's some super-secret invention better than any field glasses, intended to let me see things brighter, and magnified, and to go wherever I want it to."

"Wow! Mac must have some major pull with the Army. Maybe some major dirt on somebody in research and intelligence."

"She says this isn't connected with the military, at least not yet. It's a prototype, one of a kind, developed by one of her many contacts."

"So you get to test-drive this contraption." Cleo shook her head. "You're sure it won't explode?"

"Want me to run it by you to scan? But it isn't here yet. It may not even be here in time." Ash heard voices coming closer to the truck, and decided it was time to change the subject. "Do you know when your crew gets going?"

"Nope. Special meeting coming up. In fact, they seem to be looking for us right now. I didn't think it would be this soon." Cleo could see out the window past the driver's seat, and Ash turned to look. Ariya was gesturing toward them. Trust her to be keeping track of where they were and what they were doing.

The meeting was in the trailer. Ariya was there, along with several others who had also been captives, and Ilham, and a trained medic. Ariya translated when necessary, but all spoke at least some English and mostly kept to it for the benefit of the Americans.

"There are very few intact rooms," Ariya said, "and the few doors with locks have only simple bolts on the outside, to keep people in. Only the central block where the important men are housed has roofs. We can get people out. There are not many guards where the prisoners are kept, since they are sure of their outer walls and mines."

"We know that our commander has been drugged, and there may be others," Shifra said. "We are prepared to carry her if necessary, but we also have a means of counteracting the drug they will likely have used."

The medic nodded. "I'll take a small hypodermic needle disguised as a fastening for my keffiyeh, and medications sewn under its lining. Some of the others will have them as well in case there are more in need, or mine is lost."

"Nice idea," Cleo said thoughtfully. "I thought those scarves were only lined to make them warmer."

Ash was uneasy. "All this sounds just about plausible, but how will you keep the captives from panicking, even stampeding over each other, when the gates come down? The noise will be as terrifying as a cannon attack, or even greater, and the earth will shake. And what explanation will you give for it all?"

"Some of our people are already there, unwilling captives," Shifra said. "Once told that we come with a top-secret plan to rescue our commander and lead all the prisoners to safety, they will work with us to keep order among the others. No explanation, simply a warning that it will sound as though iron and stones are being torn apart and smashed to the ground."

Ash wasn't convinced, but Cleo chimed in, "Neat! If they've heard of the Shadow Hand, they might have a clue. If they haven't, or don't believe in things like that, they'll assume we've somehow got hold of a new kick-ass technology."

"You must trust us," Shifra said, "as we must trust you."

There was a moment of silence, until Razhan, who had taken the single chair beside Shifra, stood and went on as though everything was settled. "Our most recent information is that the raid will occur soon, tomorrow afternoon. With luck, the sentries in our hilltop fortress will be able to see the enemy's trucks raising dust along the road well before they reach the village, so we will have some warning. The villagers have already been told to hide in the hills, and our forces are ready to charge upon the raiders as soon as prisoners have been taken. They will fail to recapture the captives, but will prevent the village from being ransacked."

Shifra looked from face to face. "Are we all agreed that we must dress and act as villagers taken unawares? Are we sure our soldiers are ready?"

"There's no holding 'em back," Ilham said.

"That's what I'm afraid of." Shifra sighed. "I'll try once more to impress on them the importance of acting like villagers, not soldiers."

A tall, weathered woman who had been leaning against a wall now straightened. "What's the difference? Everyone's prepared to fight, villager or soldier. Some resistance will be expected. But we know we must seem to lose in order to win this battle."

"Then we leave here at dawn tomorrow, reach the village by midmorning, dress in the clothing that will be left there for us, and when our signal comes, climb into a large open-bed farm truck and ride along the road as though we were on the way to some shrine or social gathering and had no notion that we might be attacked."

Mac, uncharacteristically silent so far, spoke up. "The sooner you're captured, the more time you'll have to prepare the women in the city for escape, but the more danger you'll be in. We're looking at a pre-dawn smashing of the gate, when most of the guards will be either asleep or preparing for their morning prayers, and there'll be just enough light to see where you're putting your feet."

Ilham had been shifting from foot to foot. Now she burst out, "I should go too! My tough old hide rules me out as a salable sex slave, so I'd probably get killed right off, but...okay, right, I couldn't do much if I got killed first." She slumped back against the wall.

"We rely on you, Ilham," Mac said sharply, "to work with Ash, to have her back while she's taking down the gate, and mine as well while I'm watching her."

Ash had been enjoying feeling invisible, but now everyone's gaze turned to her.

The medic broke the sudden silence. "I must ask this, without offense, I hope. Are you really the Shadow Hand one hears about? Is there any truth to all of that?"

"Depends on what you've heard." Ash looked around, making eye contact with each of them. "And on what you've seen. Yes, I can do things that seem impossible. No, I can't explain why. I never asked for such power. But as long as I have it, I'll keep using it for causes like yours. I can and will tear down that gate."

There was another moment of silence, and then Ariya, who hadn't spoken before, cried out, "Ash can even tear mountains apart!"

Cleo started edging around toward Ariya as fast as she could. The girl saw her coming. "And Cleo is also powerful. She saved my life!"

"From what? Who?"

Ash wasn't sure who spoke, but she knew, watching Ariya's face, just when the girl realized the trap she'd laid for herself. How could she reveal who had threatened her?

Cleo got there, put an arm around Ariya, and faced the group. "Not that big a deal, really, just some falling rock. An accident, terrifying at the time. Right, Ariya?"

"Yes, right." Ariya sounded breathless. Cleo must be squeezing her pretty hard. Ash was also sure that Mac had been holding her breath.

Now she said, calmly and authoritatively, "I have seen Ash hold up a large helicopter about to crash, with her mind alone. I have seen—and so have Razhan and Ariya—Ash lift up great boulders without touching them and then smash them down with tremendous force. I have even seen her do this at a great distance. Cleo has seen much more, and so have viewers of YouTube videos posted by an associate of theirs. Yes, the Shadow Hand videos are real. We would not ask any of you to put your lives in danger even to save others if we were not sure that Ash can tear down the gate, and Cleo can lead you safely through the minefield to the secure zone where our transport vehicles and troops wait. And one more thing; don't be alarmed if you see something strange in the air, a drone. It would be carrying only a viewing device to help Ash see the city from a distance. No bombs."

The silence that followed felt like it might be permanent.

"Any more questions?" Ash asked.

Cleo made her way back to Ash's side and took her arm. "If not, I suggest we all get what little rest we can. I don't know about the rest of you, but I've had damned little sleep lately, and I need some. So does Ash. We're only human."

Mac's nod of approval was good to have, but nothing compared to the comfort of knowing that Cleo, who knew her best, had affirmed that Ash was no freak, but "only human."

They took to the truck again for the night, instead of sharing a tent with the others, and no one objected. If anyone watched in the night, there was no rocking of the truck to see, but inside, the long, slow, sensual couplings of bodies and minds alternated with periods of deep sleep, both almost too sweet to allow thoughts of the future to distract from them.

CHAPTER 19

"It works?"

Ash didn't answer. Mac and Ilham stood beside her on a hillside next to the truck and motorcycle, but Ash's whole being was focused on the scene playing out three miles away—and virtually right in front of her.

The two dozen women crammed into the open truck bed, dressed in cloaks and long skirts or baggy trousers, heads wrapped in colorful scarves, clung to each other and the metal sides as distant swirls of dust raced ever closer. Their truck jolted and swayed, trying to outrun their pursuers, or at least appearing to.

Ash saw Cleo standing unsupported in the middle of the truck bed, legs adjusting automatically, riding the erratic jouncing of the truck. She even saw Cleo's wild grin, like a Roman chariot driver hurtling into battle. *Better wipe that look off your face before the capture*, Ash thought—and Cleo turned, looked straight toward the hills, and flipped her the bird. The thought had been intercepted, even though she hadn't consciously sent it. Good!

She grinned. It was like the old days when a battle threatened and they braced for it with snarky exchanges, before they'd become so close that fear for each other weighed down their bravado. She wished Cleo could see her now, with the elaborate helmet and visor that made her look like an alien coming to ravish Earth's women.

"Don't let your eyes get too tired. You don't need to see this part," Mac said. "Could I…"

Of course she wanted to look for herself, after all her arrangements, but it wasn't going to happen now. "Sorry, I've finally got this thing calibrated for my own eyes. We'd better not mess with it." Which Mac knew perfectly well, having read Ash the instructions. The gear had been delivered to their camp, while the technician who would launch and monitor the drone and even control it remotely if necessary had been taken directly to the hilltop fortress nearest the village and would later be moved to a higher spot overlooking the walled city from a distance. If Ash looked upward behind her she could see the drone, a vaguely hawk-shaped speck high against the too-bright sky. Looking harder, she thought the sweep of the wings might even look like a falcon.

Mac resorted to her field glasses. "They're getting closer."

"Yes." Ash kept her focus on Cleo, who had leaned forward to signal someone in the truck's cab. Suddenly, black smoke poured from the tailpipe, and the truck slowed. Obviously some trick Cleo had rigged. The oncoming vehicles, jeeps and several vans, closed the distance fast. Within minutes, warning shots were fired and the farm truck, already scarcely moving, came to a stop.

"There's no use watching." Mac tugged at Ash's sleeve. Ash jerked her arm away. Men poured out of the jeeps and onto the farm truck, wrestling the convincingly resisting women down and into the vans. Cleo didn't resist except to huddle on the floor of the truck bed, head bent with her arms trying to cover it. Playing the role of a weak, fearful woman. *Please, remember you're playing a role, Cleo.*

Two men were hauling Cleo to her feet. Ash's already tense body stiffened even more. "You can't interfere!" Mac shouted, but Ash barely heard her. Cleo was shaking, maybe sobbing. One man jerked her head back to see her face, then jabbed a hand into her crotch. Making sure she was a woman. A buzz of rage rose in Ash so bitter she could taste it.

"NO!" Mac's second shout got through. Ash hesitated.

Another, more powerful *"NO!"* blasted into her mind. Cleo screaming at the man? But Cleo managed to twist her head toward the hills, and a brief flash of fury lit her face as the next cry burned into Ash's mind. *"NO! Don't watch, damn it!"*

Then Cleo was gone, thrown into an open van door with the others. The vans and jeeps roared off, while Ash struggled to hold herself in, to keep from yanking the vans back and clashing the jeeps together. Mac's arms around her, joined by Ilham's, helped. Not that they could restrain her mind, but they could distract her from her surging emotions—augmented, she suddenly realized, by the fury of Ishtar.

Ishtar knew nothing about strategy or tactics, just destruction. No sense of all the complexities, and all that had to be done. Or not done. Already, defenders from Razhan's troops in trucks and jeeps were racing down from the hills in a pretense of pursuit, shooting into the sky, forcing the enemies to speed away without ravaging the village or the rest of the district.

Ash stood still, trembling but resigned. Mac lifted the helmet from her head and packed the gear away in a padded case. The falcon-shaped drone high above moved eastward, as they would, getting closer to the hills nearest the walled city.

It would be many hours before anything more could be done. They would go now to wait with some of Razhan's troops at a mountainside observation post to the east.

"C'mon," Ilham said gruffly. "Ride with me, Shadow Hand— Hotshot—Ash— whatever. Nothing takes your mind off trouble like wind in your face and a rumbling motor between your legs."

Mac nodded, and Ash climbed on behind Ilham, who shouted back to her just before revving the engine, "They'd better have a damned good meal ready for us!" Then they were off, with Mac driving the truck behind them.

The roar and vibration of the motorcycle was certainly distracting, although it made Ash long for a horse between her legs instead. The food was okay, kebabs with far more vegetables than chicken, and a filling lentil side dish. The warm meal was welcome since it was considerably colder at this elevation than down on the plains.

The setting sun threw long shadows from behind the western mountains as Ash, Mac, and Ilham set up their post on the highest outcropping of rock. Ash refused the chance for a few hours of sleep.

Instead, she paced compulsively and strained to see the far distant city through a haze, both visual and mental. She knew more or less where Cleo was, but Cleo had cut her off. No communication, for now. That would come later when it was time for action.

Ash finally sat on an isolated rock and reassessed the photos and sketches Razhan had given her. One in particular hinted that the lions' heads were set into the tops of great pillars, and not carved from the same stone. She couldn't be sure. But as she strained to make out details she felt some presence watching over her shoulder, focusing on the lions just as intently. What felt at first like hot breath on the back of her neck grew until she had to shake it off. Ash swung to face it and said into empty air where no one, of course, could be seen, "Damn it, Ishtar! Don't distract me. I'll handle this my way. Ease off!"

The heat ebbed away. Ash looked around and saw with relief that there were no soldiers in view to observe her display of apparent insanity. She returned to her study of the photos, noticing a faint vibration in her fingertips when she handled them, but she was able to shake that off as well.

The huge gates shown in the photos were built of heavy wood and crisscrossed with bands of iron. When the locks were opened, the gates would swing inward. The images were so granular that she couldn't tell how the gates were attached to the pillars, but she would tear them apart in any case, whether or not she could spare the lions.

She stood, stretched, and went to join the others at the fortified overlook.

Time dragged on, until suddenly it raced with the roar of trucks and jeeps and the turmoil of soldiers packing up their weapons, supplies, and communication equipment. One after another, three truckloads jolted down the rough road to join with the distant fleet of vehicles preparing to rescue the freed captives. When and if they *were* truly freed, Ash thought, swept by a chill so keen she would have welcomed the goddess's hot breath. But Ishtar had, it seemed, "eased off," except for that faint vibration in Ash's fingers.

Mac spoke with the driver of the last jeep just before it departed, leaving behind an almost eerie silence. Then she checked her watch, said, "It's time," and strode to the truck, calling for Ilham. Ash was on her feet, the tingling spreading from her fingers across her whole body, energizing and at the same time calming. Deep inside, if she searched, she could still feel Ishtar's power lying in wait like a crouching lion, ready to leap forth with a deadly roar.

CHAPTER 20

CLEO COWERED AGAINST A FRAGMENT of ancient wall, her ears ringing. *A funny word, "cowered,"* she thought through a haze. She'd known some pretty feisty cows. Try to slam them down the way she'd been slammed and you'd be lucky to get away without being trampled. Just as well to stay low, anyway. She could take down an enemy from knee level as easily as from anywhere above, if it came to that.

The ringing in her ears gradually subsided. At least cowering had been a useful tactic, and the loud and frantic panicking before that. When the harsh female jailer had groped between Cleo's legs to be sure she was a woman, her screams and sobs and thrashing had led to being slammed against the wall, but had also provided enough distraction to let most of her companions, including Ariya, slip through the open chain-link gate in the interior wall and merge swiftly into the shifting mass of captive women and children.

Some of the would-be rescuers would make their way after dark toward the central buildings and the nearby locked prison where Nisreen must be held, while others would spread the word of the planned escape among the prisoners. Two, blending into the nearby chaos, remained close to guard Cleo, but they were wise enough not to interfere with her deliberate strategy.

The jailer, who had been trying to keep the new arrivals together near her post, yanked Cleo away from the wall and shouted obscenities in Arabic, punctuated with strikes by the short lash she carried. When a man with a wispy gray beard and a long staff approached them, she gestured toward the knife at his belt and then pantomimed stabbing at Cleo, who straightened slowly from her crouch and looked as timid and stupid as she could. The few men she'd seen since being tossed from the van had carried only knives, not guns, and knives she could easily counter—except she mustn't reveal her skills.

He approached, looked her over, then groped her chest with a bony hand. She kept her head lowered to hide the fury in her eyes, and had to close them when he pried open her jaws to inspect her teeth, as though assessing a horse for sale. Then, abruptly, he stabbed a hand into her crotch even harder than the woman had done. Shards of buried memory crueler than pain stabbed through her, a genuine panic that the woman's brutality had not ignited. Fear fought with fury. *Show the fear...hold tight the fury.* She opened her eyes, and real tears trickled down her dusty cheeks.

"On your knees, girl!" A casual swipe of his staff knocked her down. "Let this one live," he told the woman. "She will bring only a small price, though better than none. The law forbids a man to lust after a boy, but who can say a boyish girl slave is improper?"

Cleo's Arabic was good enough to let her understand most of what he was saying. When he looked closely into her face again and murmured, "Ah, green eyes! Perhaps she even has a spirit worth the breaking. A prize after all," she understood much more.

So did the jailer, who glowered. "Even you, *Effendi*—" her snide tone stripped the honorific of any respect, "—are not permitted to sample the merchandise. Especially before virginity is proven."

The man shrugged. "In the morning, the Imams will officiate at the inspection of the newcomers, and as physician I will be assisting them. Perhaps I will make an offer then." He paused for effect. "Or possibly sooner."

The newcomers. Who had already mixed in with the rest and would be impossible now for the jailer to identify. She would be punished for that. More obscenities and insults followed the man's retreating back. "Fraud! Butcher! Poisoner!" When he failed to react, she turned again on Cleo with a kick that sent her to the ground. Another connected with her head and just missed her left eye. Pain from the hip that bore the brunt of her landing shot through her. One of her watching protectors took a half step, but the glare in Cleo's right eye pushed her back into the anonymity of the crowd.

The jailor raised her foot again. That foot. So vulnerable… A simple grasp and twist and she'd be down, hard, with Cleo's thumbs pressing into her jugular. She struggled with the impulse, tensed, then rolled out of the way of the descending foot and scrambled away into the shelter of the shifting groups of women.

There were loose stones and tumbled half-walls everywhere, and in the shade of one wall she curled for a while into a defensive ball until the memories retreated. The sun sank lower. The shadows lengthened, then merged into twilight. Her protectors drifted by discreetly from time to time.

Cleo couldn't rest. The strain of doing nothing kept her tense. Just as in that suffocating cave by the wadi, but now without Ash. Where was Ash now? Better not to think about that.

By full night, several bright lights showed along the outer wall and a glow rose from the clustered buildings housing the enemy leaders. Only a very few scattered lanterns could be seen anywhere else. When one of her protectors approached again through the darkness, this time alone, Cleo was suddenly alert. The woman stopped beside her and murmured, "There is some delay. My sister has gone to help."

Some delay? Bullshit. Cleo searched for the danger and felt it. A gun raised, in the direction of the prison where Nisreen must be held. She took off through the maze of half-walls and clustered women at a limping jog, ignoring the pain of the heavy bruises on her hip and cheek, and clambered over one of many low dips in one of the walls. The other followed close behind.

The prison for prestigious captives was dark in contrast to the well-lit buildings nearby. Cleo and her companion were stopped silently by one of their own people where the shadows were deepest. "Reviving our commander has taken longer than we thought," she whispered, "and just as they began to carry her out, minutes ago, these two men came walking this way. Ariya went to distract them, pretending to be lost. She ordered me not to show myself. One wandering girl might not raise suspicion, but two could."

Between the nearby building and the prison, three figures were visible in the light from a side window. Two men, one scarcely more than a boy, and Ariya.

Distraction was putting it mildly. The older man held Ariya tightly from the back with his arm around her waist. The younger stood awkwardly holding a gun. Probably handed over by the other to free both hands. They were laughing, but quietly, likely not wishing to share their prize with others inside the building. Or to be caught "sampling the merchandise."

They had torn the keffiyeh from Ariya's head, and she twisted and writhed silently, trying to keep her cloak from being forced open. Cleo, from the shadows, caught her eye and gave her a miniscule nod. Good girl, not screaming and drawing more attention.

"I'll lure them around to the back," Cleo told the others. "Hurry the commander away and hide her near the gates—but not too near." She scooped up handfuls of small stones and the few larger ones at hand and knotted most into one end of her keffiyeh. The others she kept in her hands and sleeve as she moved silently around the back of the dark prison.

The first thrown pebble startled the young man with the gun. He glanced around and shifted nervously. The next two worried him enough that he clumsily raised his weapon. Two more and he charged around the corner, where his head met the swing of the stone-weighted keffiyeh—and in that instant of impact, Cleo felt Ash trying to reach her. No time now to answer. The other man followed—with Ariya letting herself be dragged along—and had only an instant to see his companion fall, stunned, before he was knocked out too. More than knocked out. That one, Cleo judged, would never wake. The younger would be out for several hours. She thought of taking the gun, an old rifle, but a quick examination told her that it was in such bad shape that it was as likely to kill its bearer as any target.

Ariya was already ripping her recaptured keffiyeh into strips and efficiently binding the younger man's wrists and ankles, as well as wadding up pieces to tie on as gags. Cleo bound the other, keeping Ariya from getting a good view of his shattered head.

"We should just kill them." Ariya gave one a kick.

"You don't want to see what a man's head looks like when it's been smashed open."

"Yes I do!"

"That one's younger even than you. Shut up and come on." But a seething anger rose in Cleo as she led the way around the next corner, an urge to go back and smash in the second head even though she had decided against it. What had Razhan said about their boys being conscripted by the enemy? And one had even leaked information to warn his family's village of attack.

The urge intensified into a sharp prodding, nagging at her to turn back, to smash, to kill. Was this the way Ishtar prodded Ash? Tough. *Screw you, goddess. You didn't draft me, I volunteered. My decisions are my own.* With an abrupt shake of her head, Cleo shut down the unwelcome connection. A split second later she felt Ash trying to reach her again, this time with a sharp command for her to respond and report. Cleo shot back an equally sharp retort and shut down that connection, too.

The moon had risen above the clouds, and in the distance they could just detect figures moving slowly away, keeping to the shadows. One turned to signal them, and Cleo and Ariya followed, keeping watch from side to side and frequently behind.

They met the others in a corner behind stacked water barrels, as safe as anywhere else, which wasn't saying much. The beacons high on the walls were aimed outward, but not well shielded, so some light trickled back inside and made shelter imperative.

Colonel Nisreen Khider was at least able to walk by now, with assistance, though there was still a hazy air about her. Their original plans had allowed time for her recovery. Now there was no telling how soon the dead and the merely stunned would be discovered, and Colonel Khider's escape as well.

"Ash. Be ready to act sooner than planned. Complication. Enemy killed, not discovered but might be any minute. Stand by."

The response was instantaneous. *"Got you. Ready when you are."*

"Need a little more time here." Cleo paused. *"Got you, too. Always."*

There was no time for more.

Shifra left the colonel's side and leaned close. "What has happened?"

Cleo told her in as few words as possible.

"How soon?"

"No sign of trouble yet. But we can't wait long."

A figure approached through the shadows. Ariya crept forward to meet the newcomer, whispered with her, and returned. "Only two guards, that evil woman and one other. Our people are prepared to take down both."

"Good," Shifra said. "Tell her to go back and spread the word that we must leave almost at once. Take down the guards. Finish getting the women ready."

The silence that followed morphed into a subtle stirring of the air, the faint, muted murmurings of hundreds of women alerted to the prospect of escape. If the guards on the outer wall noticed, they might shrug it off as some foolish female business, perhaps a birth, or a death. Or they might not.

Cleo scanned the top of the wall. There seemed to be only two sentries, one in each of the two lighted towers, showing no interest in what went on within the enclosure. If she concentrated, she could detect a gun in the tower on the right, but the guard wasn't holding it. She stood on a pile of rubble and stared back toward the central buildings. No change. No uproar.

"Ash. Gun in the tower to your left, my right. None in the other. Wait for my signal."

"Right," Ash sent. *"I'm on it."*

Cleo looked higher, into the night sky beyond the wall. Was that small, dark shadow drifting across the stars a drone?

Just then, Ariya returned and prodded her. "Look, over there."

A single lantern, bobbing closer, casting an occasional beam across a wispy gray beard and a hand gripping a long staff.

"Go!" Cleo gave Ariya a small shove. "I've got this one."

Ariya took off through the darkness where the wall itself cast a shadow.

Time. Just a little more time for the rescuers to get ready. What was he doing here? Coming to exchange verbal barbs with the woman jailer? Coming to find Cleo herself?

She circled in the shadows until she could approach as if coming from the inner enclosure's gate, and nearly tripped over a mound of clothing and flesh. From the angle of the head it was clear that the neck was broken, and by the short lash next to the hand, attached to an equally broken arm, Cleo was sure of its identity, even though the face, what was left of it, was unrecognizable. Whoever had taken down the jailer had done good work. A real overachiever.

She moved on, creeping forward into the widest space between the inner wall and the outer, and waited for the old man to come closer.

But he paused some distance away, cocking his head, muttering, and cupping one bony hand behind his ear. He must have heard the hum of unusual activity.

She had to get closer, which meant she had to reveal herself. Her keffiyeh was pulled over her hair loosely, and the loaded end hung down where her hand could grip it at just the right length.

"Effendi..." Her voice was tremulous, timid, child-like. She shuffled toward him, head bowed.

He raised the lantern. "Ah, Green-eyes. So your keeper accepts the offer I sent." He swung the lantern around, searching the darkness. "What makes the hive buzz tonight? And where is that greedy she-demon?"

She took a few steps more and shook her head, eyes still downcast. If she looked up, he would see her deadly rage too soon. Just a little closer, and she would straighten, stand strong, just as she had finally stood strong, fury driving out fear, all those years ago in New Hampshire. "I do not know, Effendi."

He stepped back. "Why does she hide? A trap? Has she set a trap for me?" He looked wildly around. "Now guards are coming!"

Cleo did straighten then. Lights were spreading out from the central buildings. The tunnel vision of her fury had almost blinded her.

"Ash! Take down the towers, now. The left one with the gun first."

So fast it might already have been in Ash's grip, the top part of the tower tore loose with a sharp, satisfying crack, spilling man and rifle outside the wall. With even more clamor of destruction, the whole structure separated from the wall and smashed to the ground. The other tower followed while shards of the first were still falling. *"Now the central buildings. Blast them with everything you've got."*

The old man swung from staring at the vanishing towers to see Cleo as she stood straight and fierce and as intent on Ash's work as if it had been her own.

"Witch!" he spat. "I should have known from your green eyes!"

His staff came at her so fast she couldn't have dodged if he'd been a step closer. As it was, she sprang back, then forward to grab its end on the return swing, and wrenched it away from him. The effort brought her down, though, at a bad angle. Pain shot up her leg, barely muted by adrenaline. She didn't even try to stand, just pushed herself up onto her knees as he came at her with his knife. The leverage from her position wasn't good, but she swung her stone-weighted keffiyeh hard enough to knock the knife from his hand. Then, as Ash sent two huge projectiles roaring above them, he ducked reflexively and she swung again, connecting with his head. He fell, smashing his skull against the ground, while a surge of vicious joy swept through Cleo. *There you go, Ishtar, this one's on me!*

But she still couldn't stand. When she tried, pain lanced through to her core, and when Ariya and the medic ran forward and lifted her the pain was even worse. In what little shelter they managed to find, her mind cleared, at least partially. Whatever Ash had sent arcing overhead could be heard pounding the central buildings over and over, like great hammers of the gods. Or goddesses. *"Way to go, Ash! And now...now..."* Her mind began to mist over.

"We will carry you, Cleo, all the way." Ariya's voice, strained with suppressed tears, could barely be heard over the wild destruction of the central buildings and the screams of men.

"No," Cleo said with absolute certainty, mind clear again. "Ash will lift and carry me." With an effort so intense it twisted her face, she sent, *"Gates away! Now!"*

CHAPTER 21

ASH WELCOMED THE COMING OF dusk. They could move on at last, while it was not yet dark enough to make driving without headlights impossible. Headlights might have been noticed from the distant city.

By the time the rocky bluff rose before them, darkness made climbing treacherous. The surface had been scoured smooth by centuries of sand storms, and only a series of rough diagonal cracks provided reliable footholds. Ash, with the strap of the viewing gear's padded bag slung crosswise over her head and shoulder, clung to stone still radiating leftover heat from the sun.

Mac climbed ahead with a pack stocked with food and drink for the night. Ilham came behind and stopped on a narrow ledge well below the summit, standing guard with her own pack of supplies, and her rifle.

The crest of the bluff was mostly level, with a few dips and high spots. Ash set down her bag in a hollow and knelt beside it, reaching inside to run careful fingers over helmet and visor to be sure they weren't damaged. The escape had been planned for just before dawn, hours away yet, but if things kicked off sooner she would be prepared to act.

Mac had set up her supplies a few feet away, and when she unscrewed the top of a thermos and said, "Coffee?" Ash gratefully accepted, glad of the hot brew. Even in the desert it was early winter, and the day's stored heat drained from the stone more and more rapidly now that the sun had set.

At last Ash looked up into the night sky, just light enough yet that the drone's falcon façade was silhouetted against it. She lifted the programmed helmet carefully from its padding and rested it on her hip, then gazed out over the plain below. Turning slowly, eyes now adjusted to the low light, she oriented herself in the natural world.

To the west were the hills, and then the mountains that had become so familiar.

To the south and southeast was the vast expanse of desert she had come to know well in her years with the Army.

To the north—more mountains, she thought, but too far away to be sure of, and in any case it was the northeast that drew her gaze. To the northeast there was Cleo. And the walled city, outlined in the deepening night by lights along its walls at long intervals and a faint glow from within. Ash remembered thinking that the international Army base approached from uphill at night looked like a palace from some fantastic Arabian Nights tale, but this walled city could have been the real thing, no longer a palace now.

"Do they have electricity there?" she murmured low to Mac, though there was no one else who could hear her.

"Probably a gasoline generator for lights on the wall, and in the officials' rooms at the center, but mostly oil lamps for the rest, if any lights at all."

Ash kept watching the city, imagining it in ancient times. The inner glow could have been a celebration of a royal wedding, or a festival of magic, or even an elaborate ritual where all bowed down before the goddess and worshipped her with chant and sacrifice. Had Ishtar been there? Was Ash only imagining that the inner buzzing had morphed briefly into a purr?

It didn't matter. Now, that glow could be the concentrated anguish of the hundreds enslaved there, in this war that, as so often in the past, was being fought on women's bodies.

She shook her head to clear it. Would Cleo laugh at her for getting so fanciful? They had sometimes made up far-fetched stories on long journeys together, but those had been on the raunchy side.

The real question was, would she ever hear Cleo laugh at her again?

She turned to Mac. "I need to use the helmet and visor now to get a look at the gates."

Mac jerked out of her reverie at Ash's voice. She had been deep in thought, too, perhaps wondering if she would ever hear Nisreen again.

"Here. Let me." Mac fumbled with the clasps and helped buckle them under Ash's chin. Ash could feel the faint trembling of Mac's fingers and, on impulse, put an arm around her shoulder and gave a quick squeeze. Mac returned the gesture. The sisterhood of fear for loved ones.

The visor showed her a close, brighter-than-life view of the gate, once she managed to get the settings right. The ponderous wooden doors, the iron bands leading to…yes! The huge hinges were anchored to the stone pillars by iron spikes. Anchored to the pillars, but not to the lions' heads. Looking closer—even closer—the lions were carved from a different type of stone entirely, like granite with a tawny tint. They were easily five feet high and nearly as wide, not part of the massive gray pillars themselves but bound to them by bands of metal like collars.

The buzzing now in her head became a throbbing, though not especially painful. Was it Ishtar's approval? Her sorrow? Ridicule or illusion? It didn't matter. The gate would come down, and if the lions were destroyed, what greater honor could there be for them than freeing the women?

She removed the helmet, sat down with it in her lap, and leaned against the food pack. Mac sat beside her. Still hours to go. The rising moon, nearly full, drifted in and out of bands of cloud—or, no, the clouds did the drifting. She watched the moon, the stars—so far away, so removed.

"Nisreen!"

At first it seemed to Ash that the moon had leapt partway across the sky, but in the next instant she realized that a few hours had passed. She must have dozed off. Mac turned to her, the intense relief on her face clear in the moonlight.

"Nisreen can contact me!"

"Cleo?" Ash could feel her presence so strongly it almost felt like touching, but there was no response. After a minute or two of worry and waiting she snapped impatiently, *"Sergeant Brown, report!"*

That brought an equally sharp retort. *"When I'm damned good and ready, Lieutenant!"*

At Mac's questioning look, Ash said, "Cleo *can* communicate, but she refuses to." Frustration sharpened her voice. "What the hell is going on in there?" She made the helmet and visor rise to her and settled them in place again. "Did Nisreen say anything useful?"

"Useful to me," Mac said. "Not to anyone else. She sounds weak, but alert."

Ash crouched on the highest point of rock, watching the city like a falcon seeking prey. When she zoomed in on the gate, she could almost feel the rough stone of the lion's head on the left. If she were to exert force... Yes, it would yield, when the time came. And the other lion? More resistant. Her hand tensed, tensed more, then drew back abruptly as the stone loosened with a jerk. She hoped no one had noticed the tremor.

"Ash."

Relief swept through her.

"Be ready sooner than planned. Complications. Enemy killed, not discovered, could be any minute. Stand by."

Ash's response was instantaneous. *"Got you. Ready when you are."*

"Need a little more time here." Cleo paused. *"Got you, too. Always."*

Ash spoke to Mac without turning. "A problem. They need to get out soon, but they're not ready yet."

Waiting took more strength than action could. The rocky summit offered only limited space for pacing, but Ash strode back and forth over what little there was. Mac seemed preoccupied in connecting with Nisreen, apparently on matters more personal than news of what was happening.

"Ash."

She stopped in mid-stride.

"Gun in the tower to your left, my right. None in the other. Wait for my signal."

"I'm on it." Ash focused her visor on the guard towers and the wall between, and waited. And waited. What was going on?

When Cleo's signal came—*"Ash! Take down the towers, now! The left one with the gun first!"*—Ash was so ready she moved her fingers a mere tenth of an inch and felt the wooden struts pull apart from the base by five feet. The figure inside the lookout structure stumbled, arms flailing, then clutched at a railing, mouth gaping in what must be a scream, while Ash sent the whole tower swaying like a palm tree in a wild hurricane. She felt the cracking of wood, the grating of stone, as she wrenched the entire lookout away, shook it until both man and rifle tumbled out, and smashed the whole stone tower to the ground. Then she sent the gun flying far into the night, and ripped the other tower away from the wall. The heat of battle, of power, surged through her.

"Now the central buildings. Blast 'em with everything you've got."

They were in sync now, as much as they'd ever been. Even more. Ash felt the old high. She tore loose the great stone lion head on the right, raised it high, and watched it arcing over the city, followed by the one on the left. The drone must be following her eye motions without any adjustment on her part, because suddenly she could see inside the walls. Beneath the soaring lions' heads, the masses of prisoners organized by the rescuers waited to pour out from their roofless enclosures. The few visible guards scattered in terror as the fierce stone heads sailed above them, parting the air with a roar like a double tornado, and slammed down on the headquarters—where there were flimsy, makeshift roofs until the heads came down onto them and smashed through in eruptions of jagged splinters. She raised the lions again, made them smash through time after time, then landed them intact on the rubble.

"Gates away! Now!" Cleo's command came through firm and clear.

Ash seldom needed gestures anymore, but now, standing precariously on a high point, she raised both arms. The rush of blood in her veins and hum of triumph in her head made her feel like the conductor of a Wagnerian orchestra directing a crescendo.

Crack! The right side of the gate tore away to the outside, bringing rocks from the pillar with it, and she swore she could hear the splintering and crashing from even so far away. She wrenched the remaining gate from its crumbling pillar, then made the shards of wood and iron and stone part like the Red Sea, leaving a wide, clear path. Two women came out, stepping from shadows into a beam of bright white light. Light?

A second drone had appeared, pouring light onto the roadway. It was joined by a third, zooming from side to side, and up and down, as though scanning the scene. Maybe even recording it. If the situation hadn't been so grimly real, Ash would have felt like she was in a movie. What the hell was going on?

And where was Cleo? One of the first two out Ash recognized as Shifra, with a tall silver-maned woman leaning on her for support. Could that be Nisreen? Then Ariya and the medic followed, supporting someone between them. Cleo! With arms strung around her helpers' necks for support, slowing them down. Behind them a stream of other women poured through the dust and rubble of the pulverized gateway.

"*Cleo!*" Anxiety burned the word into Ash's brain.

Cleo's thoughts rang clear in her head. *"Lift me, Ash! I'm okay, just can't walk. Leg out of commission. We can do this. I'll point the way. Make me fly!"*

The urge to snatch Cleo to safety was nearly overpowering. But Cleo would resist, and the mission would fail cataclysmically. Meanwhile the goddess brayed for more blood, for extermination of the enemy, with no room for mercy, or focus on the escaping women, or any rational thought. Ash pushed her back and seized control of her own mind. She had to listen to Cleo now, not the supernatural entity inside her head. She funneled her frustration into power, groped for Cleo, found her, and lifted her to stretch out

224

parallel to the ground. Mac moved close to brace Ash's back in her effort, and Ilham soon joined them and knelt on the stone to keep Ash's legs stable.

Cleo was clutching something wrapped in her keffiyeh. As her body rose, the scarf unfurled to reveal what had been concealed in the lining—a long white banner bearing the huge symbol of a black hand. The light from the drone shone full on it.

There was no time to wonder how Cleo had managed it. Ash carried her forward, twenty feet high, pausing, changing direction, the two of them one body, one mind, in two places. The drone's light stayed on Cleo, while a river of women, two or three abreast, followed her. Some leaned against each other, some carried children on their backs. Razhan's soldiers went up and down the line keeping everyone calm and moving as fast as possible.

Cleo looked only down and ahead, searching out each landmine. Ash wanted to scan the city, to look for guards who might mount the walls and shoot at Cleo, at the escaping women, but she couldn't be distracted.

She kept her arms raised, in case it made a difference. They were already aching, in spite of Mac and Ilham's support, and her shoulders shook with effort. Why had she practiced lifting heavy objects? Weight meant nothing now. It was time that threatened to drain her strength—time and distance—and there was still so very far to go.

Cleo must have sensed that. *"Hold me, Ash...keep me flying..."*

"I've got you. Always." Nothing else mattered. Ash braced against the strain, calling up reserves of strength she'd never known she possessed.

Her concern about the guards diminished when Mac murmured in her ear, "Nisreen tells me that the few men watching from the walls are falling in prayer, none raising guns. When Cleo rose from the earth, with the Shadow Hand banner, they cried out that she must be a djinn, or an afreet, but the women all tell each other that she is an angel."

The river of freed prisoners flowed on, following the beacon that was Cleo. Cleo kept on, pointing out each turn to be made, held up by Ash. And Ash was held up by Mac and Ilham.

"How far to go?" Rigid concentration roughened Ilham's voice. Ash looked only at Cleo, not daring to glance away to see how long the river of women had become, whether it yet had an end, when it might reach the trucks and safety.

Mac freed one hand to raise her field glasses. Ilham increased her support.

"Our transports have turned on their headlights," Mac said. "They make a stream of brightness. Only a quarter of the way still to go before Cleo reaches the safe zone." She returned her full support to Ash and murmured, "Don't forget to breathe," close at her shoulder.

The turns Cleo directed came more closely together now as the minefield became more vicious. Ash watched with such intensity that her eyes burned. *I can make it…we can make it…* Deep in her mind, or spirit, or gut, she felt that some other source of power had joined what she already had. No time to think about that now. *Keep on. Keep Cleo flying. Keep on.*

She wasn't aware of the trucks forging further out onto the plain until they stopped again at what must be the very edge of the minefield, their lights a bright river showing where safety began. Even when Cleo reached that line, Ash kept holding her up, while the stream of escapees continued, lit by the beams from the drone, until Mac tugged at her arm. "No enemies are following them. You can lower her now, gently. Razhan and the others will get her onto a truck bed and bring her the rest of the way."

Ash lowered Cleo, felt her reach the ground, felt other arms support her.

"All safe now," Cleo sent, then cut off communication.

Ash didn't lower her arms, but stretched them out to her sides, flexing the stiff muscles, rotating her shoulders, still staring out over the plains below. Mac and Ilham stepped away and began gathering their gear. It was time to move.

"What the hell!" Ilham's cry hit at the same time a blast of light from a previously unseen drone streamed past them from behind, momentarily blinding them when they glanced back at it. Blinking wildly, Ash refocused to witness her own dark shadow cast out from the rocky outcrop and projected far out over the plain, a giant, elongated figure with outstretched arms like something out of a monster movie—or a superhero one.

For half a minute a wild, intoxicating pride in her power surged through her—those magnified shadow arms and hands could reach down and lift great boulders, destroy ancient cities!—until she remembered Cleo's words. *"We're only human."* That brought her back to herself. She spun around, shielded her eyes against the drone's glare with one arm, and sent the intrusive technology spinning away. As she watched, the drone executed a graceful loop, still streaming light, then flew off toward the safe zone.

"Bastard!" She'd tacitly assented to photos and videos making her look like a big deal in Boston without showing her face too clearly, but not to this staged drama, not to whatever technician was behind it.

Ash sent Mac off with the truck to reunite with Nisreen and stayed on with Ilham, watching again through the helmet's visor to see whether any escapees in the column needed help. Razhan's troops were still among them, going up and down the line, making sure no one strayed or fell behind.

At last, confident she could leave her post, Ash followed Ilham down the steep, dark side of the bluff to the motorcycle and they headed for the repatriation camp and field hospital set up beyond the first range of hills.

As the motorcycle wove carefully along the road through the camp, the milling crowds seemed chaotic, but nearer the center they saw distinct family groups reuniting. There were smiles, but even more tears, and some of the released captives seemed to be on the verge of collapsing. Ash saw one woman huddling on the ground with a family group around her, and when the woman straightened slightly it was clear that she held a small baby in her arms. The older man and woman next to her took several steps backward.

"Plenty of that going on," Ilham grumbled. "She's probably been in captivity so long that the father can only be one of the enemy."

"What will happen to her, and others like her?"

"They'll be cared for, one way or another, but..." Ilham stopped the bike and looked back. Ash looked, too, and held her breath as the older woman took one step forward, then another, and reached out, taking the baby and holding it close. The man lifted his daughter to her feet. "That's the best way, for sure," Ilham said gruffly.

They kept on, going slower and slower as the crowd grew denser. Finally, inside the hospital complex, they walked along beside the motorcycle. Things seemed more organized there. In an expansive tent with the sides rolled up, dozens of pallets were lined up, all of them occupied, but many of the patients Ash could see didn't have apparent physical injuries.

"Exhaustion," she murmured almost to herself.

Ilham nodded, but added, "Trauma, too. Mental trauma."

"Of course. Their captivity must have been hell to endure."

"Oh yeah. And the escape..." Ilham paused, looked straight at Ash, and made a gesture with one hand that took Ash longer than it should have to interpret.

"Oh! You mean Cleo 'flying,' and...and all the rest." Of course. The lion heads roaring over them. The walls being torn down by an invisible force. The tremendous noise, the massive destruction. How brave they had been, how strong, to take the chance for freedom even through such terrifying and inexplicable turmoil. No wonder they were exhausted, and traumatized. She couldn't have done them more harm than good, in the circumstances—this was war, after all—but still.

Ilham gave her a gentle thump on the shoulder. "Better this way than being slaves. They'll mostly get over it. And as we've been moving along I've heard plenty of folks chattering, happy enough to believe that supernatural beings from their legends took a hand in saving them."

Ash was only half-listening, still gazing into the tent, a dark mood rising in her, until Ilham jerked on her sleeve.

"Hey, I see some folks I need to get to. I had friends in that hellhole. Here…" She grabbed a passing nurse and told her to get somebody to take "Shadow Hand" to Cleo's private tent.

So much for anonymity. Ash followed the young nurse, who was too awestruck to speak, pausing when she heard a familiar voice in a tent they passed. When she looked in through the narrow space where a flap hung open, Mac was there on her knees beside a cot where silver-haired Nisreen lay, one hand on Mac's bowed head, the other stroking her back. Their voices were low, but vibrating with feeling so intense that Ash pulled herself away to preserve their privacy.

The nurse was just pointing to Cleo's tent when Ash was jolted to a stop by another voice, one that belonged to the other side of the world.

"Hey, Ash, how'd you like my latest gizmos?"

"Twelve!" Ash's reaction was not exactly welcoming. "That sure explains a lot." So Twelve had been Mac's "independent entrepreneur." No wonder Ash had felt like she was in a movie.

Twelve shrugged. "I guess you didn't care for my money shot at the very end, but at least I only filmed you from behind. Even after all my videos, nobody would recognize you in a crowd. Just the same, that image would make a great movie poster. You've gotta admit the rest of the gig was well done."

"Yeah, okay, but I need to see Cleo now."

"Oh, she's all right. I've already told her about our next gig."

"There is no next gig."

Twelve went on as though Ash hadn't said a thing. "Arizona. Jian and her whole crew are already there. I'll be there later, after I do another job for Mac. She knows how to get funding! Anyway, did you know that lots of those sex-trafficked Chinese women are smuggled first to South and Central America and then over the border from Mexico?"

Arizona. Red rock canyons. Wild horses. High country ranches. But all Ash said, for now, was, "No, and I don't want to hear it. Maybe later. Right now, get lost, before I rip you into two Sixes. Or a Seven and a Five."

"Ha! Good one." Twelve turned casually away and faded into the shadows between tents. Ash watched her go. There was something different about her, a sense of purpose, maybe, and confidence that came with success.

The nurse's awe had been replaced by a repressed giggle, but she composed herself and lifted the flap to the next tent.

"Cleo," Ash began, then stopped short when she saw her on a narrow cot, one leg splinted, bandages covering the left side of her face.

She could still talk out of one side of her mouth. "Hey, what a victory! Don't look like that, I'm okay. Only scrapes and bruises under the bandages. You won't believe how hard it was, keeping in character, managing not to take down either of those assholes who hit me until the very end. I didn't even curse!"

"That *is* hard to believe. But your leg…"

"Just a crack and a torn ligament. Soon mended. We need some time to make different plans for our next campaign, anyway. Gotta keep 'em guessing." She looked closely at Ash's face. "You look pale! Better pull up a chair and sit down."

There were no chairs, but the nurse brought in a pile of threadbare floor cushions. Ash kept on standing, and gestured for the nurse to leave them alone.

"No more campaigns like that one, for sure."

Cleo must have had about enough residual adrenaline in her system to keep her cocky. "You're just jealous because I got to fly through the air like Superman, and you didn't. Did you see Twelve? She sure outdid herself with those drone contraptions once she had the chance and the backing. Maybe next time she can film me flying over the Grand Canyon."

"Only if you're flapping your own wings." Ash fell to her knees on the cushions and leaned close, stroking Cleo's uninjured cheek with a gentle finger. After a minute or two Cleo wriggled, trying without luck to sit up.

"Want some help?" Ash carefully raised her without laying a hand on her bruised body, then stood and slid a cushion behind her. "Is that comfortable?"

In answer, Cleo reached out both arms, and Ash leaned in for a tentative hug.

"I won't break," Cleo said, holding her more tightly.

"You'd better not." Ash shifted so that she sat sideways on the edge of the cot with her head on Cleo's shoulder, her lips brushing Cleo's neck. *Have I broken too much already?* she thought, the dark mood returning, and only realized that she had sent the words to Cleo when she felt the response.

"What's wrong?"

Feeling each other's thoughts skin to skin sent a wave of joy through Ash. The dark mood began to lift, but didn't dissipate entirely. She sat straighter so that she could meet Cleo's eyes, and spoke her thoughts aloud, low enough that if the nurse were close outside the tent she wouldn't hear. "Can you imagine how brave and strong the women we freed had to be? Some of them are in the hospital tent, exhausted, but some are also traumatized. Not just from all the noise and smashing and threat of mines, but the impossibility of it all, walls torn down by an invisible force, and... well, all of that."

"And me flying over their heads." Cleo began to slide down the cushion. The adrenaline was fading, her own stress catching up with her. "But if I...if I hadn't been so slow, hadn't got myself bunged up, hadn't needed to be held up like that..." Her voice wavered.

"No! Flying above, doing the impossible, may have been exactly the right thing to do, the thing that made it all work." Ash thought back to what Mac had related that Nisreen had said. "Do you know what they're calling you? The women you saved, the soldiers here, most likely even the enemies in the city?"

"Definitely not Superman," Cleo began, but her bravado gave way to a look of bone-deep exhaustion. "Tell me," she whispered.

"Some think you're a djinn, or an afreet in a rare good mood. But the ones who get it right say it was an angel who led them out of that hell."

"No..." Cleo began, but Ash put a finger over the exposed side of her mouth.

"That's okay. I guess I can put up with an angel. Angels don't absolutely have to be celibate, do they?"

For once, Cleo had nothing to say. The aftershock of what they'd done was hitting her, and tears blurred her visible eye. Ash bent, at first to conceal the tears in her own eyes, then to lay her weary head once more on Cleo's uninjured shoulder. They rested together, breathing as one, absorbing a strength from each other even a goddess could envy, and far beyond any superpowers a goddess could grant.

ABOUT SACCHI GREEN

Sacchi Green is an award-winning writer and editor of erotica and other stimulating genres. Her stories have appeared in scores of publications, including eight volumes of *Best Lesbian Erotica*, four of *Best Women's Erotica*, and four of *Best Lesbian Romance*. In recent years she's taken to wielding the editorial whip, editing eighteen lesbian erotica anthologies, most recently 2010 Lambda Award Winner *Lesbian Cowboys, Girl Crazy, Lesbian Lust, Lesbian Cops, Girl Fever: 69 Stories of Sudden Sex for Lesbians*, and 2014 Lambda Award Winner *Wild Girls, Wild Nights*, all from Cleis Press.

Sacchi lives in the Five College area of western Massachusetts, with frequent stays in the White Mountains of New Hampshire.

CONNECT WITH SACCHI
Blog: sacchi-green.blogspot.com

OTHER BOOKS FROM YLVA PUBLISHING

www.ylva-publishing.com

SHATTERED
(The Superheroine Collection)

Lee Winter

ISBN: 978-3-95533-563-2
Length: 194 pages (69,000 words)

Shattergirl, Earth's first lesbian guardian is refusing to save people and has gone off the grid. Lena Martin, the street-smart tracker with a silver tongue and a disdain for the rogue guardians she chases, has only days to bring her home. As the pair clash heatedly, masks begin to crack and brutal secrets are exposed that could shatter them both.

THE POWER OF MERCY
(The Superheroine Collection)

Fiona Zedde

ISBN: 978-3-95533-854-1
Length: 113 pages (37,000 words)

To her family, Mai Redstone is weak. When she becomes Mercy, a rooftop-climbing chameleon with at least nine lives, she finds her power. But when Mercy is called in by police to a murder case, her whole world threatens to crumble. The dead man made her childhood a hell. She is torn between giving the murderer a medal and finding the killer for her family. Mercy is a blade that can cut both ways.

CHASING STARS
(The Superheroine Collection)

Alex K. Thorne

ISBN: 978-3-95533-992-0
Length: 205 pages (70,000 words)

For superhero Swiftwing, crime fighting isn't her biggest battle. Nor is it having to meet the whims of Hollywood star Gwen Knight as her mild-mannered assistant, Ava. It's doing all that, while tracking a giant alien bug, being asked to fake date her famous boss, and realizing that she might be coming down with a pesky case of feelings.

A fun, sweet, sexy lesbian romance about the masks we wear.

EASY NEVADA AND THE PYRAMID'S CURSE
(The Cushing-Nevada Chronicles – Book 1)

Georgette Kaplan

ISBN: 978-3-96324-070-6
Length: 203 pages (72,000 words)

Easy Nevada is a mercenary with a taste for treasure, drawn to the secrets of a dangerous pyramid. She hardly expects to meet Sudanese British archaeologist Candice Cushing exploring her heritage, or a zealot bent on its destruction. In this high-stakes adventure, the women start to wonder if they're so different after all…and if that cursed pyramid has been buried for a reason.

Shadow Hand
© 2018 by Sacchi Green

ISBN: 978-3-96324-109-3

Also available as e-book.

Published by Ylva Publishing, legal entity of Ylva Verlag, e.Kfr.

Ylva Verlag, e.Kfr.
Owner: Astrid Ohletz
Am Kirschgarten 2
65830 Kriftel
Germany

www.ylva-publishing.com

First edition: 2018

Credits
Edited by Gill McKnight and Alissa McGowan
Cover Design and Print Layout by Streetlight Graphics

www.ingramcontent.com/pod-product-compliance
Lightning Source LLC
Chambersburg PA
CBHW030407020726
47493CB00003B/974